# CRUSHED

---

## THE HACKER AND THE HEIRESS

## ISABEL JOLIE

*For all the gamers out there,*

*but most especially for Josh, Emma & Ellie. You lift me to all the vital realms.*

One does not defeat demons.
One rises above them.

# CRUSHED

ERIK

The red bulb in the corner of the room flares. Life transitions to slow motion. The man on the security camera shatters the sliding glass door eight floors below. Dressed in black, he raises a suppressed semi-automatic pistol and steps over the shards of glass, then out of the view of the back door security camera. He enters the view of the first-floor security camera. His stride shows purpose.

I pick up my phone and tap out an urgent text to my team.

*Under attack. Get out.*

I slide open a drawer and lift the pistol I hoped to never have to use. The security camera flashes the intruder on the second floor. I push a button on my phone, and the wall slides, exposing a ladder. With my phone in my mouth and the gun in my hand, I climb the cold metal bars to the room above. *Kill or be killed. The Tao of Jiu-Jitsu.* The click of the panel informs me my location is now secure.

Through the air vent, I watch the wall of monitors. The assassin continues up the flights of stairs without pause. He knows his destination. I steady my breath. Sweat beads on my brow. I swallow, and the sound reverberates through my head. *Focus. Nothing good comes from divided attention.*

The door to the security room opens. The man in black enters, gun in front and at the ready. One step. Two steps. His back to me as he watches the monitors.

I point my gun. *Hold steady, same as at the shooting range.* I aim for his chest, the largest area. My best chance. I breathe in. *Steady.* My finger pulls.

The loud gun kicks. The recall throws off my aim. A cloud of dust appears on the far wall. *Dammit.*

The intruder ducks, searching for the source.

*Breathe. Steady.*

He raises his gun toward my hideout. It's him or me.

*Aim.*

A cracking sound blasts through the space.

The intruder falls back. My finger hovers on the trigger. I never pulled. Trevor, a member of my team, stands framed in the doorway. His gun points at the man on the floor.

I press my phone, and the wall panel clicks.

I climb down and join Trevor. The intruder wears a balaclava, the thin, black mask preferred by the military and assassins.

"Who do you think he is?" Trevor asks me, or maybe the room. A trickle of blood leaks from the dark hole in the center of the assassin's forehead, darkening the fabric.

I gesture to the body on the floor. "You can do the honors."

He reaches for the mask and unceremoniously tugs hard enough the body half rises. With a sickening thud, the head falls back onto the floor. Trevor closes the eyelids with his thumb.

"You recognize him?" he asks.

"No."

Trevor places two fingers against his neck, I assume out of habit. Then he checks the front pockets and rolls him over. He lifts a single piece of paper from his back pocket and unfolds it. His eyes go wide as he turns it around for me to see.

A candid photo of our team. With addresses.

*Fuck.*

"He's a professional," Trevor says. "Kane found us."

"We've got to move. Now."

# THE ILLUSION OF RANDOMNESS

ERIK

Six months later

Bells jingle as I push the vintage door. The brick walls lining the sides are windowless. The high ceilings feature ornately carved woodwork, most likely original, which would mean the ceiling is too. I don't see any glass lenses or security cameras. The floor is wood, dented and scuffed. Books line shelves and tables. There are a few small round tables for the cafe along a back wall. All are unused.

IP address location is not an exact science.

One loop, searching for a computer user, then I'll hunt next door.

"Can I help you?" a feminine voice asks.

I step past a poster stretched out on a stand announcing the latest James Patterson book. Along the back wall, there's a marble counter with a glass case for food. A young woman leans against the counter beside an old-timey cash register, and before her is an open MacBook adorned with colorful stickers. *Score*.

I step closer to get a better look.

A braid of light blonde hair, so light it's almost white, curves around her neck and down slight shoulders. Silver earrings dangle, and smaller ones line her lobes and sparkle in the light. Her eyes meet mine. Light blue irises arrest my attention.

Those blue eyes track my movements. Because I'm staring, captivated. There's a table of books to my right, and I grab one. In my peripheral vision, I see her gaze drop back to her keyboard.

She's not at all what I anticipated.

Firefly's avatar has a jet-black high ponytail and enormous anime-style black eyes. Of course, her avatar is also part Amazon, wields a Level 12 sword, and wears strappy sandal boots with flying capabilities. On the battlefield, she's brutal. For a year or two, I had suspected a dude with a female enchantress avatar played by my side. Tons of players own avatars of both genders.

Never in my wildest fantasies did I envision my gaming comrade sported white hair and barely-there blue eyes, so pale, some might call them gray. Ghostlike. She closes the lid on her laptop and exits from behind the counter. Her long, flowing, patterned skirt swishes behind her as she floats through the store, straightening a stack of books on one table, lifting a book, and moving it to a shelf. Her toe rings glint in the overhead light whenever her leg kicks out in front. Firefly, in real life, is a pixie.

The gray tank top she wears perfectly encapsulates her breasts, sharing the shape with the world. Far smaller than her avatar's bullet-shooting breasts, the real-life version before me obliterates the illustration. Unfathomable.

"Can I help you find something?"

She's close, so close words escape. I shake my head and open the book in my hand. She returns to her place as a barista, flips open her MacBook Air, and resumes typing.

Bracelets cover from her wrist to halfway up her forearm. Her arms are slender, and her nails are short and painted dark, as dark as my clothes. She smiles. Then clicks away.

The bells jingle. A delivery guy with a large brown cardboard box on a hand truck enters. He's wearing light-colored shorts and has a large tattoo on the back of one calf. It's a dragon.

*No. Impossible.*

One step closer, still carrying the book, a better visual emerges. The art is off. The lines are crude, the color amateurish. His inspiration for the dragon might have been an American Chinese food menu.

"Did you want that book?" Firefly looks up from the form she's signing for the guy with a mediocre tattoo. I hold out the heavy hard-cover book. There are cats all over the cover. Kittens and a cat.

"No." I set it down and exit. She must think I'm the weirdest of the weird.

On the drive home, instead of a winding two-way road choked with slow-moving vehicles, I see her. Her perfect, unblemished porcelain skin. That mystical white hair and those captivating blue eyes. I hear her voice. It's light and feathery. *Can I help you?*

We've known each other for over fifteen years, and I've never heard her voice before. The two of us are virtual friends. Anonymous friends. Normal in the gaming world, when every player has an avatar identity. You never know what psycho you're gunning down. Over the years, as I closed off from every other person around me, I remained real in my private texts to Firefly. At least, as real as one can be without knowing one's name. But a name is a descriptor. The substance is beneath.

My hunch had been she, or he, was a fellow coder. In recent years, I'd become fairly certain she identified as she/her. Her pronoun usage remained consistent. She never asked for a photo. I should have asked for a photo. I would've used it as a screensaver.

"Where have you been?" Kairi greets me in the hallway with a spoon in a tub of communal ice cream.

"That's disgusting." Roommates. I have told her a minimum of twenty-five times to scoop it in a bowl.

"Where'd you go?" She's like a parrot. No, I could put a curtain over the cage for silence.

"Did you miss me?" I taunt. She jabs the spoon in the container. The action grates every last nerve. I push past her into the den.

We've been locked away in this house for months. Kairi suggested this location at a time when we had few options. I'll give her one thing. It's in the middle of fucking nowhere. Theoretically, we're in the middle of a vacation hotspot. An hour and a half north of San Francisco, wine enthusiasts drive here in droves. After six months in Napa, if I never see a grapevine again, I'll be good.

In the middle of the living room floor, Trevor is leaning over one leg, stretching. My dog, Astra, is laid out beside him. Her tail wags back and forth in greeting. Trevor takes Astra on his runs, which have lengthened over the last several months. Astra, a German shepherd, is a highly trained protection dog. Trevor keeps her in fighting shape by wearing her out.

Since we arrived in California, he's thrown himself into workouts. He's former military. He treats his workouts like they are a matter of life and death. Then there's Wolf. Wolf and Trevor were on the same team. Their team disbanded after an operation went sideways in Afghanistan. I hired them both. Over the years, we've become close friends.

Wolf is at his desk. All of us have desks in the oversized living area. Glass doors open onto a wraparound deck. Kairi's mom used to rent it out to vacationers. Now she rents it to us. There is zero paperwork tying us to this home. Nothing traceable connects us to this location.

"Any news?" I ask Wolf.

"Ransom attack on a small company based in San Diego. Pleasure Lights. Ever heard of them?"

"No." I land on the reclining chair and pull back the lever, sending my legs up high. I like how the chair responds. But they make better chairs. Gaming chairs that accommodate multiple monitors. I'd replace this one but then I'd have to deal with it when we move. And we will move.

"I've got a call in an hour with the CEO. You want in?" Wolf doesn't look up from the device on his lap.

"No." I lift off my glasses and scratch my eyebrow. "Why are you dealing with a hack?" Wolfgang is building out our security division—physical security. Monitoring, security agents, the stuff I originally hired him for.

"He wants to pay them. But get this—they want to meet him in person."

"They aren't hackers." They might want to kill the guy. Meeting in a random warehouse would be an excellent call for such a plan. But no hacker meets in person. Yeah, in Asia, our old syndicate did have a few buildings to house hackers. Mainly so we could ensure they were actually fucking doing their jobs and effectively monitor their activities. But they worked for us. And management didn't show faces. "Anyone who knows shit about hacking would send crypto payment instructions."

"You think I don't know that?" He leans back in the chair and crosses his arms over his chest. The tatts on his biceps stretch.

"Any word from NSA?" We plan to take clients from all over the world. But our most important client, the one who cut me a deal to remain out of prison, the National Security Agency, is the one we drop everything for.

"We're getting a new contact. I'll be the one who goes down to meet her for in-person updates," Kairi announces as she puts her hand on the back of my chair.

"Down where?" If she says San Francisco, I will pop a blood vessel. We're about an hour and a half from the city, but there are traffic cameras all over that place. There's no way Kane doesn't have passive data collection. He's running all that data through a facial recognition program. Combing data can be time consuming. It won't be instantaneous like in the movies. But if we get on a feed he's tapping into, he'll locate us. I know he's doing it, because I'm doing it. Only, I'm doing it because I want to know if he returns to the States. He's doing it because he wants to hire assassins, just like he did six months ago. And a year before that.

"She's picking the location."

"How do you know it's a she?"

"I don't. But if I don't know someone's gender, I like to call them a she."

"Why?" Trevor asks her from the floor, and I scowl at him for giving her that one.

"Because I like to assume the best in everyone." She smiles gleefully. She's a twat. She's actually much more what I envisioned Firefly would be like if she were female. Kairi never wears make-up, her bangs almost cover her eyes, and she's always in T-shirts and sweatpants. "Now, where'd you go?"

Kairi is a low-level coder. Maybe mid-level. Mostly cut and paste. She's decent. Getting better. Her specialty is phishing. She's got a way with people. She can get a phone number from any rep from any company. She reads people, and if they see her in person, she's unstoppable. She has these freckles that give her what she calls country girl innocence. But even online, where no one sees her mug, she makes friends in a world where no one trusts. She develops sick camaraderie in a world where it's all fake first names, and everyone's on a VPN, a virtual private network, behind firewalls. It's her superpower.

She pops my head.

"Fuck." I lean forward out of her reach.

"Answer me."

"I wanted to check something out."

"You?" She points an index finger at me. "Without security?" Now Wolf and Trevor are looking at me. This girl is as annoying as my sister.

"It had nothing to do with work. I just needed out." That's partially true. But I'd also gotten a text. And I hacked the game site. On a whim. Pinged her IP address. Mapped it. Forty-five minutes away.

All three of my roommates are staring at me. I didn't enjoy having roommates in college. So much so I moved back home.

"What you do affects our safety." It's a line Wolf likes to parrot. When we agreed to splinter, we committed to each other.

"It's stupid." They keep looking at me. They're bored. We should play Overwatch. It's insane they have this much interest in my activities. Back in Bangkok, they never asked. Of course, maybe back there, they didn't want the answer. "I traced an IP address." Three sets of eyes stare at me. "Wanted to check it out."

"By yourself?" Wolf's hand balls into a fist. Jesus.

"Someone I used to play games with. When I was young." Relax.

"What game?"

"Zeitgeist." Like any of these losers have heard of it.

"How young?" Kairi's squinting at me, all detective-like.

"Young, okay?" She inches forward. "Like college. High school."

"Did you find her?"

"How do you know it's a her?"

"Because I don't see you as bi."

"There's nothing sexual about it, perv. I was just curious." There are some advanced things one could do to throw off the scent. But... "She's not a hacker. She was a gamer. Now she's not. Now she owns a bookstore."

"Huh." Kairi's tongue traces her back teeth. Her tongue piercing flashes in the light. And now I wonder if Firefly has a tongue piercing. "You know, it's pointless. None of us can risk a relationship right now. You get that, right?"

There's an unnecessary hardness to her glare. I know her words are accurate. I wasn't looking for a relationship. I don't do relationships. I was just curious. And bored.

"What's her name?" Kairi probes.

"Didn't confirm it." None of my online names are real, and it's been that way for so long I don't place value in names. And then, because I spend way too much time with this crew, she asks the question as I think it.

"How do you even know you found the right person?"

# NOT A LOCAL

The bell hanging over the centuries-old wooden door chimes. The high-pitched, fragile sound fills the quiet space. The bell jettisons me from a daydream cloud to planet Earth.

An attractive man with raven black hair and thick-rimmed glasses enters my shop. A messenger bag hangs across his chest. His black, slim fitting jeans and black V-neck tee give off a city sleek vibe. I remember this man. He came in the day before, then left without buying anything. Probably a San Franciscan on vacation, seeking Wi-Fi to do some work while his significant other has spa time.

His glasses evoke intelligence. The urban all-black aesthetic is no-nonsense. Also no fun. He's scouting for a place to get work done.

I give him my best customer-friendly welcoming smile and wait to see if he'll order a coffee or if he'll leave again within minutes like he did yesterday. Some customers assume they must order to use my space and Wi-Fi, but really, I don't care. I decorated this place in the hopes others would use it as a coffeehouse.

The man heads to the far back corner, to the table I normally occupy when I'm not behind the counter. The corner table offers a view of the front door, down the long aisle, and a full view of the barista station. The dining area sits on an elevated platform, and while there are some locations in the store that remain out of view due to shelves, the corner serves as a birds-eye perch.

My phone rings, and a circular photo of my grandfather flashes on the screen.

"Hey, Granddad. You good? Can I call you back?" Voices carry in this space, and I'm always conscious that my customers can easily hear my conversations.

"You have a customer?" The surprise in his tone is notable.

"Yes."

"Is it busy?" His question is comical. But Granddad never leaves the vineyard, so he really wouldn't know exactly how much my business endeavor has flopped.

"No. It's still early. Tourist traffic doesn't get going until later." The defensive fib comes naturally.

"The first tour bus comes through here in twenty minutes."

"Yep."

"If you had your merch here, you could make sales."

"I'll bring some books over on Monday."

"Just books? No gift items?" My grandfather believes in touristry crap. His words, not mine.

"Would you like bookmarks? Or book lights?"

"Don't you stock any of the gift store stuff? The hand towels with funny sayings? Anything like that?"

"You already have that stuff in the gift store."

"But you're young. Hip. You can pick better selling stuff."

I roll my eyes at his ridiculous statement because clearly, being younger has not given me a competitive advantage in the marketplace.

A notification alert in the top right of my computer screen announces I have a message in War of Zeitgeist.

"Go get ready for that bus. Talk to you soon."

"Love you, Vivi."

"Love you too."

The faint audio of my Spotify Coffee Shop playlist is marred by faint clinking. Keys click in rapid-fire succession as the man in the corner taps away on his thick laptop. Since it is just the two of us in the shop, I lean over the counter.

"If you need the Wi-Fi password, just let me know."

"Got it. Thanks." His stern expression softens, making him appear borderline friendly. And handsome. In a nerdy, thick-framed glasses sort of way.

I should check my message. There's nothing more to say to my customer. Yet I stare. It's just the two of us.

He points. "You've got the password on a placard up there."

True, but no one else seems to see that placard. The light above reflects on the glass in his frames, but his dark eyes flash beneath the glare. He swallows. He's waiting—for me to stop staring. He's ready to work.

"If you want anything, just let me know."

"Can I have a decaf coffee?"

"Sure. But don't feel you have to order anything."

"Excuse me?"

"I mean, just because you're sitting here, you don't have to order anything. That isn't why I asked. And if you're ordering decaf, you've probably already had your coffee for the day."

The corners of his lips lift ever so slightly. Not enough to call it a smile. More amusement at my poor proprietary skills.

"I'll take the decaf coffee and water. Thanks."

I push off from my resting place against the counter and set to work. With his coffee cup and saucer in one hand and a glass of iced water in another, I approach. He remains focused on the screen, although I sense he monitors my advance out of his periphery. He snaps the laptop closed before I reach the table. People normally keep their laptop open when I deliver a beverage or refill water.

He could be working on a top-secret document. Or watching a movie. Maybe he's embarrassed to be watching a movie. Or maybe it's at a racy part. There are so many possibilities. Maybe he thinks I'm nosy.

I offer a cordial smile and practically curtsy after placing his drinks down. My stomach flutters. The breakfast croissant from this morning isn't sitting well.

"If you need anything else, just call out." I step backward, prepared to spin and retreat.

"Are you the owner?"

"Yes?" I draw the answer out a beat or two to create an understated question. What would he want to complain about? Did he see a cockroach?

His gaze wanders up and down my body. I literally feel it, as if his eyes are lasers and they transfer heat. He swallows, and his Adam's apple flexes. His hands rest on his thighs, and I find myself taken in by his forearms. He wears a braided black leather bracelet on his left wrist, and on his right, a thick black band and a watch. It's an old-fashioned watch, with a second hand. The man's tan, lean forearms are downright sexy, as is the way his shirt curves around his shoulders. He isn't overly muscular, but his muscles are noticeably sculpted.

16

"How long have you been open?"

I flip through my mental calendar. I left my home in Paris at the start of the pandemic, days before the international lockdown. It took me about a year to decide what I wanted to do once I returned home, and then another year to execute.

"Less than two years?" I answer, unsure of my accuracy. Time has more or less blended for me, the days morphing into months with no clear definition.

"And you're the founder?"

Founder strikes me as an overly important word, but correcting him isn't necessary. "Yes." *And your complaint?*

"I like the place. It has a good vibe."

"Thanks." He is literally the first customer to ever comment on the atmosphere. "When I opened it, I had this idea. There's this bookstore in Paris, and it's extremely popular."

"Shakespeare and Company."

"Yes." I point an index finger. *Holy smokes.* "Have you been there?"

"Yes." Those lips turn up at the corners again, softening his stern exterior and making him less business and more friend. "I'm pretty sure most tourists who visit Paris stop there."

There is some truth to his statement. There are lines to enter the infamous store. I particularly love the narrow, centuries-old staircase in the back. I'd considered doing something similar in this store, but my older brother Max had counseled me to wait and see if I needed to expand upstairs. As it turned out, his advice had been solid, and now I use the upstairs of the store as my apartment, and below the store I turned into a cellar to house my burgeoning wine collection.

"I used to own a wine store near it."

"Why'd you move here?"

"My family is from here. When the pandemic hit, I didn't want to be stuck overseas. I wanted to be home."

He nods understandingly. I'd wondered if I was making a knee-jerk reaction, but when I heard borders might close, every parcel of my being screamed I needed to get home. So, I did. A friend handled the closure of my wine business. It hadn't been a bad call. Paris pretty much remained closed for over a year, and the restaurants that had been my principal source of business wouldn't have been buying from me.

"Why not open a wine store?"

I half-laugh, then stop short. He doesn't get why I think his question is funny. "There are so many wine stores here. I thought I'd stand out by opening a bookstore."

"There's no competition." There's nothing to indicate he's mocking me, so I smile at his comment. The skirt I'm wearing doesn't have pockets, so with nothing to do with my hands, I wrap my arms around my waist. "I'm glad you're here. I'd rather work from a bookstore than a wine store."

"Right?" I ask, psyched he gets it. And he smiles, too, a real smile. "What do you do?"

"I'm in tech."

"I can see it." He rocks the sexy nerd look. Those thick black frames are hot. He probably has a great girlfriend in his life who dresses him. Or maybe a wife. And he is one of those guys who leaves his band in the shower. "Are you from San Fran?"

"No." He sniffs and glances at me, then around the empty store. "Seattle, originally. Now I live nearby."

"Seattle? Big tech scene there too."

The door chimes and we both look to the front. Alejandro from Sonoma Market pushes open the door with his butt, using both his arms to carry his large white cooler.

"Gotta go. Shout if you need anything."

Alejandro opens his cooler on wheels, and I order a variety of desserts, the kinds of things that keep for several days and look good sitting under glass domes. Croissants, scones, pound cake slices, and muffins. I'd tried buying whole cakes but had to throw away too much.

Alejandro also delivers my lunch. The dill chicken salad on a freshly baked croissant is a weekly ritual. Maria adds thinly sliced tomatoes and dill pickles to mine. I lift my special order from the cooler and glance over to the corner.

"He has some sandwiches in here. I'm not sure if you'll be here at lunch, but if you think you will be, you can pick one out."

"I'm not set up for individual sales," Alejandro grumbles.

"I'd buy it. He could buy from me," I tell him, low enough our conversation remains private.

IT hottie glances over from his laptop, fingers still on the keys.

"What kind?"

"Chicken salad, chicken parmesan, turkey and ranch, turkey and Swiss, PB&J."

Alejandro stage whispers, "Those are supposed to go next door."

"You don't have any extra?" I seriously doubt that.

"What do you like?" IT hottie asks. Alejandro and I both glance over at him, but his dark gaze centers on me. My stomach goes queasy. I could maybe give him my sandwich.

"Chicken salad."

"I'll take one," Mr. IT says.

"We only have one with tomato and pickle." Alejandro frowns.

"I know." I frown right back at Alejandro. He shouldn't be rude. With a black Sharpie, I squiggle out IT on the white wax paper wrapped around the sandwich. Then I sign Alejandro's receipt for the bakery items and sandwiches. They bill me each month. My business might not be doing well, but the Rossi name does wonders in the valley. Everyone knows I am good for money owed.

"Thank you," I say it with emphasis and finally earn a friendly smile from Alejandro. He's a nice guy; he just doesn't like it when I don't follow the rules. It's not my fault, though. He makes it easy to get around them.

Once the new pastries are set out, and old ones are tossed, I settle on my stool and launch Zeitgeist. The screen prompts the question, "Are you ready to embark on the sojourn of a lifetime?" Drums bellow, and I quickly reduce the sound on my laptop. Then I click on the message icon in the top right.

*Sanguinetti:* How much you charge for coin?

Huh. I don't remember ever playing with anyone with that username. And I've also never sold my assets. I've heard of people doing so, but this game is ancient. Why would someone want to buy assets now? I click over to send a message to my one friend within this realm, Phoenix.

> *Firefly:* Someone just asked to purchase my coins. Have you had any requests like this? I think I read about Venezuelans playing a game for income. As in, the coins earned in the game were worth more than their Venezuelan money due to uncontrolled inflation. It was some old game that worked on dated machines. You think Zeitgeist is under the same attack?

I hit send and pull out my Kindle. It can take days for Phoenix to respond.

Bright yellow sunlight streams in through the front window. Good weather doesn't mean great things for business. As my luck would have it, wonderful weather is the norm in Sonoma Valley. But it doesn't bother me as much as it should. I like my quiet time in the shop. In my head, on some days, I feel like Meg Ryan in *"You've Got Mail,"* only without the dependable, entertaining friends-slash-employees, and instead of kids' books, the books I sell circle travel and wine, and coffee table books, the big, beautiful books no one really reads but displays. I do keep a section of colorful children's books on hand in case a vacationer needs to buy a gift.

As the minutes tick by, I sneak discreet glances over to my one customer. I grew up in the valley. The men around here are typically either retired or are passionate about wine. Or beer. There's a burgeoning craft beer industry in the area.

The guys I went to high school with spanned the normal range of high school stereotypes: Jocks, preps, and nerds, plus a segment like my older brother, nature-loving tree huggers. Ruddy, flannel-wearing, blue jeans, work boots kind of guys. The farmers who love the land. That really describes the type of guy who would grow up here and stay. Most of the other cliques grow up and leave. One thing I know for certain. The guy wearing all black and sexy Clark Kent frames might live here, but my hunch was right. Mr. IT is not a local. He's nice to look at, but my other hunches are probably spot on too. There's a girlfriend, or he's a psycho. He's a look-don't-touch kind of guy.

# STRATEGIC SABOTAGE

ERIK

"Where are you off to?" Kairi stands with a coffee mug in hand, one hand on her hip, all cranky and bossy. She's wearing a pair of her wildly patterned loose pajama bottoms and a gray tank top. Thick, fuzzy socks peek out from under the hem of her crazy pants. She's in her most preferred office outfit.

"Heading out." I kick the screen door footplate, and it swings open.

"I can see that. But where?" The door slams shut with a whack. I readjust my messenger bag that's slung over my shoulder and take her in. We're all suspicious by nature. It's why we're still alive.

"I found a place I like to work. I need a change in scenery. That's all."

Her eyebrows remain angled in a way that communicates she's not buying it. I let out a sigh loud enough I know she'll hear, even though she's standing down the hall.

"I'm not keeping anything from you. Don't read into it." I kick the door again, only this time I exit. The door cracks closed with a loud bang, and the gravel grinds underfoot. That's all Kairi needs to know. I'm not about to tell her I confirmed the woman in the shop is Firefly. And I now know her first and last name. She'll jump on a soapbox about how I don't need to be pursuing her.

And if I tell her that I'm looking out for an old friend, she'll call me paranoid.

She'll put her hand on her hip and give me her you-need-therapy spiel when I tell her the shop is antiquated and likely to be robbed by anyone who is curious about her cash register. If I go and tell her that I don't like that someone I can't track asked her to sell her game coins, Kairi will go apeshit asking me what I'm doing hacking into a game and remind me that there are more important projects for me to be addressing.

She's right. There are. I'm working on a decryption system that could eliminate the financial incentive for cybercriminals and make the Internet far safer. That's what I originally set out to do way back when. I aimed to join the white hat force working to keep the newest frontier safe. Turns out I joined the wrong team. *You either win, or you learn.* I learned.

I crank up the loud truck and ignore Kairi as I drive away. Kairi came into this in a completely different way than I did. She's learned a ton, but she doesn't get me.

On the day I took my first hacking job, Firefly and I crushed the Kraken Invaders in the twentieth realm. My fist bump flew sky high, in the middle of the cafeteria. And another fist came from behind me and pushed my fist forward.

*"Nice hit." I recognized the guy speaking. He was in my data science class. He sat in the back, two rows from the back wall.*
*"Hit?" I asked as I closed my Chromebook.*
*"Must've been a hit. You're drumming air. You ever want a bigger hit, come find me."*

*"And you are?"*

*"T.J. Kanagasingam."*

*There was no chance I could repeat his mumbled name. He chuckled. It was a weird, nasally laugh. His thumb hooked under his belt. I shook it off and loaded my stuff into my backpack.*

*"You can call me Kane. All the Americans do. What's your name?"*

*"Erik."*

*"Lai." He says with a grin. "That's one cool-ass last name. I wanna get laaaii-iiiiiiid."*

*"Right." I swung my backpack over one shoulder. I should've walked faster. Should've recognized he knew too much about me without reason. Should've questioned how observant he must have been to catch both my first and last name in a class that doesn't do rollcall. My suspicions should have been piqued. But I was young. Naive. My enemies were a mix of dragons, vampires, and mercenaries.*

*He caught up with me. "Seriously, man. I got jobs. They pay good. You're a codester, right? It's sick shit. Addictive like crack. Gnarly brain candy."*

*"No, thanks." The sun was bright that day. I stopped to get my sunglasses from the front pocket of my backpack. If only it had been a cloudy day, that would've been the end of it. With those short legs of his, he would've had to run to keep up with me.*

Thirty minutes later, I pull into a parking spot across from The Bookery near Sonoma Square. I slam the truck door closed, and it bangs. It's a gas-guzzling relic. Three trips into town, and it's sitting close to empty. Rust lines the door frame and speckles the hood. But it's a truck that sits around Kairi's mom's vineyard for anyone to use.

While free is nice, if we're staying in the States, I should get my own vehicle. We've been lying low, but I am itching for a change in scenery. Hence the third time I've driven down to work from a musty bookshop.

Wolf might be on to something by researching and picking a destination. He's hot on Santa Barbara right now. He's been searching for commercial space to build out our headquarters. Because now we're legit, and we'll have clients.

There's a chill in the air as I jaywalk across the street. I wonder if she'll be there again today. She's the proprietor, but surely there are days she lets staff take over.

One car slows, and I nod in its direction, appreciative. I've lived in cities where you take your life in your own hands by crossing the street in an unmarked spot.

I reach The Bookery doors and slide off my sunglasses. The bell chimes, announcing my entrance. There are no customers. No one is in the store—at all. A faint coffee aroma fills the space. A door behind the coffee counter swings open.

Firefly halts and the swinging door slaps against her back. Her thick mane is braided once again, and it drapes over her shoulder, curling over the curve of her breast. Loose strands twist below her jawline. Those pale blue eyes zero in on me. No, that's not accurate. I zero in on them. Maybe it's because I've spent years in a majority brown-eyed world, but I can't look away. They are so light, like ice or sky. Not at all what I imagined, not that I spent time imagining what he or she looked like. Her lips are pale pink, and like her eyes, almost void of color. My breathing becomes shallower, and I force a deep breath through my lungs.

"You're back." She sounds surprised.

"Do you mind?" I head to my table.

"No. Of course not. Can I get you something to drink?"

"A regular coffee." She has a board filled with whipped cream options, but I don't do foo-foo. A vision of a dollop of whip cream on each of her nipples comes out of nowhere. My brain is mutinous.

"I have some beans from South Africa that are going to have a stronger taste and some from Venezuela with a milder taste. It's probably more along the lines of what some people consider breakfast coffee."

"I'll take the South African. A splash of soy."

"Coming right up."

The place is empty, and therefore I hear her moving, lifting a mug, pulling on a lever. I hear every step of her boot against the wood planks. My Chromebook powers up, and I focus on the progress bar. I not only hear her approach, but I sense her nearness.

"Would you like some water?"

"Maybe later?"

"Sure thing. Just call out if you need anything."

"Does it bother you?" She halts in her tracks and her braid swings over her shoulder and down the middle of her back.

"What?"

"If I sit here all day? Using your Wi-Fi?"

Her pale pink lips curve upward. "Not at all. Makes it look like I have a customer."

She returns to the barista counter. She leans against it, her own mug steaming while reading from a device. It's small and lies flat on the counter. She uses the tip of her finger to swipe. I think it's her phone. I resume plugging the charging cord into the outlet in the wall and getting my workstation set up for the day. I toggle the VPN, hovering to ensure I am connected securely.

The front door swings open, setting off the chime. An older man with gray hair and a full beard, and a woman, presumably his wife, enter. The woman leaves the man in her wake and heads straight for the counter. As she orders her coffee, the man sits down in a leather chair and thumbs through a book. I'm reading an article from *Wired* that someone on my Twitter feed shared, but it's nonsense, and I can't help watching the customers. The woman walks around, perusing the books. She ordered her coffee in a to-go cup, and she sips it as she reads the spines on the shelves.

"Oh, Tom, look at this." She sets her coffee down on the edge of a shelf and lifts an enormous book. "It features all the wineries in the Sonoma area. And look, we've been to most of these."

"Bring it here," he says to her. She does, and he snaps a photo of the cover with his phone. "I'll order it on Amazon."

"But…" I can hear the hesitation. "Shouldn't we buy it from here? While we're here?"

"Joan. That book weighs twenty-five pounds. It'll make our luggage overweight. I'll order it now, and it'll be waiting for you when we get home. If you want a trinket, we can go back to the hotel store or that Christmas store."

"I want to stop by the sock store to get the boys' socks."

"Fine. We've got an hour before the bus leaves." He gets up, and they move as a unit.

Firefly gives no indication she heard the conversation, but I can't help but wonder how her business is surviving. Which reminds me, when I asked if she needed money, trying to understand why she would entertain a text from a complete stranger, she didn't really respond.

I open Zeitgeist, careful to angle my monitor to the wall. I mute the audio and skim the old texts.

> *Firefly:* I researched. They opened a market a few years ago. Apparently, there's an exchange, but it's a bidding system. Like eBay for virtual goods. Anyone approach you?

> *Firefly:* Something's going on. Just had another offer. Crazy. Can other players see how much is in my treasure chest?

Next to the counter, she rests her chin on her hand, all her attention focused on whatever she's reading. She's in her own world, so I respond.

> *Phoenix:* Ignore offers from strangers. They'll assume
> you dropped out. You did, rt?

When I quit playing, she said she quit too. It's a time suck of a game. There's a ding on her computer. I'd go insane if I had notifications turned on. She smiles at her monitor and types. I wait.

> *Firefly:* Would you be jealous if I played?

> *Firefly:* Just joshing. No, I haven't played in ages. It's wild
> players are contacting me out of the blue. I'm reading
> the most amazing book right now. The person is
> traveling the globe, seeking the happiest place on
> earth.

> *Firefly:* If you could live anywhere in the world, where
> would you choose?

Apropos. I kick back, thinking about locations. I've lived all over the world, admittedly for fleeting amounts of time. I liked Seattle, where I grew up. But the threat of being recognized is too great. Kane and I have overlapping friend circles.

I suspect she lived in Paris. A VPN can shroud location, but I don't think she uses a VPN. Multiple times I pinged her in the same general area in Paris. During part of that time, I lived in Hong Kong. Part of the time in Bangkok. And for some of those years, I moved frequently.

When threat levels rose perilously high, I sent my twin, Cali, to live on an isolated island for her safety. She now lives near DC with her husband. Cali swears she likes the area, but I think the traffic would be exhausting. Tokyo is an enthralling city, but...I'll get a much bigger kick out of watching her response if I answer her this way.

> *Phoenix*: Anywhere in the world? I'd say Napa. California.

Chimes announce a new arrival, and we both look. Wolf fills the door. The guy is enormous. A former SEAL, he's ripped. He's also my favorite sparring partner when I want to practice jiu-jitsu. He can beat me in any other sport—running, swimming, biking, shooting—but when it comes to martial arts, I've been a student since the age of four. I can take him. But he's always a challenge.

"Hey." I hold up my coffee mug in greeting. He pulls out the chair across from me, whips it around so it's backward, and straddles it. Out of the corner of my eye, I notice Firefly is captivated. *Huh. Is he her type?*

"Who's the platinum blonde?" His question is low and discreet.

"What?" I grit out. The asswipe chuckles.

"Down, boy. I take it you confirmed she's your gamer?" He leans over. "You gonna out yourself?"

29

"No." I close the laptop lid. Her phone rings and she steps behind the swinging door. "She can't ever know." He pointedly looks at my computer. "She's not going to figure it out. I won't let her."

"Why? Because of Kairi?"

"One, Lara." It's unbelievable I have to remind him. "Two, no."

"Hey, I get it. It's a code with you guys. First name only. But she's not a hacker, right? She's a gamer. She'd be floored. You might get some."

"No." I shake my head. He's pissing me off. Kairi's right. We can't be too cautious. I asked him here to check the place out. "She has a cash register out in the open, and she works by herself."

"Does she know I'm doing this security review?"

The door swings, and she re-enters. She approaches our table, and he keeps his lips zipped.

"Can I get you something to drink?" she offers.

"No, thanks." They check each other out right in front of me. Unbelievable. I should just leave.

"Do you need anything else?" My mug is almost empty, so I pass it over to her. She looks at me like she expects me to say something. What did she ask me? I can't remember, so I tell her thank you, and she goes back to the barista station.

"Did you give any more thought to Santa Barbara?" Wolf gives no indication he grasps how annoyed I am. At him.

"Was I supposed to?"

"Yes. Why don't you come with me to lunch? My laptop's in the trunk."

"I told you to do what you want."

"But I think you'll like the place. We need offices. That place of Kairi's worked initially, but we're shredding each other's last nerve being on top of each other. Plus, Farmville is not your speed." He slips a phone out of his pocket and slides it across the table.

"What's that?"

"A phone. Your burners drive me nuts. This one's secure."

I check it out. It's an iPhone. I prefer BlackBerry. He's already set it up. And there's a directory with our team's numbers. I have all the numbers memorized. I don't need an address book.

"How safe?"

He explains this iPhone is supplied by the NSA and has EncroChat installed.

"That's still around? Didn't the feds bust a ton of people using that?" I glance over at Firefly, but she's not paying us any attention. I'd love to untie her braid and let her hair fall loose around her shoulders.

"You're not public enemy number one. You'll be fine with this. At least keep it on you so we can reach you. Especially if you're going to be working remotely." I get messages through different messaging services our team uses on varying browsers. They can always reach me.

A delivery guy straining with a large box enters. It's the same delivery guy from the other day. I drop the phone into my bag. One more device to charge.

"You want me to take this down to the basement for you?" the guy asks her.

"No, I can get it." Firefly answers without hesitation, her tone light.

"Are you sure? It's heavy. I almost used a pulley."

"Well, if you wouldn't mind."

"Not at all, Vivi."

I don't like how he looks at her or how he says her name with a high degree of familiarity. The name on the domain address for The

Bookery is Vivianne Rossi. He called her Vivi. How well does he know her? And what's in her basement? Books?

A throaty noise from Wolf reminds me he's still sitting at my table.

"Want me to scope out the basement too?" The smirk on his face annoys me. My negative energy is high this morning. I should've run sprints. "Why don't we leave now for lunch? It's late enough."

And leave while she's down in the basement with that guy? Absolutely not. He could attack her down there. She's a sitting duck.

"No worries. We'll wait until she's back up here," Wolf says. The guy is so intuitive it's frightening.

# SOCIAL SECURITY

VIVI

"Be careful," I call after the man with a Kevin name tag as he navigates the stairs with a box so large there's no way he can see each step. It's super sweet of him to do this. I didn't pay the extra charge for delivery to the basement. He's such a friendly guy. He probably doesn't comprehend how much trouble he'd be in if he slipped on these stairs and his bosses had to use their insurance to cover the value of this shipment. "Careful," I repeat.

The musty basement odor strengthens the farther down the stairs we go. I recently converted the finished basement into a cellar, and I'm slowly filling it up with my private collection of California and French wines, thanks to regular winnings at the online Chicago auction house.

Now and then, I'll have a few friends over and light candles, and we'll share wine and food down here. There's something about eating in a cellar, especially one with a barrel brick ceiling. That's memorable. I direct Kevin to the oak table in the center of the room, and he heaves the box onto it.

"More wine?" Kevin asks.

"It's my thing."

The tip of his nose bumps the glass on one of the wine refrigerators doors. "You in wine clubs or something? I feel like I deliver to you every week."

"Does anyone live in this area and not join a few wine clubs?" I could tell him the back story on this shipment, but I seriously doubt he wants to hear about the historical sales value of these wines and why I believe I got a deal. My granddad would wax poetic about the vintage, the weather that year, the winemaker's philosophy and approach, and keep the poor guy trapped in conversation for forty-five minutes.

Kevin explores the space, his hands in his pockets as he peruses the perimeter of the room. Natural stone, original to the house, lines the walls. The ceiling is a feature I added. My guests love to peruse the exquisite wine labels.

"Thank you so much for your help. You ready?" I gesture to the stairs. "I've got to get back up."

"Oh, yeah. How many bottles would you say you have down here?"

"I have no idea. I really need to start keeping up with that, huh?" I comment more to myself than to Kevin as we climb the stairs, me leading him up the stairs this time.

"Nah, I guess not. If you're gonna drink it, why catalog it?"

I do keep a record of all the wine I buy and sell. I need to for insurance, but I don't feel the need to explain myself to Kevin. And while I don't know the total bottle count off the top of my head, I have an Excel sheet on file that has the number readily available. But there's room for improvement in my organization. I might have a list of my bottles, but locating them would be a time-consuming matter. My system would not impress Granddad.

I close the heavy door behind Kevin, and he nods a goodbye.

"Thanks again, Kevin," I say to his retreating back.

Mr. IT and his oversized friend are at the corner table speaking in hushed voices. I resume my position behind the counter, flip open my laptop, and covertly watch the two men. They're both good-looking. The one dressed in black, the one who always dresses in black, is serious. His lips remain in a flat line as he converses with his friend. Or colleague. I don't think lover. They don't look like lovers.

His friend's back is to me, but given he's straddling a backward-facing chair, Mr. Tech appears to be the older, more mature person counseling a less disciplined friend on a matter of importance. Maybe he's the boss.

The door swings open, and a couple enters. They are married. I can tell by the way they surround each other and point at books. The matching wedding bands. That's another dead giveaway. The woman glances at me. She feels me staring.

I turn my attention to my laptop and enter my screensaver password. I ignore a mustached man waffling in front of the counter as he's reading the menu board and click on a message notification.

> Phoenix: Anywhere in the world? I'd say Napa. California.

I blink. The world slows, and I scan the store. There's no way. Out of all the places in the world, he could say—Somehow, he figured out where I am.

*He's messing with me. Right? What are the odds?* For all I know, he could be one of my customers. He could be Mr. Tech. After all, he's the first person to ever stake a spot in my bookstore.

His oversized friend rises and heads down the back hall to the restroom. Those dark frames tilt down, and his fingers type in a flurry.

Huh. Let's see. I type out my response.

> Firefly: Have you been there? Or is this based on travel blogs?

It's not the most original comeback, but all I need is to hear the notification. His fingers are flying over the keyboard.

His friend or colleague returns from the restroom, and Mr. Tech turns his laptop so the other man can see his screen. If he's Phoenix, he doesn't care at all about the notification. Or he's not Phoenix. A much more likely scenario.

*Ding.*

The high-pitched noise alerts me to a text. My fingers tingle. Mr. Tech and his bodybuilding friend are in deep conversation. If this response is from Phoenix, then he's not Mr. Tech. Which, of course, he's not the same guy. My imagination is bonkers. I need to rein it in. Try some focus vitamins.

I scan my screen. There's no message in the Zeitgeist app. Disappointment boomerangs inside me. The message is an actual text from Max.

> *Max: Can I go in on Granddad's birthday gift?*

I call my brother back. He answers on the first ring.

"I got him a gift, and yes, you can go in on it." We do this every year. Max doesn't particularly care to shop.

"What'd you get him?"

"You know how Granddad wanted a 1971 La Tache?"

"Sounds familiar."

"Well, I found two bottles."

"How much did you spend?"

"Don't worry about it. Just pay me what you were going to spend on his gift."

"You're going to blow through your trust fund."

"No, I'm not." Simply because he's the big brother, he thinks he knows all. My business instinct might not be fine-tuned, but I have my sources for revenue. Not that it's any of his business.

"Celeste said she's been trying to get you to meet her for lunch to go over the party menu." An engine revs in the background.

"I've told her more than once that I work. I can't just leave for lunch in the middle of the day."

"You don't have any employees yet? You can't be the only one there. What happens if you get sick? Or need a day off?"

Max is not wrong. I should hire employees. But the workload is manageable. And managing staff can be time-consuming.

"Vivi?" He yells the question. The tractor engine roars. He's pressing the accelerator, speeding to his next destination somewhere in the vineyard.

"I told Celeste to go with whatever she wants."

"Me too. Gotta run." He ends the call without a goodbye.

Our grandfather's eightieth birthday is in a couple of months. We're doing our traditional birthday party in the vineyard, only this year it's a surprise, and we've invited all of his friends. Celeste is insistent we make a big deal about this one, and she's using the same space we let others rent out for weddings and parties. My grandfather is a social guy, but he prefers his crowds to be a manageable size. I have a nagging suspicion my sister is going to overdo it. In her defense, it's not hard. He's lived here his whole life. He, and by extension, we, have a lot of friends in the valley.

Mr. IT's water glass is empty, so I carry a pitcher of water over to refill it. I can see his friend outside with a phone to his ear. As I pour water into the glass on the table, he continues typing, focused, and I take the opportunity to glance at his screen. Just the top right-hand corner where a notification would exist. But his screen is black, and he's coding.

"Are you looking at my—"

"No," I blurt as he covers his crotch. "Oh, my gosh. No. No."

Frick. He thinks I'm looking at his crotch. But looking at his monitor is worse. So, I back away. One backward step. Then another. My heart is racing.

I hit a hard wall—of man. It's his friend. I spin around him and resume my spot behind the counter. I refuse to look at the corner. I pick up my phone and text my friend Chloe. A man thinks I was staring at his crotch.


*Me: I need alcohol. You free tonight?*

*Chloe: Do you have cock tales???? Because I do!!!*

*Me: With who?*

*Chloe: This amazing guy. A Tinder find.*

There's no such thing as an amazing Tinder find.


*Me: What's his name?*

*Chloe: Bruce Williams. And he's so nice. He's on a business trip for the rest of this week, but he's back on Friday, and we're going out.*


Bruce Williams, huh? I open the TruthFinder app and enter his name. There are too many.


*Me: Where's he live now?*

*Chloe: Here! In Sonoma.*


I enter his location. That narrows it down.


*Me: Do you know his birthdate?*

*Chloe: OMG. Are you doing a background check?*

*Me: Y*

*Chloe: What is wrong with you? Why are you so paranoid?*


Because that is the world we live in. Why isn't she paranoid? She spent three months dating a guy with a fetish for dropping his pants and exposing himself. He was on the sex offenders' database. If she used

TruthFinder, she would have saved herself three months of dating a perv.

*Me: What's his horoscope sign?*

*Chloe: Nice try. CUL8R? 7?*

*Chloe: And when are you going to try Tinder? Or one of the dating sites with a psychological profile? You can have them reviewed, and background checked before hello.*

*Me: 7*

*Chloe: LMAO. At your wedding rehearsal, in my speech, I can say, "He had her with his background check."*
*Chloe: Not "He had her at hello." Get it?*

Chloe has been my best friend since elementary school. She's way too trusting and far too desperate to find a man. She needs me. I find a phone number for Bruce Williams in a White Pages directory. Then I enter it into TruthFinder. And lo and behold. Mr. Williams has an alias. And based on the data, it's looking like Bruce Williams is the identity without a social security number.

# SOCIAL ENGINEERING

ERIK

"Could this be Kane?"

Wolf's question unsettles me. We're always asking if T.J. Kanagasingam, or Kane for short, could be behind something. That's because we know how extensive his global syndicate has become. Although truth be told, Spectre is hardly the only crime syndicate. Although it might be the only one named after a James Bond film. Kane's bond fetish is legendary. Some people have a password methodology they use. Kane has a naming methodology. And while Spectre isn't the only crime syndicate, and it's not the biggest, it is the one we know best because we used to be a part of it.

The reason Wolf is on edge is that he's in charge of our physical safety, and he's always worried we've been located. Being physically located is a hacker's biggest fear.

I scan through the latest complaint from IC3, a division of the FBI. Since the US government pays our newly formed company to monitor the Dark Web for threats, they send us these reports to help us help them connect the dots. The vast Dark Web is full of anonymous, untraceable hackers. Some are more skilled than others.

Small-time con artists with a touch of tech-savvy steal a solid portion of the $4 to $5 billion stolen from Americans annually. It's the big-time players, the crime syndicates—think new-age mafia—that get our attention. It's a brave new world, and these powerful corporations often have alliances with governments with agendas that don't align with our own. It's become a big enough problem that governments back smaller companies unofficially to gain additional insights and to fight unofficial covert cyberwars.

I scroll through the list, scanning the dollar amounts of each complaint.

"Over half of these complaints are from the sixty-plus demographic. You'd think those old people would get wiser." My comment earns a scowl from Wolf.

"They've got money, and they aren't tech-savvy. Easy prey." Wolf doesn't care about the people who fall for phishing scams, and his fingers tap the corner of the desk. I get it. To him, their lives are safe. Their bank accounts might be less full, but they're still breathing. Wolf's wired to care about lives.

As I scan the list, I notice there's an increase in government impersonation scams, but it's not a surprise. We're approaching tax time. One dollar amount catches my eye.

"Is RAT on to this $60 million case?"

He shifts his chair over so he can see my screen.

"You can ask Trevor. I think he was on the phone with the Recovery Asset Team when I left this morning. That's who you're talking about, right?"

I nod. His disdain for acronyms doesn't make sense to me, given he's got a military background.

"I think they've located the funds and blocked them. They've asked

Kairi to search for a connection between that attempted heist and any syndicate or government. Trevor wanted me to mention it to you."

"I assume the FBI is all over the employee who actually processed the wire transfer?" So often we expect complicated schemes, and all they really did was bribe an employee.

"Kairi will have the full update. Like I said, she was on the phone when I left."

I continue scanning the report. Wolf taps his foot, anxious to leave. The delivery guy is long gone. Vivi is alternating between her laptop and her phone. She's animated. Her cheeks are flushed.

Were they flushed before the delivery guy took her down to the basement? There's something about that guy I don't like. He wears a uniform for a delivery service I've never heard of. The carrier's hair is slightly greasy, and he wears a gold chain.

"What do you think she's storing downstairs? Books and supplies?"

I ponder Wolf's question. She had to sign for the delivery, but I could see that happening with any number of different items.

"You want to get down there?" I ask him.

"Well, I'm going to need to come here at night to install the system, right?"

"She lives above this place. You can't safely break-in at night." He frowns at my information.

"You know, we could pull a scam from the IC3 list," he says as he rocks back on the back two legs of his chair.

"Sit down. You'll fall backward." The man can be such a child. "Which scam?" My gaze returns to the list. The FBI categorizes all fraud.

"Sweepstakes scam? Tell her she won a security system? Make it sound like all we ask is for her testimonial for our service?"

I scratch my neck, thinking about how to pull it off. It's not a bad idea.

"What kind of system are you thinking?" I ask. I like cameras. Then I can check and make sure she's safe at any point during the day. And I can even put her on rotation with my security team to ensure she's safe. But I did that with my sister, and she pushed back big time. Turns out not all women like cameras on them. Cali's angry tone reverberates in my mind. She was beyond pissed. "At a minimum, she needs a camera over the store entrance and the back exit."

"Where's the back exit go?"

"A courtyard."

"A view of the back wall of the building via camera would be useful, should anyone attempt to break in off the main street. That would be sufficient for most businesses, but now that I see you're into her, I'm assuming you're going to want an alarm system and probably a camera upstairs near her apartment entrance. Maybe inside the store, too, with a view over the cash register?" He crosses his arms and leans back again, his weight lifting the front two legs a couple of inches above the wooden floor.

"I'm not into her." His comment irks me. Why is he talking? She might hear him. "You're going to break that chair."

I've never been into a girl. I don't do relationships. Back in Asia, I was a member of clubs with like-minded people. People who wanted sex and no expectations—not even a name. There's nothing like that out here.

"I haven't seen you so concerned for someone since you put me in charge of Cali's safety." His comparison of my twin sister to a gaming partner is absurd. There's no comparison. It's in my blood to protect people. I originally began hacking in an effort to make the Internet safer for all people, not just the people I care about. And yes, maybe my experiences have contributed to a heightened sense of awareness of the dangers around us, but I am right.

The shop door swings open, and the jingle announces Trevor. He's in a T-shirt, cargo shorts, and Tevas. He spots us and heads over. Wolf stands as he approaches.

"Lunch," he commands.

I gather up my laptop. Vivi's light blue eyes meet mine as I step off the platform. I slide our dirty glasses to her across the bar.

"Have a good afternoon." She licks her lips and smiles. I want her to speak again so I can glimpse inside her mouth, see if she has a tongue ring. She has so many piercings on her earlobes. They twinkle beneath the store lights.

"Dude. You coming?" Her cheeks flush. Her skin is so pale. I want to reach out and touch her, to compare and contrast her pale tone to my olive tone.

The bells jingle, and someone coughs. I don't want to break our locked gaze. When I do, I glare at the two buttheads who have the patience of a small child.

The moment we're on the sidewalk, Wolf starts in.

"You've got to decide how we're doing this. I recommend you come out and tell her you've got money to burn, you're obsessed with security, and you'd like to ensure her business and her wares are safe, so you're installing a state-of-the-art system at no charge."

He's direct and pissy. The smallest offense sets us off. Wolf is correct. Our live-work arrangement needs improvement. It's one reason I set out to find another location to work. Wolf might think it's girl-related, but he's wrong.

"You've seen what you need to see?" I ask Wolf.

"Well, except for downstairs and upstairs. But the only way we're getting that is through you telling her, a scam, or I break in. You could take her out on a date, and I could break in while you're out with her." Wolf smirks.

"Neither of you has asked me, but my initial reaction is to side with Kairi. Staying away from her is the safest tactic," Trevor butts in. He's doing the scanning thing he always does outdoors, searching for any evil in the shadows.

"I'm not near her. She doesn't even know my name."

Wolf coughs into his hand. Trevor and I both look his way.

"I'm taking off for a couple of days. Alasdair is staying behind. When I get back, if this is still a project, I'll tackle it then."

"You driving down to Santa Barbara?"

"I want to check out the space before we sign. Vet the area. I'll be back next week."

"Okay. FYI, I'm putting a new batch of servers in Reykjavik."

"Okay," Wolf responds. He understands the ins and outs of hardware. I'm the hardware guy. I ensure we have a complex network that makes it impossible to be located. Every hacker needs to have an array of tactics at their disposal to avoid location. Now that we're flipped and we're black ops for the US government, it's just as important no one ever traces us. Maybe more important, depending on what line we're crossing.

"Do you think we can find space near here to rent?" Trevor asks.

"What?" I can't keep up with Trev today. His question is left field.

"I like what you're doing. Getting out of the house. I don't do a lot online, but I field security agent applicants. Beef up our on-call directory."

"If you took up a spot on a different table, I don't see why there'd be an issue. It would make her place look busier. No one would ever look at the two of us and think we're colleagues." My disparaging comment takes aim at his state of dress, but it flies over his head.

"We both look like coders."

No, I do not look like a coder. A Lululemon fan, possibly. An assassin, maybe, but not a stereotypical coder in a shitty tee.

Trevor pops in his earbuds and joins in a call with the IC3. He's one of our liaisons. I do not have the patience.

Our contact at the Internet Crime Complaint Center has a theory that a new crime syndicate has come on the scene, but his observations don't jive with what we're seeing in the Dark Web boards and groups we monitor. His theory that a new group based out of Nicaragua is interesting, but I see the country as more of a source for cheap labor to fuel sock puppet operations and low-level scams. It's hard for me to imagine an executive strategic team based out of the country.

After lunch, we say goodbye to Wolf. Trevor and I return to The Bookery. He's busy with the IC3, and I'm back to writing code. He's got his laptop, and I've got mine. Our surroundings fade out as I focus on the task at hand. I've been like this my entire life. When I get into a project, whether it's coding or a game, everything else falls away. It used to drive my sister batty.

A gentle touch to my shoulder pulls me out of the black hole, and I squint as light infiltrates my viewing field.

"I'm closing up soon." Those blue eyes are patient. There's no sign of annoyance. I rub the back of my neck and become aware I need to go to the restroom, so I stand. "You must love what you do."

Her loose strand falls forward, covering one of her eyes, and I reach out and tuck it behind her ear. I am not a touchy-feely guy. An electrical shock zaps my finger, and I jerk it back.

She smiles. "Static electricity."

My hand falls over my laptop lid, closing it down.

Her upper tooth digs into her lower lip, and she gives me a small, timid smile. Her perfume is musky. It's faint. I've never smelled anything quite like it. Trevor watches us from a table six feet away. I want him gone.

"I've never seen anyone so glued to a task."

"Did I not hear you?" People say that to me when they think I'm ignoring them. She said something, and I didn't hear. I hate I do that. It's one reason I depend on security systems. I need to be alerted loudly if danger approaches.

"Yeah." Her smile widens.

The bell over the door rings, and she straightens as her gaze moves beyond me.

"Do I owe you?" I hold up an empty plate. I don't have any idea why it's on my table.

"No. Trevor paid." Of course, he did. He probably ate cake or a cookie. He eats continuously. And she knows his name. He must have had a conversation with her.

The moment I return from the restroom, Trevor gives me an annoying know-it-all smirk.

"Yes?" I say.

"She's special."

She is, but what is he seeing in her? He didn't play on a team with her for years. He doesn't have a text exchange with her that spans almost fifteen years.

That smirk remains until we're out on the sidewalk. The second the shop door closes behind us, he chooses to annoy me further.

"She's the first person who has ever pulled you out of a coma and didn't get their head bitten off."

He's absurd. All of my colleagues remain in possession of their craniums.

# KILL CHLOE

VIVI

I'm midway into the latest Louise Bay novel about a hot British billionaire when the bell chimes. With great reluctance, I set my phone down and put on my customer service face. Yes, I'll admit, part of the reason I opened a bookstore is because I love reading. The requisite customer interaction isn't an aspect of the business I sufficiently weighed.

Chloe enters, smiles, then pauses at the table near the front door where I've set out the new releases and Napa Valley travel guides. She picks up a colorful title and carries it with her. As the book hits the counter, her attention circles the two men in the corner.

"You have customers," she comments.

"Well, cafe customers." I imagine these two men would only buy e-books. Although, they say the world of novels only exists because of women since men never read fiction. So, maybe they don't even possess an e-reader. The theory delivers a touch of sadness. I don't technically use my e-reader. I'm positive it's sitting at home without a charge. But, on my phone, I have multiple e-reading apps. And yes, I also own a bookshop. It's a quandary.

"They're cute." She doesn't whisper, and I wish a barista bar wasn't between us so I could give her a swift warning kick.

"Do you want coffee?"

"Yes, please," she answers while continuing to blatantly check them out. "Are they tourists?"

"I don't think so." I pour the honey into Chloe's cup, just the way she likes it, and lick the remnant off my finger. Probably so against health code, but she's not watching me. As I slide the mug over to her, in a conspiratorial tone, I fill her in. "The guy in the dark gray shorts and black V-neck? With the glasses? He's been coming regularly. The other guy is his friend. They work together. Tech. He said he lives in the area."

"Which one are you placing dibs on?"

"Neither." I let out a half-laugh.

"The guy with the glasses. He's so your type." Yeah, she's right. I love a good sexy nerd. Always have. I dream of a nerdy literature major.

"He's probably gay," I tell Chloe. I don't believe it, but saying things like that helps to temper expectations.

"No." She shakes her head. "My gaydar has not flared. Why do you say that?"

"Because. This is my shop. Our lives. Do you really think a good-looking, single, available, straight guy is going to pick my bookstore to work from?" Thinking back to the book she interrupted me from reading, I add, "I'd have a better chance of taking a nannying job and the guy being a hot, single dad."

"Wealthy. Don't forget wealthy."

"What?" I ask.

"If you're going to trope dream, don't forget wealthy."

"Would you quit staring over there?"

"Neither of them has looked up from their laptops. We're safe."

"That may be true, but people can feel someone's eyes on them."

"No, they can't."

"No, they can. It's scientifically proven."

"Uh-huh. The same way it's scientifically proven you can use your mental waves to move a stone?"

I went to Canyon Ranch one time and came back all excited that I could move a crystal by focusing on it, and Chloe has never let me live it down. She called bullshit and then pointed out that my hand holding the chain attached to the crystal was vibrating and therefore moving the stone. She's my best friend, but sometimes I don't like her.

"Stop staring. Look at me." She rests her hand on her palm and stares at the two guys, ignoring me. Well, on the bright side, it'll be easier for me to break my news while she's jonesing for a stranger. "I did some digging on your Tinder date."

She turns her head. Of course this gets her attention.

"And?" I could swear her pupils increased in size. I hate to have to be the one to tell her this, but it's better she finds out early.

"He's married. His real name is Bradley Lilith. He has three children."

"Do I want to know how you found this out?"

"Does it matter?" Yes, it's human nature to want to shoot the messenger. But, in this case, the blowhole hunting for hook-ups under an alias is the one who should be shot. And he messed with the wrong girl. I'm not a gun-toter, but I know how to hack an Instagram account. He's going down. I've outed him on Insta and FB. Next up, Tinder. I just need to locate a tiny dick pic to post on his caption.

Chloe sips her coffee, then mutters, "Damnit. Another jerk." She picks up her phone and taps away.

"I'm calling dibs on the cargo pants guy."

"His name is Trevor." He hasn't shared a last name yet, though. I don't have enough data to clear him on TruthFinder. "Aren't you waiting for David James to come back to town?"

David is a good friend of my older brothers. Chloe had a massive crush on him when we were freshmen.

Chloe sighs. Her wheels are turning. She's staring at Trevor, no doubt weighing him versus David versus whoever is in the queue on her dating app.

"Yeah, you're right. He's supposed to move back soon." She taps her cheek thoughtfully. "But that doesn't mean you shouldn't do something about your dream nerd."

"Like what? He's not into me. His friend talks to me, but he doesn't. I'm not his type."

"I doubt that. He probably assumes you're not available."

"Yes, the absence of rings on my fingers could definitely give him that impression."

"No, you have this vibe about you. All the guys in high school used to mention it. You just aren't very approachable."

"Thanks." I'm not even sure what to do with that comment.

"Therefore, you should ask him out."

I spit some of my coffee across the bar, and it splatters her crisp white blouse.

"Hey, I have to go to work later."

"Sorry. But I am not asking him out. He's a patron. Of my shop. A customer."

"Well, then, it's time we set you up on Tinder." I give her my 'hell no' expression. "Or there are a lot of services. Eharmony. Do some research and take your pick."

"Thanks, but no thanks."

"Then I'll create a profile for you."

"No. Way." I grind out the words and speak loudly enough that Trevor looks our way.

"What are you going to do? Hideaway in this bookshop for the next decade? Thirty is looming. And forty comes lickety-split after that. You've got to get out there. Live." This is coming from the girl who almost dated a married man with a fake moniker. "With an app, you can background check away. Find someone who isn't from here, doesn't care one iota about the Rossi name. You know, I'm going to help you. I need to take a dating breather. I'm going to help you find someone." She flutters her hand and returns to staring down the two men.

"Let me get this straight. You're striking out on dating apps, so now you're going to parlay an identical dating strategy onto me?"

"Aren't you lucky?" She grins. "Ask him out on a date."

"No."

"Yes." She pushes her coffee mug my way and points a stiff index finger at me. "Ask him, or I do something."

"Bitch."

She smirks. "You've been back for ages. At first, I accepted you were trying to get your business open, and you needed to get your feet on the ground. But now you spend your days locked in the building. It's like we're still in quarantine, except we're not. You've got to break out of that introverted shell."

"I am an introvert. There's nothing to break out of. That's who I am." She can be so incredibly frustrating.

"He's your type. And who knows how long he's gonna be coming into your shop to work. Ask him out. You can't really ask him to coffee, but ask him to do something."

"Don't you have to be at work?" Hope that she has a pressing need to vacate the premises fills me. She's not whispering, and I don't know why she seems to think there's a wall between us and the back corner tables. I work from over there—when no one is in here. I can hear everything that happens in this store from that corner. I can even hear people walking by on the sidewalk.

"Ugh. I do need to go to work. It should be slow. I'll create your Tinder profile for you."

"Did Bruce teach you nothing? If not for me, you would've been dating a married man. With kids. Three of them."

"One rotten apple doesn't mean the whole barrel is bad."

The bell chimes as she departs. She can be infuriating. I rinse her mug in the sink then set it in the dishwasher. The bell chimes again, and I whip around in time to see the door close behind Trevor. Mr. Tech, or as Chloe referred to him, the sexy nerd, remains focused on his laptop screen.

Over the next hour, customers trail in, seeking something nonalcoholic after a day of wine tastings. I sell a few vineyard maps and reflect on my grandfather's suggestion that I sell more gift store items.

The minute hand on the clock over the door clicks to the twelve, and it's officially six p.m. It's closing time. I wipe down the counter, prepared to go rest a hand on Mr. Sexy's shoulder and break his focus, but to my surprise, when I look up, he's standing before me.

"You've already paid." I smile to soften my words. It sounds a little bitchy, but I don't mean to be. Therefore, I smile.

"Vivi, we haven't officially met. I'm Erik." He shoves his hands into his shorts pockets and stares at the ground. "My friend says I should ask you out on a date. Would you be available for dinner tomorrow night?"

I'm going to kill Chloe.

# PERSONAL DATA

ERIK

"Did you ask her out?" Trevor says as I toe off my shoes.

"Ask who out?" Kairi butts in.

I ignore them and open the refrigerator.

"That is disgusting. Put your name on the bottle. It's now yours." I ignore Kairi, down the last of the milk, then head to the sink to rinse it out before dropping it in the recycle bin. "What is your problem?"

She's got a hand on her hip, all attitude.

"I don't see a need to get out a glass when I'm going to finish—"

"Not that, dumb ass. Who's the girl?" She crosses her arms. Trevor's footsteps pound down the hall, and he enters the kitchen with a smug smile.

I've officially hit my max with roommates. I need to live somewhere else. Their mere presence raises my blood pressure. We've worked together for ages, but living together is a recent predicament. These guys are closer to me than my blood relatives, but I am over cohabitating.

"He's got a thing for that shopgirl. And it sounds like she might have a thing for our man here, too."

"What shop?" Kairi directs her question to Trevor.

"The Bookery? On Sonoma Square."

"I don't remember that store. I haven't been down there in years."

That would be the reason she doesn't remember it. The store's website domain was claimed less than two years ago, but I don't offer the information. Instead, I glare at my two roommates, debating how to best address the fact that the time has come for me to move out.

"Her name is Vivi. She has a friend named Chloe. Is that going to win any name game points?" He hops up on the counter to sit.

"Holy shit. Vivianne Rossi?" Kairi asks.

"She's blonde, blue eyes. Breasts like…" Trevor holds his hands up as if he's cupping breasts against his chest, and Kairi reaches for him, pulling his hands down, her face scrunched up, expressing her disgust.

"Yes, she's younger than me." That information gets my attention.

"How much younger?" I ask.

"Oh, at least four years. I was a senior when she was a freshman. I didn't know her well, but I'm friends with her brother. The Rossi's are like an institution in the valley. I had heard she moved to Paris."

My IP trace had confirmed her location in Paris for several years. *Four years younger? I've been playing Zeitgeist with Firefly since I was a sophomore in high school. That would've put her at like, what, twelve? Eleven? Is she not Firefly? Did the original Firefly trade her avatar? But even if she did, it wouldn't affect the messaging app.*

My brain churns, processing this information.

"And Chloe…" Kairi raps her thumb against her chin. "The name is familiar, but hell, it could be familiar because of a Hollywood actress."

"Chloe's kind of hot. But she seems immature. Going on and on about Tinder. Which, man, you never answered the question. Did you ask Vivi out?"

"We're going out tomorrow night."

"Good." He grins, and by doing so, grates my raw nerves.

"What happened to us agreeing we shouldn't date anyone right now?" Kairi asks.

"No, Kairi, trust me. If you saw him with her…"

I exhale, pick up my messenger bag while Trevor blabs, and exit the room. After I locate an apartment, I'll tell them I'm moving out. At my age, I shouldn't have roommates. This was all supposed to be a temporary situation. Then it became more permanent when my brother-in-law opened the doorway to an agreement with the US government around the same time we had to run for cover. The feds overlooked my past transgressions in exchange for my working for them. I didn't desire a future on a most wanted list, so I agreed. Kairi, Trevor, and I had been busy getting all the kinks worked out. Living together facilitated a non-stop work environment. But I need space.

I don't disagree with Kairi. My life is complicated. Dating isn't a thing I do. I didn't overhear the conversation that Trevor did, but when he texted that I'd better ask her out or she'd be on Tinder — that was all the encouragement I needed.

Romance scams are one of the leading cons out there. It's my job to know this. Sickos pretend to be someone they're not, all the while looking to siphon off money from some sucker looking for love. Most of the pervs that hit the FBI report strung along dozens of unsuspecting people. No, that's definitely not a world I want Firefly, Vivi, or Vivianne mixing in.

Besides, I'm curious. I've been curious about her for as long as I can remember. Or since that day when I got an anniversary notification that she and I had been teammates for one year. No one survived as my partner for that long. We'd virtually high fived. And then she messaged me. Lowkey gaming strategy. Jesus, had I really been playing Zeitgeist with her since she was eleven or twelve?

Blasting away bad guys had served as my favorite form of decompression for years. Television bored me. I liked the interaction of a good game. Back and forth.

"You got my right?" Boom.

"Still got a tank?" Explosion.

A whole pack of fire-eating zombies appears? "Open that sorcery book."

Fun times. Carefree. Then one T.J. Kane appeared.

*"Have you ever thought about making a difference?"*
*"Like what? Teaching?" He tucked in his shirts, and his pants were high-waisted. We were in grad school. Quite a few of our classmates had teaching on their radar.*
*"No, man. Dream bigger. Way bigger." I chugged the beer. I'd agreed to one beer, but I wanted to get back home and fire up Zeitgeist. "Join the war."*
*"What war?" Enthusiasm poured off him. I expected he was about to tell me about a killer new game, and I wasn't opposed to learning about anything cutting edge.*
*"The war for net safety. For an even playing field. White versus black, and I'm not talking race. I'm talking intent. And you can make money too."*
*"How?"*
*"You take jobs. You can code. Like, actually code. You're not a cut and paster. You'll make more than me."*
*"What kind of jobs?"*

*"Friendly attacks. Look for weaknesses. As you get a rep, you can scan code for backdoors. ID malicious code. It's like gaming. With levels. Challenge. Only you get paid. Sometimes crypto."*

*"Friendly?"*

*"Yeah. Companies hire you."*

*"How much?"*

*"Ranges. Start with five hundred. Pretty quickly progresses into the thousands. It's sick money for a few days' work. I'll show you."*

───

"You know, you didn't really have to ask me out."

The closed sign clicks against the glass. My palms are sweaty, and I wipe them against my jeans.

She's dressed for a date. She's wearing a long white dress that hugs her curves and a cardigan with a floral pattern. Thin silver necklaces shine in the light, and her shiny hair bounces with loose curls. She's looking at the ground, and when she finally lifts her gaze and I take in those light blue irises, my chest aches. It's an uncomfortable sensation, and I soothe it by pressing my palm to my sternum.

She stands there, watching me, and I remember the first thing she said when I arrived. It's the only thing she's said to me.

"Do you not want to go?" I don't understand her comment. Why would I have to ask her out? Did she see Trevor's text to me? Is she monitoring my texts?

"No, it's just…" Her voice trails off. "Let's go. I'd like to get to know you." She locks the door, and I scan the overhang. There are no security cameras. Wolf hasn't performed his magic yet. But that's because he's waiting for me to see if I can get her to approve it.

"Have you ever considered security cameras?"

"No. There's really no theft around here." She drops a large keyring into her pocketbook.

"There's theft everywhere." It's not acceptable to be that naïve. It makes her a sitting target.

I guide her across the street to where I parked. Movement in a car parked one block down, on the side of the street of her shop, catches my eye. A man sits in the driver's seat. He looks away. The hair follicles on the back of my neck rise.

I open the passenger door of Trevor's dark gray Tesla and watch the vehicle as Vivi gets in. The man sits still. I slide into the driver's seat and watch the man out of the rearview. He doesn't appear to be doing anything.

"Do you like this car?" Vivi asks. I'd planned on taking the vineyard's pickup, but Trevor insisted I take his car. It's still relatively new and has that new car smell.

"I do. It's not mine. But I think I'm going to buy one. I like driving it. Watch this," I say as I reverse and head down the street. I've already entered the restaurant's address into the navigation, so I hit the button, and the car takes over, driving us around the square. The man in the car remains parked. Good.

"It's driving for you." She smiles. "Yeah, I know a lot of people with Teslas."

So, the self-driving feature didn't impress her. *But does she know about this?*

"My balls are hot," I tell Siri.

"What?" Vivi's smile widens, and I think she might laugh.

"Did you notice the temperature just dropped?"

Her fingers rub the seat leather, and she nods.

"Now. Watch." I tell her. Then I address the car. "My balls are cold."

The wavy lines for the heated seats light up on the dash. I point because I don't think she notices.

"The seat warmers just came on," I tell her.

"No way." She's amused. I think it's a cool feature. I could go on about how to open the charging port by saying 'Open Butthole.' I really do like this car. I'll order one tomorrow.

"Do you always wear black?" she asks. That's a change in conversation.

"I'm colorblind. Everything I buy is black or gray. That way, I don't have to worry about something not matching."

"Being colorblind just means red and green get confused, right?"

"Technically, but I'm still off on colors. I used to do web design. Things I thought looked great would get shrieks of disapproval. My perception is different. I like black. No one ever tells me I don't match. It works for me. Easy. And everything comes in black."

"So, I suppose your Tesla, should you order one, will be black on black?"

"Nah. There are too many dusty roads around here. I'll probably go titanium."

She looks out the window, watching as the car heads out on a highway.

"Where are we going?"

"A place a friend recommended. SingleThread. She said it has three Michelin stars."

She fidgets with her dress, pooling it beneath her fingers and rubbing it. The movement is mesmerizing.

"That's a pretty long drive from here," she says.

I tap the nav so it extends on the screen, and we can see our estimated arrival.

"It's not too far. Any music you want to listen to?" I tap the screen.

"You know, I think I'm craving Mexican. Any chance you'd be down for staying around here and going for El Molino?"

"Sure. Do you have the address?"

"I'll direct you. I know these roads like the back of my hand."

I'd prefer to use auto drive, but I take over driving from the car since she wants to get there with archaic turn by turn directions.

When we arrive at El Molino Central, it's packed.

"Do you want to maybe just order takeout? We can go back to my place. I have a patio behind the store, and it's a nice night."

"Sure. You think they'll sell us a margarita pitcher to go?"

A devious grin flashes, and she signals for me to follow her. "They're not supposed to, I don't think, but I know a guy."

Twenty minutes later, we're leaving with two enormous bags of food — and two different kinds of margaritas in jugs.

As we pull onto Central Avenue, I park behind the car I'd seen earlier. The man is still in it. I consider tapping on the door and making him drive away, but I decide instead to memorize the license plate and pretend he hasn't piqued my suspicions. He's staring down the side-walk. There's no indication he's checking his rearview mirror or is generally aware of his surroundings. If he's scoping her store, he's an amateur. But even amateurs can be dangerous.

When we enter The Bookery, she locks the front door behind us, and I follow her straight through the shop, along a narrow hall, past the tiny restroom, to the back door. There's a fence with a wooden door that presumably leads to the back alley. Comfortable chairs surround a fire pit, and plants fill out the perimeter. One thing stands out to me about this space. Anyone could walk in from the back alley and then straight into her store without being seen. It's a significant security threat.

While she fusses with lighting the fire pit, I text Trevor the license from the car outside and ask him to research. I also stealthily take a photo of the back wooden fence, so Wolf and I can discuss it later.

"Did you just take a photo?" She's smiling, and it's a teasing smile, not a mocking one. Her blonde hair wraps around her neck, and I'm tempted to reach out and tug the thick braid. Instead, I shove my phone in my back pocket.

"You've got a nice space out here." Lights hang from the corner posts, the old-timey Edison lights spaced out about one foot apart. She clicks a switch on her phone, and they twinkle to life, and low music blends into the hum of the night. She sets us up at a small round table that's near the fire pit but over to the side.

"So, how old are you?" It's a left field question. But my thoughts are circling around the fact we met online when she was twelve. I want to know more about how that came to be, but without her knowing I'm Phoenix.

"Twenty-eight. And you?"

"Thirty-two." Now a completely acceptable age difference, but not when she was twelve. "So, what kinds of things do you do for fun?"

"I read. I drink wine." She lifts the milk jug that's filled with a classic margarita. "I love you wanted a margarita. Do you know how rare that is around here? I love wine, don't get me wrong. But it's nice to switch it up. We do have a budding craft beer scene around here, but—"

"I'm not really a big wine fan." She gasps at my admission, those stunning light blue eyes wide with disbelief.

"What?" I ask, slightly uneasy. I don't see how that's a big deal. I don't drink much alcohol in general. I like to be sharp and aware.

"I don't think I've ever met someone like you." She says with a smile as she sits and places her cloth napkin in her lap.

"Admittedly, I'm new to the area, but there have to be others—"

"No." She shakes her head. "It's criminal to not like wine in these parts."

"But you have craft beer."

"Yes, but beer lovers also appreciate wine." She sips her margarita, then realizes it needs salt on the rim and is up in a flash.

While she's gone, I check my phone. Trevor has texted back.

*T: You with your crush?*

I start to text back a denial but then stop myself. Maybe I do have a crush on her. Big deal. She's beautiful. Gorgeous. And she's been a friend since I was sixteen years old — which is half my life. No one else, other than my twin, can say that. That doesn't make her a crush; that makes her important to me. And I hope that guy sitting outside in a car doesn't mean I've brought a shit storm to her doorstep.

*E: Anything on the tag?*

*T: Is this urgent?*

*E: If I'm being followed*

*T: Hold.*

The lights in Vivi's upstairs apartment flicks on. I can see her shadow moving around. From what I can tell, she's the only one in this area with a live-work situation. The businesses on each side of her are dark.

*T: Registered to a local address. Not reported stolen. Could it be he was just waiting for someone to get off work?*

I think back to the guy. It's possible. If someone locates us, it's going to be a more sophisticated assassin than the guy sitting in a beat-up sedan. He looked unsettled when we made eye contact, but maybe I inadvertently gave him a stony expression. I've been told I can look like a mean mother fucker—Wolf's words, not mine.

*E: Maybe.*

*T: Chill out. Enjoy your date.*

Trevor is a good friend. He injects chill into everything he does, even though he takes his job seriously. It's the reason we work well together. He keeps me level.

The door swings open, and Vivi carries two glasses, the rims now coated with rock salt. She also balances a small dish with sliced lemons and limes.

"Salt-rimmed for our margarita. If you don't like it, that's fine. But I have the most amazing salt. It has a slightly hickory taste. It's perfect with the margarita."

"Sounds good to me." When she sits, she removes her cardigan, exposing the smooth slope of her shoulder. Her white dress drapes over the shape of her breasts, and there is a hint of the outline of nipples through the fabric. She lifts her drink, and a scripted tattoo along her inner wrist catches my attention.

"What does your tattoo say?" Under the dim light, the tattoo shows as a dark gray line across her ghostly pale skin. For the briefest of seconds, I flash an image of my lips pressing against the soft skin. I shift in my seat, and only then do I notice she doesn't want to tell me about it. She licks her lips and holds her fork in a way that hides the tattoo from sight.

"Something silly. I got it when I was seventeen. My parents were furious."

"Is it legal to get a tattoo that young?"

"No. Some friends and I drove down to Tijuana. They don't care about age there. We were supposed to be spending the weekend in San Diego. I was grounded for like, well, the rest of my senior year of high school."

"So, I take it it's something you'd undo if you could?" Now I'm curious about what it says. I want more insight into Vivi as a rebellious teen. The sorceress I knew didn't share those kinds of details.

"It's silly. I had a crush." She loads a tortilla chip with salsa and bites it, then covers her lips graciously as she chews.

"So, it's an ode to a boy?" When I was in high school, I never had a crush. The gaming world had been my obsession. Which evolved into coding. And my obsession evolved into what some might call an addiction. She flutters her eyelids, and a light pink haze colors her cheeks, the pale skin across her chest, and above her breasts. "Did he break your heart?"

"No, actually. He never did. I just didn't know him. It's silly."

"A celebrity crush?" My sister Cali had crushed hard over the lead singer of some band. He was way too old for her, but she had his poster up and went a couple of years stalking his haunts in Seattle when she was in college.

"No." She asks me about where I went to college, and when I tell her University of Washington, the tattoo is forgotten. Our conversation is easygoing. Her questions are benign.

"When you were growing up, did you ever want to leave here?" I'm curious about this point because I've spent six months here, and I'm on edge. When Kairi suggested this location, I didn't know the lay of the land, but this is Vivi's hometown.

"Absolutely. And I did," she says before the tips of her fingers cover her lips as she chews.

"Oh. Where'd you move?" I know the answer, but I want to hear why she moved there.

"Paris."

"What'd you do there?"

"Importing and exporting."

That answer throws me. "Really?"

"Wine." She shrugs like it's self-explanatory.

"Did you like doing it?"

"No." She giggles. "Mind-numbingly boring. I suppose that's why when the pandemic hit, I was so willing to leave Paris behind."

"Paris not for you?"

"Oh, no. I loved Paris. Truly. But the importing business...so dry." Her eyebrows lift, emphasizing her point and her lips glisten enticingly.

We have a ton of leftover food, and she wraps it up. I help her and carry the plates and glasses up the stairs to her apartment. The apartment over the store is accessed by a narrow staircase and a wooden door without a peephole. She twists the knob easily, and it occurs to me she didn't lock it behind her when she came downstairs.

"Do you have a security system?" I blurt as I step over the threshold and take in the brick walls and large windows with iron grids. The dark wooden floor bears scratches. The space feels historic, but it's also warm and colorful.

She turns right to the back, and I follow her into a closed-off kitchen that looks out onto the courtyard in the back.

"No. There's really no need. Like I told you, Sonoma's safe. It's not the sleepy little town I grew up in, but it's not a big city. It's no Seattle or Paris." She opens the refrigerator and pushes our take-out containers onto a packed shelf.

"If I sent someone over to set up a security system, would you be okay with that?"

She spins around, and her brow is wrinkled. "What?"

"I'm in security. That's what I do." It's the closest I've come to lying to her yet. It's also the closest I've come to telling her the truth. "And I'm gonna be honest. You need some improvements."

"Seriously, I think I could leave the front door unlocked, and all the books would still be there in the morning."

"Yes, but what about your cash drawer?"

"Do you know how few people pay in cash?" She rinses out our glasses in the sink, and I step closer, annoyed she's not taking me seriously. That's when I see the side of her forearm. The kitchen light above is bright, and I can easily read the script.

*The Firefly and the Phoenix*

69

I was her crush, and she doesn't know it. Her shoulder presses against my chest as I crowd her against the sink. I breathe her in. She has a light, sweet fragrance. It's reminiscent of the honeysuckle vine that grew in our backyard growing up. The warm memory of simpler times engulfs me when she lifts those cloud-like irises. I wrap one arm around her lower back, and my left hand traces her jaw. And then my lips fall to hers.

My peripheral vision fades to black, the same way it does when I code. Only my brain is lost in a fog. Her soft lips press against mine, and a crackle of heat fires a completely different set of synapses. Sensations spread across my skin like wildfire.

She opens softly for me, tentative. Her silky soft strands slip through my fingers, and I angle her face upward and rock against her softness. I lift her up onto the counter, cupping the curve of her ass, and feast on her mouth like a starved man. My cock strains painfully in my jeans, and I pull her to me, her thighs against my hips. I grip the edge of her dress and explore her bare leg, the smooth, soft, supple skin, all the way up to silk. My thumb slips under, and my other hand, locked on her breast, twists her nipple through fabric, and she gasps, "Holy shit."

The breathless words breach the silence and hit me like an arctic blast. The side of her refrigerator, the sink nozzle, the hood over her stove all return. I blink, and my brain whirs back to life. Short bursts of coherent thought intrude. *I can't. She can't be in my world.*

My dick throbs against my zipper, arguing. Those light blue eyes catch mine, confusion laced in her expression. The cool night air wafts through her cracked kitchen window. My rapid breaths slow. *I can't.*

I close my eyes, blocking her from sight. I hold an arm out, feeling for the wall, then the stairwell.

"Erik? Are you okay?"

"I should go. Thank you for the date."

I find myself at the bottom of the stairs, on autopilot.

"Wait, Erik Young. I have a question for you." Young? Oh, that's right. She insisted on asking for my last name before she'd go on a date with me. The cool metal doorknob in my palm mitigates the dizzying sensation threatening my brain. I drank too much. Those margaritas must have been wicked strong. "Are you sure you're okay?"

"Fine. What do you want to know?"

"What's your birth date? I'm big into horoscopes."

# GOOGLE

VIVI

The soft whir of a phone vibration hums. I follow him through the store, completely confused. We were hot and heavy, and then it was like ice. *Did I touch him wrong? Did he remember something? Someone? Is he married like the Lilith jerk? Or did he get a conscience about a girlfriend?*

"Lock the door behind me." His back is to me as he turns the knob. The Bookery door creaks open, and the bell chimes. His head turns left, then right. He steps out onto the sidewalk and pulls the door closed behind him.

I breathe out, emptying my lungs of oxygen, taking stock. *What the frick just happened?*

I need to do some research on this guy. If he's married, and he just took me on a date, I'll unleash a fury of biblical proportions on him. That's so not cool. And exactly what some tourist yokel would try to pull. Someone whose wife is all out spa-ing it up and assuming he's working during the day. I've seen plenty of couples do that. I've just never had the misfortune to be hit on by the hubby.

But there's no wedding band shadow. He has olive skin, though. I shake my head. No, anyone wearing a band all the time would have lighter skin under the band when removed…right? Maybe he has a girlfriend? He's new here. Maybe he's in a long-distance relationship? But why ask me out on a date?

Armed with a birth date and a college, I search TruthFinder. I get a list of results, but none live in our county. He always pays in cash. He borrowed a friend's car. There may not be any documentation yet tying him to this location. Which in and of itself is suspect. I need his home address. I could ask him for his street address, but that's weird. Especially after the way we left things. He may not even want to go out with me again. He might have thought I'm a bad kisser. But no, I saw ample evidence of his attraction.

Still, there's nothing more I can do until I see or hear from him again and probe for more information. I flip around on my TruthFinder app, just in case there are options I'm unaware of. And that's when I notice my prior searches.

Bruce Williams. Bradley Lilith.

His real-life Instagram profile is open, meaning I can look through all his posts without his permission. There's a cute black poodle. A little blonde girl with pigtails. There's a photo of a woman breastfeeding a baby with a younger version of the girl in pigtails, but this time she's wearing a headband. Men like this deserve to pay.

I flick back over to his pseudo-Insta account. The one he gave Chloe when he was seducing her. He doesn't have dick pics in his feed, but it's clear he's using it to woo. There's a photo of a shiny black sports car. Him finishing a Spartan race, but you can't really see his face, just a muscular chest and a muddy hand clutching a finisher's medal. I wonder if the loser snagged the photo off someone else's feed. I've outed him on Insta. But Tinder? That's where he hunts for prey.

I pour myself another margarita, get comfortable on the sofa, and let my fingers attack. *Click. Click. Clickety-clack.*

With hellfire raining down on one lowlife, I pour myself another drink and call Chloe.

"How'd your date go?" Her quick answer to my call is unexpected. She had a date tonight, too. She didn't give me this one's name, so I didn't check him out.

"Fine." It's my auto-response.

"Well, mine was not," Chloe blurts, and I hear a hard *bam*. It sounds like a cabinet door slamming shut.

"What happened?" I try to remember what she said about the guy.

"No chemistry."

"Did something happen?" You can't be mad at someone for lack of chemistry. I hear a clink. "What're you doing?"

"Pouring myself a glass of wine. I need it. And no, nothing happened. He just sat there, staring at me. We had nothing to talk about. It was so awkward. And he had these black hairs randomly located across his upper lip. Like, I wanted so badly to find some tweezers and pluck them. I couldn't figure it out. Like, was he trying to grow a mustache and couldn't? Did he shave with a dull razor and missed some hairs? It really got to me. I couldn't stop staring. By the time we finished our appetizers, it was all I could see. His lip." I hear her moving around. "He went to kiss me goodnight. You know you hear about chemistry between people?"

"Yeah." I pull a pillow onto my lap, content to let Chloe let it all out.

"I had the exact opposite. Like vile, vomit-worthy repulsion. Bile rose in my throat. I'm not even kidding. His hands were clammy. Gross. Just gross. I can't even. I should've stuck to my dating hiatus." She pauses for a breath, and I stare out the window at the night sky. Several bright stars twinkle in the distance. "Where'd you go on your date?"

"Ah, well, we were supposed to go to SingleThread."

"Fancy. What happened? Don't tell me he thought he could just walk in without a reservation."

"No. He had a reservation. Or at least I think he did. But I suggested we go to Molino. It was packed—"

"Saturday night," she interrupts.

"Yeah. So, we ordered food and brought it back here."

"Who were you afraid of seeing at SingleThread?" She knows me well.

"It's not that I was afraid. But I didn't want to be introducing him to people right and left. Even if I didn't recognize any of the diners — which is probable, given it's tourist season— I definitely know several of the waitstaff, the sommelier, the bartenders."

"You're anti-social."

"Eh." I prefer introverted, but I will not belabor the point. "Just wasn't what I was in the mood for."

"And how did what you were in the mood for go?" I grin for the first time since Erik backed away. "Come on now. I've seen you ogle him. You got him back to your place. Did you take him upstairs to your cozy little bachelorette love shack?"

"Puh-leaze." We both giggle. She's been giving me hell for choosing to live in my own apartment and not back at our family's home. But I'm almost thirty. Why would I live with my grandfather? I've never understood why my brother and sister do. Our little giggle fit ends, and I spill. "It was weird, Chloe."

"Uh-oh. What did he do?"

"We were having the hottest kiss of my life. Like, we went from first kiss to his hand up my skirt in a nanosecond. It was like…" Heat emanates, just thinking about that kiss and his hard pecs and how much I wanted his fingers.

"So, chemistry…"

"Off the charts. He's a great kisser. But then he backed away like I was diseased. Or, no, that's not right. He just looked shocked…maybe? Like he couldn't believe what we were doing? I swear, I mean, you know my mind can go crazy—"

"Hell, yes, it can."

"Yeah, well—"

"Daydreamer. Your imagination is like none other."

"Chloe," I snap. Forcing her to listen is sometimes challenging. "I had this feeling, like maybe he's married or has a long-distance girlfriend. It was like this moment of 'holy shit, I shouldn't be doing this.' And now all I can think of is all the reasons he might react like that."

"Okay. So, a cheater. I get that theory. Remarkably close to my most recent Tinder debacle. But he seems like a nice guy. And his friend was there. And didn't you say he said Trevor told him to ask you out? If he's in a serious relationship, his friend would know. What other theories are percolating?"

"Well, this other one is truly crazy."

"Let's hear it." I have a vision of her sipping her wine on her front porch. Her neighbors probably think she's an alcoholic.

"Okay. So, do you remember the tattoo I got when I was in high school?"

"How can I forget it? I got one, too, remember? 'Born to be Wild' is etched on my skin. Dumbest fucking tattoo ever."

"Yeah, well, mine says Firefly and the Phoenix."

"From some game you played. As dumb as mine, but at least yours has a nice ring to it." Her comment brings back a memory of her dropping her bra at the tattoo parlor. We were both way too drunk, and she thought the tattoo artist was hot. He had black hair pulled back in a ponytail, silver rings all along one eyebrow, and she wanted him to squeeze her boob.

"You can get it removed," I remind her for the ten-thousandth time.

"Nah, it's below my boob. As I age, it's going to sag and fully cover it. Enough about tatts. What's the theory?"

"Well, I could swear I saw him focus on my tattoo. Like, read it. And then he was kissing me. It was…" Hot. Inferno level hot. "What if he's Phoenix?"

"Oh, my fucking god," Chloe shouts at an ear-piercing decibel level into the phone. "If he's Phoenix, why not tell you?" She sounds like she's just submitted evidence to a jury.

"I don't know. I told you it was crazy. And, the other day, I had this idea he might be Phoenix. Just this gut hunch. I can't remember why exactly. And I texted him in the game app. He had his laptop open. No ding. Nothing to indicate a notification came through."

"Maybe he doesn't use notifications. Those dings drive me bananas."

"Yeah, I thought of that. But no. He didn't even blink. No screen identification. And come to think of it — no response. Not a surprise. Phoenix and I can go weeks without responding. It's how we've been friends for so long."

"You've crushed on that virtual guy long enough. It's time to get out there into the real world."

"I'm not crushing on him. I don't even know what he looks like. I just can't help but wonder…And I, too, have been out there. I just went on a date."

"And now your overactive imagination is pretending this guy is game boy. Or he's married. Or has a girlfriend. I'm surprised former felon hasn't entered your list."

"True." I sigh. "That's actually a problem. I can't locate Erik on Truth-Finder. He could be a felon."

"My therapist is really good."

"Shut it." I stare down the hall at the kitchen, wanting a glass of something but not having the energy to get up for a refill.

"I'm kind of serious."

"I don't need a therapist." But I am curious about Erik. He showed up out of nowhere. New to the area. He pays in cash. I chew on my thumbnail.

"You know, he's spent every day working from your bookstore ever since the first day he walked in. And it's been what, two weeks now?"

"Yeah, roughly."

"Well, let me throw this idea out there. Maybe he likes you. And the kiss was hot, yes?"

"Yes."

"Maybe he didn't want things to get out of hand. Maybe he wants something more with you. He could be one of those guys who believes real relationships don't stem from sex on the first date. So he cooled things down in the only way he knew how because his desire for you was so overpowering, the only way he could stop himself and water down his burning inferno of need was to walk out the door. He couldn't speak because the only words flowing through his brain were 'I burn for you.'"

"All right, now you're just being dramatic for the fun of it."

"Yep." She cackles. "I guarantee you, he'll be back. And he's not married. His friends wouldn't play along. You know, there's always the most obvious answer."

"What's that?"

"That he's a giant geek, and he freaked when he had someone with your hotness caliber, and he had to leave before he blew his load because he's that out of practice."

"You think he's geeky?"

"Yeah! He's got those glasses, and he's all serious and focused. If I was in college with him, I'd totally try to copy his answers on a test."

I can see her point. Not that I believe he's out of practice. Nothing about that kiss implied he needed to dust off his skills. That's just Chloe's humor at play, but she's also right. He emanates intelligence. And those muscles. Lean but hard and firm. He's disciplined. He said he works in security. Is he military? Police? FBI? CIA? If he comes back into my store, I'm going to snag his license. If he's FBI, there might be a badge or ID card. His license might also have an updated street address, but even if it's his old address, that'll be a Google goldmine.

# SAFE

ERIK

The cool, dry air combines with the faint hint of perspiration coating my skin. I should be freezing, but I focus on the dirt path. The moon lights the way along the dirt and gravel road. Rows of grapevines border each side of the shallow ditch. My dog, Astra, lies down in her lion stance, paws out in front, ears pricked forward, alert.

If you want to be a lion, you must train with the lions.

The words in my jiu-jitsu master's gravelly voice play in my head. I bend my legs in position and tear off on my fifteenth sprint, running as hard and fast as I can, my lungs burning as I breathe through my nose. Controlled. My quads and thighs burn. My watch beeps, and I slow, gasping, hands on hips, until a bead of sweat drips from my forehead, itching, and I swipe it away. Then I drop onto my hands and feet for another set of twenty-five push-ups.

"I take it your date didn't go well?" Kairi calls from the head of the road. She holds a flashlight in her hand, but she doesn't need it. A clear night sky shines above.

"Went fine," I grit out, determined not to lose count.

"Got a call that you never even showed. What happened?" She sounds concerned. I hit twenty-five and sit back on my heels, then swipe my palms together to clean off the excess dirt. "It's after midnight. What's going on?"

"Just getting in a few extra sprints." Today wasn't my day to lift. I don't like long-distance running. It bores me. But I like sprints. I like to push myself until my lungs and muscles burn.

"Should I go get Trevor?"

"Why?" I wipe my brow and stand.

"You look like you could use a little jiu-jitsu practice." I trudge up to her. She knows me. I like to lose myself in anything that requires focus.

"We've got practice planned for the morning. I just needed to burn off some energy tonight." I'm done with my workout. If I don't get some sleep, Trevor will kick my ass in the morning. We have a mat near the equipment shed, and we get in a good session about three times a week.

"So, what happened?" She's going to keep asking. She's like my sister Cali in that way. Nothing gets dropped.

"Nothing. Vivi wanted Mexican."

"Are you fucking kidding me?" Kairi goes from concerned to pissed in a nanosecond.

"What?" I grunt.

"You don't stand up a reservation at SingleThread. I called in a huge favor to get you that table last minute on a Saturday night. Did you even tell her what you had planned?"

"You know you're screeching, right?"

"What the fuck, Erik?" She slaps my bicep, and the noise pierces the quiet nightscape. When we first moved here, the quiet drove me nuts. Now, I'm used to it. It offers advantages. No one can sneak up on us. "What Mexican did you get?"

"Molino?" I say, trying to remember the full name.

"Are you kidding me? You gave up dining at a restaurant with three Michelin stars in favor of something you can eat any day of the week?"

"It's what she wanted." I could tell Vivi didn't feel comfortable going to SingleThread. Not everyone likes ritz. But there's no reason to share that level of detail with Kairi. "Thanks for getting me the reservation. I appreciate it."

"You'll never get another one from me."

"Don't be like that."

"Nope. I really can't believe it." She's shaking her head and looking down the road I was using as a track. Astra is now sniffing the ground near a grapevine. He lifts a leg and does his business. "So, how was Molino?"

"Fine. Good food." I didn't care for the margaritas so much, but I don't like sweet.

"And the date? Vivi? Did you guys hit it off?"

The feel of her soft hair in my fingers, her smooth skin, the pressure of her thighs around my hips, my groin pressed against her core — it all floods back. All the benefits of a sprint routine blown away with one question.

"Yeah."

"Great." She angles her eyebrows as she evaluates my answer plus my presence outside in the middle of the night. It doesn't add up. I'm aware it's suspicious, but I don't want to get into it with her. "Why don't you invite her out here for dinner next time? I'd like to meet her. Even though I remain officially on record that you don't have any business dating someone."

"You know her." Now she's following me as I head into the house. Astra trots beside us, tail wagging. He's ready to go to bed.

"High school doesn't count. I barely remember her. I'd like to ask her how she's doing. She's had some rough years, from what I remember." Yes, Vivi and I both lost parents over the course of our friendship. It's probably one thing that drew us closer. Made us more than just gamer friends. In all honesty, I might have dropped our friendship when I stopped playing. But her parents died.

"So, does that mean you'll invite her?" I stop. I say nothing. Where'd she come to that conclusion? Trevor steps out of the shadows, joining us as we approach the back door.

"You and Vivi, huh? Maybe now you'll admit I did you a solid by pushing you to ask her out."

"I'm not asking her out again. Kairi was right." I snap open the screen door, and it slams behind me with a whack.

"Why?" Trevor and Kairi ask at the same time. It figures. I tell Kairi she's right, and she questions it.

"You guys know as much as anyone we can't be in a relationship." I sit down and unlace my running shoes. They both stand in front of me, arms crossed, judging.

"A few months ago, I might have agreed with you. When we first arrived here, sure. But there's no sign we've been traced. There's no sign Kane is even looking for us."

Sometimes it's like Trevor has learned nothing from jiu-jitsu philosophy. It's like he's never studied Sun Tsu. Kane will wait until we don't expect him. Then he'll strike. He will leverage time to his advantage.

"And that guy who was outside The Bookery tonight? That car is registered in Sonoma County. He's a local. Chances are he was just waiting for someone. Like I said." Trevor scratches behind Astra's ear. He's cocky. Nothing ever scares Trev.

His theory is logical, but I don't buy it. The guy was scoping her store.

"One day, we'll all be able to date again. Have relationships." Kairi's words break my train of thought. I slowly look up, wondering if I heard her right. The love of her life was killed in front of her, in front of all of us, less than two years ago. "When it's safe," she clarifies. "This situation isn't doable indefinitely. But the risks are high. Lara is proof." She turns to Trevor, seemingly pleading with him to agree with her.

"I'm planning on moving out," I announce. I place my dusty, smelly shoes on the shelf in the coat cupboard.

"Let me guess. You're probably looking into those apartments near Sonoma Square, maybe a unit with a view onto East Napa." Trevor wears a know-it-all expression as he toes off his shoes. Everything around here is so dusty, we have mutually agreed to go without shoes inside.

"I haven't actually looked yet." I didn't know there were apartments available for rent right there, but now that I do...

"Hey." Kairi's hand falls to my forearm, and she lightly squeezes. "I'm serious. If you're going to date her, at the very least, you can't let her know who you are. You can't give her anything that could lead someone to us. And you can't do anything – anything at all – that would make someone believe she's important to you."

I understand what she's saying. I do. I haven't met my nephew yet, all because I believe Kane has people watching, and he knows my sister.

He's found us once. And he hired an assassin. Twice. We underestimated our risk before, and Kairi's girlfriend paid with her life.

I climb up the stairs to my bedroom, and when I feel Kairi's gaze on my back, I call down, "Goodnight."

Trevor shouts up, "Want to move our mat time to five-thirty? Or six o'clock?"

"Six works."

"You working from The Bookery tomorrow?"

I turn down the hall and don't bother answering. But, yeah, I'll work from there. I like the space. And I want to keep an eye out for that guy. Who cares if he's a local? Locals can be criminals, too.

As I close the door to my bedroom and twist the lock, I see her. The memory of those whisper-light blue irises isn't one I want to let go of. I've seen the real Firefly now. I've had a taste. She's intoxicating. There's no harm in working near her.

I'm thinking of her thighs, and her heat beneath the silk as the warm shower water pours over me. I tug on my hard erection, playing with the tip, imagining it's her fingers, her grip around me. Then I envision her lips wrapping around my cock, the warmth of her mouth, and the suction. My finger shifts those silk panties to the side, and I thrust deep inside her. She's warm and tight. She rocks her head back, mouth open, gasping, and a breathless, "Holy shit." I pulse out my release, then rest my palms against the tile. Water drains over my hair, down my face.

One of the core tenets of jiu-jitsu is to know thyself. *Know thyself.* I've got a problem. My body wants her. But I want her safe.

# UNLOCKED

VIVI

My sister's name eclipses the news article on my phone about a congressman's lewd past. *Are all men sorry wankers?*

I accept the incoming call and break away from the disturbing article.

"Morning." Celeste rarely calls me on weekday mornings, especially Mondays, which she claims are manic.

"Excuse me," Celeste says, but it doesn't sound like she's speaking to me.

"Celeste?" I ask, then endure silence. If she's having earbud issues again and wasting my time—

"Sorry. I'm in the Emergency Room. We're not supposed to have cell phones in the waiting room, and I didn't see the sign."

"Why are you in the ER?" I scan the room for my pocketbook and shoes.

"Granddad fell this morning."

"What?" Our grandfather is getting up there in age, but he's like an ox. He's a farmer.

"His foot slipped on the tractor step. He went down. Hard, apparently. They think he may have fractured something. He's in x-ray right now."

"Holy frick. I'll be right there."

"Can you leave your store?"

I roll my eyes at her question. I typically make less than a hundred dollars a day in revenue. I'm technically losing money to keep it open.

"I'm on my way. Are you actually at the hospital? Why not Urgent Care?"

She fills me in on her location as I slide on shoes, grab my pocketbook, and head out the back door to my car. When I arrive, she's standing outside the doors with a cigarette between her fingers. She's not a regular smoker.

"Thanks for coming. He's in the worst mood."

"Well, he's in pain, I imagine."

"That, and he's mad at me." Her voice intonation reminds me of our teenage years when she'd feared getting grounded.

"Why?"

"Because he didn't want a doctor. But he couldn't move! Like, you could see the pain in his face. And he would only sit there."

"Celeste…he's angry he's hurt. He's not angry at you."

"No, he's mad at me. He wouldn't listen. So, I called Max. He came in from the vineyards. He took one look at Granddad and gave him a choice of being carried or of leaning on him to get to the car. There was never any question if he'd go to the hospital. He didn't argue with Max at all."

"Eh, well…Max is a big guy." It's a weak excuse, but it's not like our family dynamics are new to her. I do share her frustration that it took Max for Granddad to do what he needed to do, but that's life.

"He didn't come to the ER. He has a new crew today and didn't feel comfortable leaving them. So, the whole drive into town, Granddad lit into me about how dare I call Max, that he had important things to do."

"Like you don't." My sister is a sommelier, one of a few hundred in the world. She's also our winemaker. She's as busy as Max, plus some.

"Yeah, well…tell that to Granddad." Emotion seeps through her words.

"When did this happen? It's barely eight."

"Before six. Granddad had his phone, and he called me. Thank god he had his phone. Who knows how long he would have been out there stuck below the tractor. He has a gash on his head, blood…it was bleeding pretty bad. He can't move his right leg. He just wanted me to set him at the kitchen table and leave him. Can you believe that?"

"Yes." Because that's our grandfather. Stubborn as all get-out. "Ugh. I hope he's not seriously hurt. He'll be a nightmare if he's bedbound."

"No shit." We both burst into laughter. It's not funny, but it's a laugh or cry situation.

I'm sitting with Celeste in the waiting room when a doctor in scrubs emerges from the hall. Celeste sits up straighter, clearly recognizing him. Upon seeing Celeste, he smiles and gestures for us to follow him. They have a private conference room for doctors to meet with patients, and he opens the door for us. It's a small room, but now with HIPAA laws, they're getting smarter about protecting patient privacy. Which is when we discover that there's a limited amount of information he can share.

"If you get your grandfather to give us permission, we'll be able to tell you more. Given his age, I do recommend that you talk to him about putting his close family members down on his form. It might also be smart for him to provide a medical power of attorney to someone. Just in case. You never know what could happen."

I understand what he's saying. I would have thought Max already had medical power of attorney for Granddad. But he hasn't said anything yet about how our grandfather is doing.

"Is he okay?" I ask, interrupting his public service announcement.

"I'm going to bring you to him. I'll tell you in front of him what's going on if he agrees."

That's not an assurance that he's okay, but I understand he's bound by confidentiality laws. But, given he came in due to a fall, how is this necessary?

We follow the doctor down the hall. I assumed this man was a doctor, but his name tag states he's a physician's assistant. He looks to be around my age. He pulls back a curtain. Granddad lies on a hospital bed with a bandage wrapped around his crown. The material reminds me of an ace bandage, but it's lighter. His legs are covered by a blanket, but they look the same size, so I don't think he has a cast. My grandfather scowls.

"Granddad." I say the word in an overly chipper tone, and I swear the man glowers. Pissed off doesn't adequately interpret his expression. "I hear you're doing okay." I didn't actually hear that, but it seems like a good thing to say.

"Then why do they want me to stay overnight? I'm not doing it. I'm going home."

Oh, dear. *Why would they want him to stay overnight for a broken bone?*

Celeste and I exchange confused looks, and we stare at the PA, who notably is standing at the end of the bed, away from my grandfather. I reach for my grandfather's hand. He can be a grumpy SOB, but he's all bark, no bite.

"It's a recommendation." The PA shrugs. "We can't force him to stay. But he took a hard hit to his head. He definitely has a concussion. And we can better manage his pain if he's admitted. He fractured his hip bone." There's a lot the PA doesn't need to say to us. Our grandfather is seventy-nine. He might look like he's twenty years younger, but at seventy-nine, it's a good idea to take precautions.

"Granddad, come on, now. One night isn't going to hurt. And then we'll know you're safe. And the pain meds. Don't turn down the pain meds." I exaggerate every word, the same way he did to me when I'd fractured my wrist and had been on a homeopathic kick and didn't want any chemicals in my body.

He tugged on my hand, wanting me to get closer. I lean down, confused, and he wiggles his finger for me to get closer. I smile as I realize he wants to whisper something in my ear. When my ear is next to his lips, he whispers, "Will you sneak in wine? Good stuff?"

I belt out laughter until I catch Celeste's expression. She looks hurt and betrayed. I smile at her, trying to communicate that it's all right, that he didn't share anything heartfelt or deep.

"We should have a room ready for your grandfather soon," the PA says.

"Great," I say.

"This man tried to tell me I might want a plastic surgeon. Thinks I'm going to have a scar on my forehead. Can you believe that? As if at my age a scar is a worry."

"It'll just make you sexier." His lips turn up at my comment, not into a smile by any stretch, but I'll take it.

"Granddad, I'll go back to the house and get you whatever you need," Celeste offers. "Toothbrush, anything else?"

"I'm not moving in. Jesus. You want me to live here?" he growls at her.

"She's being nice. And thoughtful." I admonish him like I'm talking to a little boy. "Do you want your iPad? Are you reading a book right now? We can bring in food, right?" I look to the PA for confirmation. I don't really know what the rules are for food at the hospital.

"You can bring him lunch or dinner. But I'd recommend keeping the food light."

"I want a burger and fries from In-N-Out." He glares at the PA, daring him to contradict his request. "And since I'm staying here, needlessly, I'd like a strawberry milkshake too."

"A nurse will be here to take you up to your room shortly." The PA smiles. He doesn't have a dog in the fight, so why does he care if my grandfather chooses to ignore his dietary recommendations?

My phone rings, and I pull it out to check it as the PA walks away.

"It's Max," I tell Granddad and Celeste.

Granddad takes the phone from me and assures Max he's fine. The conversation is over in under sixty seconds. Celeste and I exchange glances. I'm not sure what she's thinking, but I'm thinking we need to have a sit-down discussion with our older brother. I don't think we're set up yet to best deal with medical issues.

Granddad hands me back my phone. There is a text from an unknown number. I swipe it.

*Hey, this is Erik. Everything okay?*

Ah, so he did show up at The Bookery for work this morning. I really should hire an employee or two so I can deal with emergencies like this without having to close the store.

*Me: Yes. Family emergency. I might be closed tomorrow too. If you want to work from the store, my back door is unlocked.*

As soon as I send the text, I second guess it. I barely know this guy. I've entered all kinds of details on TruthFinder, and I don't think I have a match. He has no social media history whatsoever. And while I can't stop thinking about that hot-as-fuck first kiss, he weirded me out. I'd be all over Chloe if she acted as trusting as I am acting. It's not like there aren't other places offering free Wi-Fi.

Celeste taps away on her phone. I'm certain she's getting important work done. My grandfather is resting on the pillow, his eyes closed. We're just hanging out, waiting for Granddad's room. So, I open the Zeitgeist app and pop a question over to my favorite sounding board.

> Firefly: Is it weird for an adult male to not have a social media presence?

# JUST IN CASE

ERIK

"You getting a migraine? I have prescription meds. You're welcome to them."

I massage my temple and brow. The pressure intensifies, and my nostrils flare. I reread her message over and over, and the words don't change. I am not hallucinating. *Her back door is unlocked? What the ever-loving fuck? Does she not know someone was scoping her place? No, she doesn't, because you never made that clear to her.*

"Dude. Your veins. That one on your temple. And neck? Lay back, man. You need to breathe." He reaches for me, and I jerk.

"I don't need to lie down," I snap. Then regret it. Not because Trev can't handle a mood, but because now he looks wary, like I'm a ticking time bomb.

I pinch the bridge of my nose, close my eyes, and take stock. *Okay. Her door is unlocked. That actually gives us a chance to put some cameras in place. And we can get in front of her store without her seeing as well. It won't take us long. We'll get set up, and I'll lock up after.*

"What cameras do you have?"

"Huh?" Trevor reaches toward my brow like he's trying to feel my temperature. I push off the sofa and glare at him.

"Security. Equipment. What do you have?" I don't have time for bullshit.

"All right, man." His laid-back California vibe comes to life, and he heads down the hall. "Come on. I'll show ya'. You gotta breathe. Maybe we should move down south with Wolf and the guys. You could get in some surfing each morning. That blood pressure thing you got going, it's not going to work for the long haul."

I follow him downstairs to a walk-out basement. It would be a basement, except only half of the room is surrounded by wall and, on the outside, earth. The other half is windows and door, and then there's a patio with a table and chairs. It's not really a first-floor room. It's just the way they built this house into a slope. I never come down here, but it's apparent from the shelves and stacks of boxes that this is where Trevor has been storing the hardware.

"What you need?" he asks. He shoves his hands into his shorts and waits.

"What would you recommend? Should we call Wolf? This is for The Bookery. She's not there today. I want something over the front door and back door, minimum, maybe a cam over the cash register with a view of the stairs that lead up to her apartment." I'd love to have cameras in her living space too. I believe the more security surveillance, the better, but I once went overboard with my sister, and she had a problem with it. I get her point. It'd be one thing if I was the only person watching the cams, but I wouldn't be. And, as Cali pointed out, even if I was, some might think, well, Cali thought it was creepy.

Trevor texts Wolf. I read through the descriptions on the boxes while Trevor taps out a message. When he's done, he drops his BlackBerry into his oversized cargo pocket.

94

He steps up to the shelf and pulls a white box off, and passes it to me.

"You like her, huh?" he asks as I open the box and examine the contents.

"I do." She's one of my oldest friends. I'm protective of all my people.

"What's going on with her?"

"What do you mean?"

"Why's she out today? Why'd she give you permission to put security in her place?"

"She has a family emergency." His question makes me realize I still don't know what's going on with her. When I pinged her location, she was in the vicinity of the hospital. She said family, so it's not her. But an uneasy sensation stirs in my gut. *I could access the hospital's database and check the records...or I could just ask her. Quicker to ask.*

"She doesn't know you're putting cams in her place, does she?"

"Nope." He removes the box from my hands.

"Then we'll need different hardware," he says. He stands in front of the wall of product, arms crossed over his chest.

I pull out my burner phone and text her back.

*What kind of family emergency? Do you need anything?*

The thud of boots on stairs announces Wolf's arrival. I choose to ignore the fact he once again forgot to remove his shoes. We've picked out product, agreed on strategy, loaded our bag of tools and a battery-operated handheld vacuum to clean up any dust we create, and we're in Trevor's Tesla before she texts back. I sit in the back seat, letting

Wolf, who is considerably larger than me, take the front passenger seat.

*No. Thanks for asking. They're admitting my grandfather. He took a spill this morning. It's just a precaution. Sorry to upend your workday.*

"Hey, you decided on a Tesla, right, boss?" He calls me boss because that's his chosen nickname for me, not because he actually reports to me.

"Yep. I like them."

"When's it coming in?"

"Haven't ordered it yet." I looked for apartments, but I'll need a car too.

*No problem. Glad all is okay.*

I send the text, then stare up through the glass roof. The white clouds overhead are light and airy. A fall shouldn't be life-threatening. He must have hit his head or something like that. If they're admitting him, they're afraid of something. When my mom was in the hospital, she should have been fine. I had one of the best heart surgeons in the world flown in to do a standard procedure. There are no guarantees.

An urge to go to the hospital, to check things out, to hover just in case, builds. The urge is nonsensical. In her mind, we barely know each other. We had one date. But maybe the urge isn't entirely illogical. It sucked not being in the hospital with my sister and dad. Helping from afar never feels like enough.

Trevor claims an open street spot a few doors down from The Book-ery, and we all clamber out of the car. I scan the cars parked on the street. They're all empty.

"You guys wait here. I'll go around back to let you in."

Within minutes, I'm unlocking the shop's front door. The door chime echoes in the dimly lit store. I pass Wolf a stepladder that had been leaning against the back of the building.

"Why don't you start with the camera out here? You think you can get it up in the eaves where no one will notice?"

He doesn't answer, just studies the space.

"What about electrical?" Trevor asks.

There are overhead lights and exposed wiring connecting them.

"You guys go do the inside. I've got it out here," Wolf says. He never tells us how he's going to do it, and we don't ask. He's dressed in workman's boots, jeans, and a black T-shirt. Anyone passing by will assume he's hired.

It takes us a little over two hours to get cams set everywhere I want. I lock her back door. If she doesn't have a key, then I'll tell her I'll break in for her, but there's no way I'm leaving a door to a business unlocked. *I've got to sit Vivi down and crush her naivety.*

As we climb back in the car, Wolf asks, "So, where to for lunch?"

"It's mid-afternoon," I say. The guy eats like it's his mission. For every glass of water I drink, he eats a Power Bar.

"You guys aren't hungry?" he asks.

Trevor nods when I shake my head. Trevor's pulling out of the parallel spot and doing a three-point turn to head in the opposite direction when I spot the suspect. He's walking with another man down the street. I tap Trevor on his shoulder.

"That's the guy," I tell him. He looks over and nods.

"Yep," he confirms. "He probably lives here, which is what we originally thought."

I let it drop. While Wolf and Trevor talk about Santa Barbara and potential plans for a move, I pull out my iPhone and access the video feed. The two men stop in front of The Bookery. One guy presses his face against the glass, shielding sunlight with his hand. I'm about to tell Trevor to turn around when he steps back from the door, and they continue down the sidewalk. *Maybe Trevor is right, and he lives in the area.*

Trevor drops me off at the house. Kairi's waiting outside. They've decided to go to a sports bar and watch something or another and have an early dinner. I gather my things, climb into the old farm pickup, and drive to the hospital.

She probably won't need me. But I'll be there, just in case.

The lobby is more of an open-air atrium with seating areas off to the sides of a central welcome desk. Large windows line the front wall. Electrical outlets are near the wall, but there are none in the floor to accommodate visitors in the central areas. I scan the crowd, searching for a platinum blonde braid or a colorful skirt. When I close my eyelids, I see those blue eyes. Doing so is a poor substitute for the real thing, but at least I'm in the same building she is in. That counts for something.

I find an empty sofa against a wall and plug in my laptop. As I wait for the laptop to restart, I double-check with the welcome desk. I tell them that I want to send flowers to a patient and ask if she can give me the room number. She smiles and tells me that she can't give out patients' room numbers.

"Can you confirm if someone is a patient here?"

"What's the name?"

"Mr. Rossi. His granddaughter is Vivianne Rossi. I'm her ride home. I'd like to send flowers up to the room."

"Looking to make a good impression, are you?" She gives me a knowing smile. "He doesn't have a room number assigned yet, but if you order flowers from our gift shop down the hall, they'll be able to deliver them when he does get his room."

"Thank you." She smiles at me like I'm the most thoughtful man in the world. Meanwhile, I look at her with disdain. She gave up information too easily.

I go back to my computer and pull up the hospital florist. As expected, I can order flowers online, and I do. If given a choice of interacting with humans or ordering online, I will always choose a user interface.

When I type in her grandfather's last name, the motion of the keys, R-O-S-S-I, a memory flashes. I recently learned Firefly's name, but I've seen that last name before. I know that last name.

*"Two hundred thousand dollars!" Kane pumped his hands in the air and moved his body in a jerky motion that would've hit TikTok fame —and only because it showcased a man who cannot dance. "We are in the big-time, baby! Yesssss!"*

*"What do you mean?"*

*"We just got paid. And from a vineyard, no less. I am telling you, man. There is no end to the money we can rake in on ransoms." He held both hands out and circled his arms while attempting to moon-walk backward.*

*"A vineyard?" An uneasy feeling in my gut grew. We'd started off going after greedy corporations. Places that offered shitty employment benefits and low wages. Companies that needed to go down, like coal and oil. But when I thought of vineyards, they didn't strike me as overly greedy or bad for the environment. But I could see how they wouldn't be tech savvy and could be easily breached. But easy to breach didn't mean we should.*

*"Rossi Vineyards. Walk in any grocery store, and you'll see their cheap ass white wine. I've had one too many hangovers from their high sulfite, high sugar crap. And they just paid, my man."*

*I did a quick search while Mr. Kung Fu Dancer jerked his body around the room in a bizarre celebration dance. One article in* Wine Spectator *came up about a rumored customer data breach at Rossi Vineyards.*

*"They paid you two hundred thousand to protect customer data?"*

*"Yep. Oh, now, don't give me that judgmental, I-am-too-holy-for-your-shirt look. This family has more money than the gods. More than the Vatican. Ohhhh. That is an idea. You are brilliant. We should go after the Vatican! They're all child molesters. We're gonna get the rich as fuck child molesters next."*

*I closed my laptop. The view from our skyscraper suite in the Bulgari Hotel in Shanghai made me queasy. But aside from that, when I looked at the dancing Asian man, I felt nothing but disgust.*

*At first, my hacking projects were only a challenge. Like climbing a leader board. Building my hacking and coding chops. Years went by as my skills improved. I broke into sites and was paid by sites to do so. All to show them their weaknesses.*

*Kane had the idea to go after some of the less ethical firms. The ones that paid the executive team a hundred times multiples more than the employees who did the work. Seemed fair to me. But the man dancing before me in his Gucci loafers and his belt buckle with two bright gold G's...he'd gotten bitten by the biggest G of them all—greed.*

# SEXY GAMER GIRL

Granddad anger-clicks the remote, flicking from channel to channel with the impatience of a spoiled child. I settle back and exchange texts with my brother and sister, giving them updates and reassuring them I'm good hanging here for the rest of the day. I alternate between reading and watching television if my grandfather keeps it on a channel long enough to catch my attention.

Finally, a doctor comes in and asks him about pain.

Granddad grumbles, "Hurts like hell."

My grandfather prefers that his doctors be close to retirement age, or at least a Baby Boomer, and this guy looks young. I sit on the edge of the seat, prepared to stand and intervene if Granddad goes berserk on him. The doctor reads his chart, listens to his chest, and looks into his eyes. Granddad's frown screams angry to me, but the doctor doesn't get the same read.

"Mr. Rossi, I think we need to increase your pain meds."

My grandfather does not dispute the young man's conclusion, and within half an hour, he's resting in a relaxed semi-conscious state. I text the good news to my siblings. Max responds immediately. Celeste has meetings this afternoon with an east coast wine distributor, so I don't expect her to respond. Max sends me a text.

*Max: I'll bring him dinner. What do you think he'll want? I'll bring you dinner, too.*

*Me: Just bring him something semi-healthy. He'd probably request fried food, but the doctor specifically said he shouldn't eat anything heavy. He had a burger, fries, and milkshake for lunch.*

*Max: LOL.*

No, Max, it's not funny. The afternoon passes in slow motion. Nurses come in and out. I finish the e-book I'm reading. Chloe calls, and I pick up with a whisper.

"Hey."

"Is your grandfather okay?"

"He's fine. Just keeping him overnight. How'd you know?"

"Susie Parsons saw my mom, and she heard it from god knows who. But everything's okay?"

"Yeah."

"Who's manning your store?"

"It's closed."

"Maybe now would be a good time to hire some of that part-time help you've been considering."

"Where would I find someone?"

"Well, given I know an entire world of waitstaff people in the area, I bet I can find someone."

"They'd make more money waiting tables."

"Yes, they would. But plenty of them don't get enough hours and have to pull a second gig. José's girlfriend is pregnant. I know he's looking for something extra."

"Isn't he a bartender?"

"Yep, and only works nights. He was trying to make it as an artist, but now he needs something that pays. Want me to ask him?"

"Sure. Tell him I'll pay twenty an hour. You think that's enough?"

"I'll ask. And my neighbor has a daughter who is home working on a thesis. I can walk over and ask her too."

"That'd be great. Thank you."

"Running a shop by yourself is borderline insanity." Sadly, it hasn't been that difficult until now. Not once that I can think of has there been a line at the register.

Chloe and I hang up, and in what feels like minutes, I receive a text that José would love to work at The Bookery.

*Me: Great. Can he meet me tomorrow morning? I'll take him through everything.*

When she responds that he'll be there at eight-thirty, the tightness around my ribs dissipates. This is good. I can be back here in the morning and help if they discharge my grandfather. And if not, I can corner the doctor to find out why.

My grandfather is a healthy man. He's spent most of his life in the vineyards, and his weathered skin is permanently tanned. His bushy black eyebrows are peppered with white. He has a receding hairline, but he's still got a head full of hair. It's one hundred percent white. Outside, under the sun, that shock of white combined with his native olive coloring gives him an invincible, almost god-like quality, invoking wisdom and power.

In this hospital bed, the lines along his brow, his eyes, his nose, and around his lips appear deeper. He might be dehydrated. The blanket draped over his form shrinks his legs and his torso. The prominent veins on the back of his hands exaggerate his frailty. I don't like seeing him in this bed – not at all. He keeps us together. No one can live forever, obviously, but he's a pillar of strength. It's easy to believe he might be the one to do it. I want him to do it. I can't imagine visiting the vineyard without him appearing with dirt stains on his pants and work boots.

Chloe and I hang up, and I click over to Zeitgeist. The circle in the corner alerts me to four messages. Two are from the same player who wants to buy my game assets. I ignore his name and click on Phoenix.

> Phoenix: Plenty of men don't maintain social accounts. Are you talking about FB and Insta?
> Phoenix: How did you meet this man?

Phoenix's texts always excite me—because I am juvenile and ridiculous. It's ridiculous. He's a virtual friend. But his last text reads as a touch jealous. Or big brother. Protective. Am I reading too much into a text doused with brevity? Yes, I am.

*Firefly: Why do you assume it's me? I could be asking for a
friend.*

Within seconds, he responds.

*Phoenix: Are you?*

*Firefly: No.*
*Firefly: Have you heard of TruthFinder? It's an app I use
when I date men. It'll give me their history.*
*Firefly: It's crazy cool. I busted a married man attempting to
date my friend recently.*
*Firefly: Not sure of your dating status, but I highly recom-
mend this app to anyone dating off the Internet. Lots of
slime out there.*
*Firefly: Even for men. It's a good app.*

*Phoenix: Good to know.*

He doesn't text more. Phoenix is always so fricking brief. I'd like to
know his dating status. But why? It doesn't matter. He probably lives
on another continent. If he had any interest in meeting, he'd say more.
He'd pick up that ball, and he'd throw it. He doesn't. He could be
married. He could have children. He could be a woman. But I don't
think so. Regardless, he's not interested. There's no ball throwing. I go
back to reading my book.

A tapping sounds against the wooden door, and Max pushes through. He's holding two white paper bags, and judging from the size, he brought enough food for half the floor. Grease has soaked through the sides of one bag. So much for healthy.

"How's he doing?" Max whispers.

"He's been sleeping for hours. Ever since they upped his pain meds."

"I'm not sleeping. I'm resting." My grandfather's gruff tone hints at his strength, but his eyes remain closed.

"Are you thirsty? Are you comfortable?" I ask the questions that come to mind, knowing as I do so he's probably going to bite my head off.

"Max, what'd you bring to eat?" His eyelids flutter open, and he fumbles with the remote near his hand. The bed comes to life, lifting him up, angling him into a sitting position.

"Mexican. Everything we need for a build-your-own taco bar. Plus guacamole and salsa. The nurses confiscated the tequila."

"Did you really—"

He shakes his head, a sly smile answering my concern. I can just see us getting kicked out of the hospital for violating the alcohol policy. Leave it to the Rossi's.

"Did you get queso?"

"What do you take me for? Of course. How else are we going to clog those arteries?"

"Flour tortilla chips and queso. Now I know which of my grandchildren loves me the most."

I gasp, and Max chuckles. No, I've only been sitting with him all day.

"You." My grandfather points my way. "It's time for you to get out of here."

"Right when the food arrives?" I ask, half-joking. I'm starved. There's no way I'm leaving without food.

"You can eat. Then you go. I've got some business to discuss with Max, and then I'll kick him out. I'm no invalid. And I've got an entire staff of nurses at my beck and call. I don't need you kids going crazy and uprooting your lives."

"I'd hardly call one day at the hospital uprooting our lives," I admonish as I piece together a soft taco heavy on pico de gallo, sour cream, and shredded cheese. Max has arranged a basket of chips and a bowl of queso in front of Granddad. I frown because the man needs more than fried chips and cheese.

"Can you get me some water? A bottle, not what they have in that pitcher." He grimaces, and I leave the room in search of a bottle of water.

When I return with several bottles of water from the vending machine, I discover Max brought iced tea, and they've both pretty much finished eating. I set the bottled waters down on the side table so Granddad can reach them and pick my taco back up.

"I'm serious. Get on out of here," my grandfather says.

Max is sprawled in my chair, and he's graciously packed up my laptop and charger and put it into my tote bag for me.

"I've got it, Veev. I'll call you later?" Max says.

"Okay." I glance between the two men and decide they must have something to discuss that they don't want me to hear. Probably nothing that I would care about at all, but something to do with business and something I don't need to worry about. I can hear either of them explaining it without even asking them to. I'd like to say it's a male thing, but it's not. If Celeste were here, she'd be allowed to stay. They all work together. I'm the one who turned her back on the family business.

The elevator dings and I exit into the mammoth lobby with sky-high ceilings. It's dusk outside. Headlights and taillights in the parking lot glow in the distance. A nurse pushes someone in a wheelchair in front of me, and I slow my steps. I'm not in a rush, and I glance around the lobby on my way out.

One dark head of hair, bent over a laptop, earns a second glance. My heart thrums with recognition. I blink. It's definitely him. He raises his head, and his dark gaze meets mine. It's Erik. Erik without a social history.

"Erik?" I ask, the single word meant to convey *what are you doing here?* He's studying me, his focus as laser-centered as when he looks at his laptop screen.

"Are you okay?" he asks.

"Yeah." The concern in his question throws me, and I think back to my texts. *Did I imply something urgent?*

He trips forward over something by his feet. I'm too far away to help, so I simply watch. His laptop is still in his hands, and it's connected to a charger. As he lunges forward, the white cord snaps and flies into the air.

He doesn't fall flat on his face. He doesn't even fall on his knees. Within seconds, he's regained balance, but his lips are turned up on the ends. He can laugh at himself.

I smile and repeat his question. "Are you okay?"

Serious Erik returns in the blink of an eye.

"Your grandfather? He's good? Are visiting hours over?"

"No. My brother's up there with him, and they kicked me out."

"He's okay? Is surgery needed?"

"No. He's staying overnight in an abundance of caution." I use the words that have been stated to us a few times during the day. "Plus, he gets better meds here. I think that's the only reason he ultimately agreed to stay." I know my grandfather, and that's definitely the only reason. "But what are you doing here?"

He pushes his glasses up on the bridge of his nose and goes about pulling the recharging cord out of the wall and packing up his laptop. He's avoiding my gaze, and I step closer, curiosity piqued.

"Erik?" He pulls the strap of his computer bag over his head, and it falls across his chest.

"I was concerned. And hospitals have good Wi-Fi."

"You've been sitting down here working all day?" His hand falls to my lower back, and with a gentle press, he nudges me to the front door.

"Not all day. I figured there was a good chance you wouldn't stay the night. And you might need food." He raises his right arm and pushes the circular revolving door in the center of the entrance and follows as I step forward, so he and I are both sharing a division of the revolving door. It's an expansive division, so we easily fit. The door emits a whooshing sound as it turns, and I wait until we're on the sidewalk, to the side of the front entrance, to say more.

"Max brought my grandfather food. I ate some of it." He nods, and a thought occurs to me. "It's nice that you're here, but it's also rather bizarre." He shoves his hands into his pockets and kicks a rock on the ground.

"Unexpected things can happen in a hospital. I just…if you needed someone, I wanted to be here." He sounds vulnerable, and it hits me. He's had a bad hospital experience. A waft of guilt for being negative about his presence fills me. It's incredibly sweet.

"So, I've had dinner. But if you want to come back and hang out, I'd be down for that. We could order take-out if you are hungry." I'm not up for much more than chilling on the sofa. I want to kick off my sandals and sip a glass of a strong red. I'm thinking zin or cab.

"You drove, right?" he asks.

"Yes. My car is over there." I point in the general direction of my midnight blue Range Rover.

"Okay. I'll meet you back at your place. I'll bring in some extra, just in case you change your mind and decide you're hungry. Maybe I'll order from the tapas place? The one that's on the far side of the square?"

Back home, I pick out a nice bottle of Zinfandel and swirl it in the decanter. I'm an introvert at heart, and after spending a day at the hospital, I'd normally resent having someone push their way into my off-time. The absence of resentment is unusual, especially given we went on one date that ended with him bounding out the door. Inexplicable excitement simmers.

He's a good-looking guy, sure. When he works in my store, I appreciate the view. He's intriguing. I suspect if we'd been in school together, as Chloe pointed out, she'd cheat off his paper, but I think I would've clamored to be a teammate on his projects. He's quiet and reserved. And I like the way he looks at me. It's not nerves that he stirs, exactly, but there's a fission of energy. A pulse of awareness that I get when I develop a thing for a guy. He's not from around here, and that's definitely a plus. And there's an air of mystery.

I swirl the deep maroon wine and watch as a film clings to the glass on the way down. I inhale cinnamon and clove. I close my eyes as the first swallow hits my tongue with hints of black pepper and jam. The burn in my shoulders dims.

The doorbell from my back door rings, and I check the Nest app on my phone. The top of Erik's head shows on screen. He's holding a brown paper bag. I hustle down the stairs and swing the door open.

"Hi, there." My mood is worlds better than when he encountered me in the hospital. "Come on in. I just opened a bottle. Would you like some?"

"Water is fine for me," he answers.

"What?" I close the door. This could mean this attraction will die down extremely soon. I didn't devote my life to wine, like my family, but I'm not going to spend evenings with someone who won't even taste it.

"I'll have a little. I don't normally drink wine."

"You did say that, didn't you?" I ask.

"Are you a big wine drinker?"

His question confirms he has no idea who I am. I suppose I can put up with a non-wine drinker in exchange for someone who likes me for me.

"I like to have a glass or two each evening." If I'm eating with my grandfather, we'll have a glass for lunch.

"I like *sake*. But I don't drink it often. And I drink it only when I'm eating sushi or fish. My issue with alcohol is it curbs the senses."

"You think? I feel like it enhances the senses." We step into my apartment, and he approaches the table and begins pulling out item after item from the bag. In my kitchen, I grab a placemat, plate, and utensils for him.

"How much food did you get?"

"I told you, I got extra in case you're hungry. Besides, you eat leftovers, right?"

I do eat leftovers. It's easy to heat them when I'm working downstairs.

"Young. What kind of name is that?" He looks a little taken aback. "I mean, what country of origin?"

"It's spelled Y-E-U-N-G. My father's side of the family is from a small country not too far from Taiwan. Macau. Have you heard of it?"

I haven't. So, is he Polynesian? Asian? "Were you born in the US?"

"Yes." He takes a sip of water with a knowing smirk as he sets the glass down. "You're probably too polite to ask. But I can tell you're wondering. I'm mixed race. My mother is Caucasian. My father is Asian. But he, too, was born in the US. My dad's parents were born abroad and immigrated here." Ah. He's definitely Asian, but I see the mix too. His skin is a light olive color, and he has dark eyes and an angular jaw. I find his thick-framed glasses to have an intellectual appeal. In many ways, he's the strong, silent type. It's hard to imagine him relaxing.

"What about you, Vivianne Rossi?" His use of my full name jolts me.

"How do you know my full name?"

"Let me count the ways," and he holds up a hand to tick off the number on his fingers. "When you sign in on the Wi-Fi in The Bookery, the pop-up page includes the name of the store and your name."

"It does?" I ask. He nods and holds out his index finger.

"Yes, it does. You can change that if you want to."

"How else?"

"Two, you have a set of business cards on the counter. It's in that brass holder over by the sink. Anyone paying at the cash register can see it."

"Oh, yeah. I used to have them on the cash register, but the only people taking them were people who wanted to sell me something. I don't know why I had them made. Eventually, I'll go to conferences, and I guess they'll be useful there."

"What kind of conferences?" He takes off his glasses and sets them on the table, then rubs the bridge of his nose. He's apparently done with counting.

"Book conferences. Trade shows. I haven't been yet, but…what other ways?" I'm curious. It's not like I keep my name under lock and key. Everyone in the valley knows me, but this is interesting.

"It's on your website for The Bookery."

"It is? That's bizarre. Why would I put that there?"

"You have to have an owner name tied to the domain."

"So, where do you find that?"

"Well, on your site, it's on the bottom of each page, along with your store address. But otherwise, a person could go to the domain registry. Do you not want people to know your name?"

"No, it's fine, I guess." Weird. The person I hired to create my website didn't ask me about any of this.

"Can I ask you a completely different question?"

"Sure."

"How are you still single?"

"Now, that's a flirty question. I like it. I could ask the same of you." And I could. I'm guessing he's around my age, but he's fit. He dresses in a casual, sophisticated manner, even if he is colorblind, and he's thoughtful. Men like that aren't readily available. Well, straight men like that aren't. From what I understand, gay men are often in shape, dress well, and are also considerate. Chloe, from time to time, goes onto the male seeking male boards to scope out the men who've joined the ranks of our team and to dream a little dream—her words, not mine.

"That's not an answer," he points out.

"Well, I've moved around. That didn't help, I suppose. But...I'm only twenty-eight. Lots of people my age are single." He's verging on sounding like my grandfather. *There is nothing wrong with being single at twenty-eight.*

"I know, I know." He closes up containers, stacking them as he does so. "It's just your...Are you a gamer?"

I scoop up the remaining items from the table and follow him into my kitchen, a smile plastered on my face at his left field question.

"I was. Do I give off a nerdy vibe? Was that going to be your theory as to why I'm still single?"

I open the refrigerator and shift a few containers to make room for the white cardboard boxes he's holding.

"There's nothing nerdy about you, Vivi. Nothing at all. Those eyes. Perfection."

"I wear contacts." Embarrassment heats my skin. Stupid, brain fart comment.

"What color are they, really?"

"Oh, no, my contacts help me see. They, these, my, are real."

He inches closer, and his presence sucks the oxygen from my lungs.

"I could look at them all day." His fingers brush my cheek, then coax a stray strand behind my ear. My heart rate skyrockets. "And a sexy gamer…how you made it through college single is unfathomable."

His lips brush over mine, and the room spins. I lean into him to steady myself. I lightly touch his arm and trace the curve of his bicep. His shirt molds to his firm, well-defined chest, and while I've stolen plenty of glances at his fit form, touching the muscle is another level of electric.

My back hits the refrigerator as he presses his hard body against mine, and I stand one-legged, lifting a leg to give him better access. There's no doubt my panties are drenched. Between my legs, an intensifying need throbs. He caresses my waist, then my ass, and then pressure intensifies on my thighs as he grips them and lifts.

My head hits the back of the cabinet door when he places me on the kitchen counter. There's a hunger in his gaze that fuels insanity. *But is this so insane? He's cute, and who really cares? He's single. I think he's trustworthy.*

Cool air brushes across my breasts. My dress pools at my waist. My bra is gone. And his wet mouth circles my nipple. He lets it go to administer attention to the other one, and the icy air over my damp, tender skin feels so good I tease and pinch the peak with my fingers.

"Fuck, you are sexy." His fingers push aside my panties. "The sexiest gamer girl I've ever met."

"I rocked ROBLOX."

His fingers thrust inside, and his thumb works over my clit. I want off the counter. I want on him. But I also don't want him to stop.

"I'm sure you did." Hot air circles my ear as his fingers prove especially dexterous. I'd bet he's got skills with a joystick. And that thought makes me really want his, well, joystick. But up on the counter, I can't reach for him without interrupting him.

"Erik," I pant.

"Yes." His teeth graze my earlobe, and the sensation travels down my spine.

"Fuck, that feels good."

"Yes." He grins against my throat. His fingers stroke, and my back arches.

There's a nagging nuisance in the back of my mind, reminding me he has no social media history. But his fingers are in me, and the motion pretty much obliterates that tiny concern. I am so close, on the edge.

And then he's gone, no longer kissing me. I open my eyes at the same time his tongue replaces his fingers. My thighs fall over his shoulders. One hand holds on to the edge of the top of the refrigerator, and the other palm falls flat on marble. My fingers tense against the cold, hard counter, and fuck, I don't want him to stop.

I groan and moan and basically angle my core into his face. He is exquisite. His tongue is masterful. His fingers. Oh, fuck, and then I'm done. I spiral and scream and tug on his hair and almost slide right off onto the floor.

"Holy blasters," I gasp. He places sloppy kisses against my thighs. My dress gathers at my waist. I don't have any idea if he ripped my panties off or if they're just scrunched to the side. But when his lips find mine, I give him a grateful kiss because that was fantastic. I taste myself on him, and I pull him to me, my arms over his shoulders, my hands in his hair. His hair is all kinds of tousled and messed up, smooth and thick.

He puts me back together while he's kissing me. My dress falls back over my legs, and he pulls the straps up over my shoulders. The bra lies on the floor near the oven. He doesn't bother with it. I slide down to the floor, and he places one solid press of his lips to mine.

"Now, bedroom?" I attempt to raise one eyebrow to imitate a seductress. He smirks, and it looks like he's trying not to laugh, so I'm not sure at all I got the look right.

"Not today, my sexy gamer girl."

# WITNESS PROTECTION

ERIK

"Well, look who decided to come home." Kairi's sprawled out on the sofa, and Trevor has her feet in his lap with a bowl of popcorn. If I didn't know better, I'd think they were a couple. An old *Arrow* episode plays on the screen.

"G'night," I say and head to my room. I'm still semi-hard. It took all my willpower not to carry her into her bedroom. I don't think I've ever wanted sex so badly.

"You've got sex hair. Whoa. Were you with the Rossi girl?"

"None of your business." I'm two steps up when I realize I forgot to take off my shoes. I toe them off.

"It's not smart, Erik. There's got to be sex clubs you can frequent in San Fran."

"She's his little gaming friend," Trevor reminds her. I grimace. I should've never admitted to either of them I'd known her. "Zeitgeist Battle. His avatar's name is Phoenix."

"You still play?" Her tone smacks with incredulity.

"No. He hasn't played it in years. They text."

Kairi sits up and crosses her legs. "Did you know she lived here when we moved here?"

I stand on the stairs with my back to them. If I go up the stairs and ignore them, it'll be breakfast conversation. She might even try to hack into the game and screw with my avatar. There's a level of boredom these two reach that leads to childish pranks.

I return to the club chair. My shoes hit the floor with a loud thud after I toss them into the shoe pile.

"Don't fuck with her," I warn.

"Did you tell her your last name?"

"Not my real one. No." Kairi's expression is etched in concern. There's a degree of fear in those eyes that, after Lara, she wore all the time. I don't like that the fear has returned. "There's no way for her to figure it out."

"I don't understand. You've known her for fifteen years—"

"In a game."

"And you never told her your real name? How long have you been hacking?"

"We met in a game. I told you. At an age when I didn't care about her real name. When we got older, she texted and said she liked that we were anonymous. She made me pinky swear we'd stay anonymous."

"That's weird," Kairi says.

Trevor springs to my defense. "It's really not. When you're in a game, there are tons of folks you play against that you never ask for real ID."

"Maybe when you're kids. But now you're like, you're just using the game's messaging app, right? Knowing you, you probably liked it because it's safer than anything else. No one thinks to hack messaging apps within games."

"As kids, I never questioned her real identity. I didn't care. Then her parents died, and our online friendship took a different turn. But by then, I was concerned about security."

"And she never probed you for your real name?"

"Nope. We agreed. It's not important, anyway. What's in a name?"

"Do you still text in the app?" Kairi is showing more interest in my personal life than she's shown in anything in ages. It's actually nice to see. Returning home has been good for her.

"Some. Not often."

"Don't you find it odd that she hasn't pressured you to meet up? Or have a video call?"

"No. Why?"

"Well, duh. She's a woman. If I had a fifteen-year friendship with an unidentified male, I'd probably sport a crush, and I'd probably be curious about what he looked like."

"You mean female, right?" Trevor asks. Kairi ignores him. We all know she's a lesbian.

"She has a tattoo…" I say the words without considering my audience.

"A tattoo of your avatar?" Kairi sounds giddy. No, that's not it. She's making fun of me in her understated way.

"No. Of our names. Maybe at one point she had a crush." Maybe she's harbored a secret crush for a long time, and that's the answer to why she's been single. But that idea is ludicrous. "She's never pushed to know my identity."

"Maybe she already knows it," Kairi says, and I freeze. *Could she?*

"But how?" I ask. I want to hear Kairi play out her logic.

"I don't know. Is she a hacker?"

"Not at all," Trevor answers.

"This game you play…is there any way to hire someone to find out the real identity of a player? If there is, she has the money to hire someone to do it for her."

"Really? Are we talking about the same woman?" Vivi lives in a relatively small apartment above a bookshop that's in the red. Her car is a Range Rover relic. The tailpipe is all rust.

"Vivianne Rossi. Blonde, blue eyes, right? Northern Italian through and through. Whether she ever found out who you were, who knows? But I could see her wanting to remain anonymous. In the wine industry, her family is infamous. Maybe she likes having a friend who doesn't care about her family at all."

"Infamous? She's part of the Rossi Vineyards Rossis?" Spectre hacked Rossi Vineyards. I had hoped she wasn't related. But if she's that wealthy, I suppose Kane was right and paying ransom didn't hurt them.

"Yep. One and the same. Her family is an institution in this area. Maybe that's why she liked the anonymity."

"She used to live in Paris. I'm sure she has friends who don't care about wine." To hear Kairi talk, sometimes you'd think the world revolved around wine. In my opinion, the whole life on a farm thing is overly romanticized. And make no mistake, vineyards are farms. "Regardless, being anonymous works in the game. I'd prefer to keep the channel private and secure. If we're discovered…" *Shit, if we're discovered, we'll need to disappear.*

"It's been six months. Do you really believe he's still after us? Because I'm beginning to question it. We moved on, and he's got bigger projects on his plate. Spectre hits FBI lists as frequently as ReVil and Blasphemy these days." Trevor looks sincere. He doesn't fucking learn.

"The enemy strikes when it's unexpected." He should know this.

"And we acted without orders, and against orders, so he's going to chop off our heads." Trevor's sarcastic wit turns Kairi pale. "I'm sorry, I didn't mean…" Trevor reaches out and touches Kairi's knee. The love of her life wasn't beheaded, but the slice across her throat performed the same function. "I was just trying to say I don't think he's following Sun Tzu."

"He is. And when you assume he won't strike, that's when he will."

⊏⎯⊐

"Still working from here?" Trevor's dripping sweat from his morning run. A light spray of dirt coats his lower legs and socks. He's barefoot, and there's a white line revealing the portion of sock covered by his running shoe and the portion coated in dust from the trail.

"Yep." The monitor I have trained on the cameras near The Bookery flicks from the front of the store to the back of the store, to the cash register.

"Not going into town today?" It is obvious I'm not, and his duplication of a similar question is wasting my time.

"Tesla's sending someone out to hook up another outlet for charging. I need to be here today." My new car arrived, and I could share the charger with Trevor, but I figure paying for an additional station will be a benefit to Kairi's property. When we're not here, her mother rents this place out.

Trevor chugs a bottle of water and wipes his brow while watching the monitor.

"You know, just because you can see her remotely, it's not the same thing as being in the same room with her."

"Obviously." I resume reading the latest FBI update, hoping he'll take the signal.

"There has to be some personality disorder associated with someone who prefers to live behind a computer screen and not in direct contact. Before you had these cameras, you were in her store every single day. You had to be there. Now that you have these cameras, it's like you're content to sit here and stare. It's not healthy."

"Is that your professional diagnosis?" I have no idea what I'm reading, a sign that he's distracting me. He needs to leave the room.

He sighs heavily. His feet create a repetitive thud, decreasing in volume as he ascends the stairs.

Vivi hasn't been at The Bookery most of this week, anyway, but I don't need to share that with Trevor. She hired someone to work in the store. He appears to be honest. He reads when he could clean or do something useful, but other than that, he's a good employee. He has spent some of his downtime on a laptop. I can't see the screen from the view on the monitor, which makes me curious.

The camera rotation flicks to the front entrance of The Bookery. A familiar man in a baseball cap passes the store, and he pauses a beat, peering inside. The closed sign hangs over the glass panel of one of the double doors. His head angles up to the rafters above. The lid of the cap darkens his face, rendering it unidentifiable.

My view flashes to the back door, and I quickly jump onto the system to take over the screen view. The inside camera flashes to Vivi approaching the front door, passing the register. The skin on my fingers buzzes as the intersection of Vivi and the man outside nears.

I return to the front door view and run down my list of options. They are limited. A call to 911 would take minutes. Ten to fifteen before arrival. I'm over thirty minutes away.

He's almost out of camera view when my front door view returns. The sign on the glass flips. Whoever he was, he didn't want to be seen by her. And he was scoping the place. Who pauses in front of a business and looks around for security cameras? Thieves.

Or someone on Kane's payroll. Maybe he's learning the lay of the land. Determining the best location to strike. He would only strike The Bookery if he's somehow connected me and Vivi. If he's already made the connection, then she's not safe. I've stayed away from her, checking in via text so she doesn't think I'm freaking out from our make-out session. The time apart has helped to clear my head and evaluate risk and response plans.

"Hey, did you see that latest ransomware threat IC3 sent over?" Kairi enters, freshly showered and coffee in hand. She's wearing pajama bottoms and a T-shirt.

"Just an overview of the weekly report. Is the company going to pay?" The FBI prefers no one pays ransom threats. Paying the blackmailers only incentivizes them to continue with their crime spree. That's why I've asked to work with a special group within the National Security Agency on encryption software that will allow us to covertly hack into crypto accounts and reclaim stolen funds. If we eliminate the financial incentive, then we'll make the Internet a far safer space.

"They're gonna pay. They've asked us to track the transaction."

"That's pointless," I mutter. What's the point of tracking it if we can't reclaim it? My attention zooms on the screen showing the front of The Bookery. The man Vivi hired comes into view, and he pushes the door open. I check the time. He's five minutes late.

"Yeah. But I think these guys left a crumb trail. They were sloppy when they hacked in. I spent some time last night on it."

"Good." I close my laptop and unplug the wire from the wall.

"What are you doing?"

I stare at the cord in my hand. *What am I doing? I have a Tesla guy coming within an hour.*

"Erik, are you okay?" Kairi asks. I plug my laptop back in. My eyes burn, and I rub them, shifting my glasses up to my forehead. I let out a sigh. I don't want to worry Kairi, but she's part of our team, and my team is my family. Withholding information weakens our defense.

"I think Kane has someone scoping The Bookery. The guy could just be looking for me."

"If he asks Vivi about you, what will she say?"

"She knows me as Erik Yeung. I work from her store sometimes. She doesn't have my home address, or at least not a real one. She doesn't know I live with you. She's met Trevor and Wolf. If someone showed her pictures, she'd be able to point us out, but she's suspicious by nature. She might not easily buy into someone's story if they walked in flashing pictures." Or she could concoct a crazy theory and decide we're gangsters or serial killers or mafia. I found a backdoor into the TruthFinder app and created an extensive profile and identity for my new name. Took me most of the night after she shared her data mining source. But there's nothing in there that would endanger us... although I did grab some real photos from my past to give it a little depth.

"If he's scoping the place, they already know we're in the area. It seems to me the biggest risk is if they tracked you back here."

"The truck." I snap my fingers. "We need to check it for a tracking device. I've been parking it outside of view from her shop. And I drove Trevor's car once."

"I really have to say I think you're paranoid. If he's going to track us, it'll be online. That's the world he knows."

"You're being naïve. He has access to anything he wants. Now, this guy I'm watching — he's not skilled. He's an amateur. He could have scouts out all over the country. That would be one reason he's hired lower levels."

"Listen to you. Lower levels. It's not a game, Erik. If he knew where we were, he'd hire a sniper, and then, I'll grant you, it's game over." Kairi's lower lip protrudes, and even though she's looking in my direction, she's not seeing me. She's playing scenarios out in her head.

"No. Your scenario is too over the top. It's more realistic you've got a thief on your hands scoping out businesses in the square. You're so hyped up on Vivi. Have you even noticed if he's looking at other businesses too? Those businesses might be prime theft targets. I'd bet some of them…not a bookstore, but some of those gift stores and art galleries and such…they could have stuff worth stealing."

"People really steal physical stuff?" The idea is savage. I know I wanted a camera over the cash register, but her theory bothers me. Physical theft is so small-minded. High risk, low reward. There's so much more to be gained through cybercrime. For example, the small-scale ransomware that Kairi's investigating will bring in over one hundred thousand for the ransom crew, all for a couple of days' work and little to no chance of getting caught.

"Erik, have you ever considered that the only reason we're currently alive is because Kane wants us working for the other side?"

"What?"

"I don't know. It's just a thought."

"He tried to kill us."

"Yes, but we got away." Her voice trails, and I know she's thinking of Lara. I think of her, too, but what I remember is Kairi holding her lifeless body, refusing to let go, blood everywhere. Kairi, I hope, remembers Lara in life, not in death. Doesn't matter. There's no point going down either path.

"Okay. So, we've determined that this guy could be a common thief, scoping the whole square."

"The valley attracts money, and therefore it attracts thieves."

She shrugs and sips her coffee.

"Or it is connected to Kane." She gives me the look. I go on. "We consider this unlikely, but if it's the case, then he's got low level, and by that, I mean low skill—"

"I know what you mean."

"Don't roll your eyes." She can be such a nag. "Let me work this through. He's got low levels out scoping areas. Maybe he figured out your real name, tracked your origins, and he has someone out showing photos, trying to figure out if we, or one of us, have landed in this area."

"Have you seen this guy show photos to anyone?"

"No. I'm playing this out. Stop interrupting me." I sit away from my desk, out of view of the monitor. "In that scenario, is Vivi in danger?" That's the question.

"I seriously doubt it. But, in my more realistic thief scenario, she could be since she's the only one in that area who lives above her store. That place is a ghost town once the restaurants close."

I don't like the idea of Vivi being in danger. I don't like being thirty minutes away if something happens to her. It's that same feeling of desperation when my sister lived on an island, and I could have a team watching her, but we were helpless if something happened. It's why I bought the house next door to hers and rotated agents in and out of it.

I could hire security to be nearby. That would be the most secure plan. For me to stay away and hire someone to watch from afar. But she'd probably notice security, and it would be problematic. Then again, I hired security to trail my sister for almost a year, and she never noticed. But, no. That was easier. She assumed the house next door was a rental house.

"I think I'm going to take one of those apartments closer to the square." I say it aloud as my plan crystalizes. I'll be as close to Vivi as I can. I won't put agents on her, but I'll be close by.

"You really like her?" Kairi asks. There's no anger or fear. Now she seems in awe. As if it's unbelievable.

"I do." I won't deny it. She's an old friend, and she's sexy as hell, and I'm inexplicably drawn to her. My body is drawn to her, and she distracts me all the time. She's not perfect because perfect would not be a distraction, but I do like her. I hope Kairi and Trevor are right, and I'm simply paranoid. Because it'll crush me if she winds up living on the run or under witness protection, all because one day, out of boredom, I let my curiosity go.

# CRUSHED

VIVI

It's been nine days since I've seen Erik in the flesh. He hasn't made any updates to his social posts in that time. Now that I have the correct spelling of his last name, TruthFinder did find him. He's not the most devout social poster, but he is a typical guy. There are no gaps in his history. There's also a noticeable void in prior relationships. If his modus operandi is to hook-up and disappear, then that absence is explainable.

It's Sunday morning, and Chloe is over. She is telling me about David James' Facebook post. I sip my coffee and listen. He is looking for renters for his apartment in Minneapolis.

"He might be moving back," Chloe concludes.

"Or he's just moving to a new apartment." She's sporting a dreamy, hopeful look, so I expand on the obvious. "In Minnesota."

"Yeah, you're right. So, how're things with Mr. Sexy?" Her question brings him to mind, which is a bit frustrating because while I don't care about a rental in Minnesota, the distraction in and of itself was welcome. I'm tired of constantly thinking about him. I have determined he isn't the type to call, so at least I'm not waiting for the phone to ring. But he does text, albeit in terse format.

"Fine?" I don't want to complain. I don't want to be that girl. "He hasn't been working from here. But I also haven't been working as much. It's possible he's come in, and I haven't been here. I've been making it out to visit Granddad every day."

My messages with Phoenix have hit a daily stride. Over the years, we've gone through periods like this. Where we text back and forth constantly. But he's mainly concerned with what's going on with the price of gold within our game world. He keeps harping on about how I shouldn't sell.

"Do you think you'll go out again?" Chloe asks.

"He hasn't asked. He hasn't been around. It's not looking hopeful." This past time when we hooked up, it wasn't awkward, not like with our first kiss. If I'm honest with myself, I am surprised I didn't hear from him. The way we left it, you'd think I'd fall in the sure thing category. I practically begged him to bone me, and he walked away.

"You've been super busy, Viv."

"Yeah. I have. But, if he was into me, I would've heard from him by now." You can make a million excuses for a guy, but at the end of the day, if he's into you, he's gonna call, and he's gonna make time for you. I'm a big believer in the into-you theory.

"But you have heard from him?" Chloe's question is cautious. She's not certain, and I can tell she doesn't want to make me feel worse.

"Via text. Let's be real. If he was into me, he would've asked me out or dropped by."

"I wouldn't give up yet." She nudges me and clinks our coffee mugs. "If it's meant to be, it'll be."

"Puh-lease." Yes, that's another true-life theory, but it's not like I'm meant to be with a guy who used my shop for free Wi-Fi. I just liked him. And he's been the star in so many of my recent sex fantasies that I would've liked to explore that a little. Chloe is looking at me and chewing on the corner of her lip, a sure sign it's time to change the subject. "Any new interesting dates for you?"

"A guy from Healdsburg. Meeting him at a winery for a tasting in a few hours."

"That's like an hour drive." My nose scrunches in disapproval. Dating someone that far away would be wicked annoying.

"Have you not noticed that our options are limited?" Chloe defends, reading my mind.

"I bet if we went out to one of the microbreweries there'd be a single crowd."

"Name the date, and we'll go. I'll prove you wrong."

"Fine."

"Fine."

We both sip our coffee and grin. This is our routine. We never get mad at each other for real.

"How's Grandpa Rossi doing these days?" She's amused because she knows full well he's a grumpy pill.

"Driving us all batty. He's doing a ton of the stuff he's not supposed to do, and we can only yell at him but so much. He's in pain, which makes him pretty horrid to be around. Nothing makes him happy. You can't do anything right. I've never been happier I don't work with him. I don't know how Max and Celeste are staying sane."

"Family business is tough. But I think an aging parent, or grandparent, is tougher. I remember how hard it was when my mom had to convince her mom not to drive anymore."

"Oh, lord. I hope he remains a safe driver. We'd pry his license out of his cold dead fingers."

Chloe laughs. "Yeah, I don't see Grandpa Rossi going down without a fight."

"You want more coffee?" I hold out the pot in offering. She declines, and I refill mine. "Let's go sit outside." The Bookery would normally be closed on a Sunday, but José convinced me to remain open. I agreed, but only once he committed to working. I refuse to give up my day off.

We descend the stairs and wave to him. The Bookery hasn't yet opened, but José got here early to fulfill online orders.

When the back door closes behind us, Chloe asks, "How're things going with José?"

"Amazing. He's been listing my books on Amazon."

"That's weird. Don't they already have everything on sale?"

"Yes, but he has me listed as a used bookseller. So, titles that I'm on the verge of having to return to the publisher, he's been listing as used in excellent condition. And they've been selling! It's crazy. I never would've thought about it. He's also selling some on eBay. He's like this marketing wizard."

"That's great. You're glad you hired him?"

"So glad. He's the best hire ever. I owe you."

"I'm just glad you finally caved. You had no business trying to do this all on your own."

"Well, he's been a godsend. It's been two weeks, and my sales are better than they've been all year. This coming week, we're going to sit down and go through upcoming listings and place an order for new titles. He has ideas on what will sell."

"I wonder how he knows about selling books." Chloe kicks her feet up on a metal patio chair across from her seat, exposing her pale skin to the sun.

"Apparently, his aunt has a business on eBay. People drop off stuff for her to sell for them, and she takes a commission when she sells it. I guess she also has a virtual bookstore and sells used books on Amazon because people drop off books too."

"Nice. And here I thought I was just recommending a friendly neighborhood bartender."

"No, he's fantastic. And he's going to bring in some of his paintings to hang on the walls. He offered to pay me a commission on sales, but I told him no way. I'm happy to have some colorful local flair."

"Take the commission. Every dollar counts when you're starting a business."

"Please. Like I'm going to take money from him. It would be like taking money from his baby."

"Do they know if it's a boy or girl yet?"

"Girl. He's getting excited. It's cute." A red-winged blackbird flies overhead, and we both pause, watching the bird dip and land on a limb.

The creak of my back door sends the bird off into the sky.

"Vivi, someone is here to see you. Is it okay if I let him back here?"

"Yeah. Sure. How's it going out there? You need any help?"

"No, it's slow. I'm using the time to post books."

"You are the bomb. Thanks, José."

The screen door slams behind José, and within seconds it creaks again, and Erik steps through. He's in black jeans, a black T-shirt, and black sandals. Those dark eyes zero in on me, and the effect is like an oxygen vacuum.

"Hey," I say. I can't believe he's here. On a Sunday. Chloe makes a noise in her throat, reminding me I owe an introduction.

"Hi, ahm, Erik, this is Chloe. Chloe, Erik."

"I've heard a lot about you." *Oh, my god. She did not just say that.*

"Really? Good things, I hope."

"They'd be better if you came around more." *A lifetime of friendship flushed down the drain.*

Her comment has Erik shoving his hands into his front pockets and rocking back on his heels.

"Ignore her," I tell him.

"Actually, look at the time. I've got to run. My date this afternoon is over an hour's drive away. You two kids have fun." Chloe exits my backyard gate, smirking all the way. She has no fear of my shit list.

"It's strange seeing someone else behind the counter." He takes a seat on the edge of the chair Chloe vacated.

"José. He's been a lifesaver."

"What's he working on? Is he doing your books now?"

"No. Nothing like that. Turns out you can sell books online. There's a used market. Who knew?"

"But you don't have used books."

"No…but I can discount, and…Do you care about this? What brings you here?"

"Well, I'm a neighbor now. Thought I'd stop by and check in."

"Neighbor? You moved?"

"Two miles away. Walking distance."

"These past two weeks? You've been moving?" Huh. I'd just figured he'd been putting space between us. "You didn't say anything. Have you been in packing hell?"

"Not really. I don't have much. But you could say I've been in apartment hunting hell. There are no good apartments in this area. In Napa, some, but…"

"So, what did you end up with?"

"A house. Furnished. Pool in the backyard. I wouldn't call it nice, but it works. Low ceilings. So much around here has low ceilings."

"So, it's not your forever home?"

"No. But it'll do."

"Well, it's cool you ended up close by. Why here and not Napa?"

He rubs his hand over his mouth. "Why'd you choose Sonoma?"

"I liked it. This building came up for sale. I wanted to be far enough away from our family place that they couldn't expect me to show up all the time, but close enough if they needed me. And Chloe...she lives in the neighborhood. I can walk to her house." If you move much out of the town centers, you're either looking at less than stellar apartment living or homes with grand views. I wasn't quite ready for a house and yard.

"Well, I'm nearby now. If you need anything. I also have a heated pool. What are you doing today? Do you want to see it?" Other than laundry, I have nothing on the docket.

"We can walk?"

"Sure. Or, if you'd rather do something else..." He spreads out his palms and splays them open, telling me he is open for anything.

"You think you can just show up, and I'll be free to..." I stop talking because my life is so dull he absolutely can just show up. Celeste took Granddad over to one of his friend's for lunch and wine tastings. Max is probably working on a project in the vineyard.

My plans had been to sit outside and read, or maybe go for a walk. Erik tilts his head, and his lips turn up on the ends. The sun reflects sharply in a couple of spots on his thick, black hair. He's an interesting person, and I like hanging out with him. It's just a Sunday afternoon. I have nothing to lose.

"It's a nice day for a walk. I'd love to see your new home." I never saw his old home, but he made it sound like it was far away.

"Great. Are you going to change?"

I glance down at my loose, vibrant-colored pajama pants and my tank top.

"Yes. You want to sit out here, or you want to come up?"

"I'll follow you up."

The back door creaks as I open it.

"This needs some WD-40," he says.

"I know. All the hinges around here need to be coated. I just keep forgetting to buy some."

José's upper back curves over the counter in an arc. A stack of books sits beside my laptop.

"Watch your posture," I tell him. I'm guilty of the same thing, but I hate seeing it on someone else. Erik squints from behind us, staring at the monitor. "I'm going to head out this afternoon. Is that okay?" I don't know why I ask. He's an employee doing his job. He knows I don't plan on working Sundays.

"I'm good. It's slow. I'll text you if we get a Sunday afternoon crowd." In this town, on a beautiful day like today, all the tourists will be at vineyards, and the locals will either be chilling at home or on hikes or something outdoorsy. But it's conceivable tourists post-vineyard tasting might meander around the square upon their return, especially if their vacation ends today and they fly out in the morning.

I hear the soft thud of Erik's footsteps behind me as I climb to my apartment, and as I turn the knob, a memory of his last time in my space brings heat to my skin that has nothing to do with the climb to the second floor. He pushes the door closed behind us.

"Make yourself at home. I'll go get ready."

"Was he using your laptop?"

"Yeah. His is really old."

"You gave him access to your entire life?"

"I'd hardly call it my entire life."

"Really? So, if he clicked over to your bank, your password isn't auto memorized on the browser?"

"No, it is. But I trust him. After all, I'm leaving him with my cash register."

"I have an old laptop he can use." He walks away from me as if the discussion is over. It's a nice offer, but it won't work.

"It's easier just to let him access sites through my computer." I kick off my fuzzy slippers by the door.

"I'm going to pretend you didn't say that." He's rubbing the back of his neck, and tension radiates around him. Instead of going to my bedroom, I step up behind him and press along his shoulders. The muscle is hard and tight. He freezes, and I lift his hand out of the way and knead his shoulders.

"Do you carry your tension in your shoulders?" Probably very common for someone deskbound all day. My masseuse could really help him with this. A low grumble vibrates under my fingertips.

He twists around, and his fingers slide beneath my cotton tank as he pulls me up against his chest. His chest muscles are corded and equally as hard as those shoulder muscles. His mouth falls to mine, and there's nothing soft or gentle about his kiss. His tongue probes, and our teeth clash. The energy in the room goes from a low-level buzz to an amplified, frenetic crescendo.

My back slaps down on the sofa, and he follows with the heat of his body capturing mine. I cradle him in my core, lifting my legs and wrapping around him. Fully clothed, his hips rock against me with pressure and friction.

He breaks the kiss, gasping for air, and raises up on his forearms.

"Do you have any idea how fucking sexy you are? You should not walk around downstairs in this." With firm pressure, he moves his hand from my ribs up and over my breast, pushing the tank top up and over. I raise my arms while watching the rapid in and out movement of his chest. As my tank goes flying, he lets out a coarse groan.

"God, you're gorgeous. So perfect." Before I can respond, his mouth is back on mine. He pinches a nipple, hard, and I squirm. Then he trails kisses over the sensitive skin beneath my ear, down my neck, and yes, he sucks in a nipple and need melts my core.

I tug on his shirt, wanting it off. I want to explore his body, too. He has way too many clothes on. He pauses in his ministrations and pulls his shirt over his head. His glasses come off too, and they clatter across the floor.

"Can you see?" He's just as good-looking without the thick frames. His dark eyes meet mine, and I tug on his hair, wanting him closer. The absence of glasses is more intimate. No one else sees him like this.

"I can see." He slowly lowers himself, his bare, muscular torso touching me for the first time. His skin is cool. I wrap my arms around him, holding him close. Our kisses are calmer now, even as the rhythm of our hips promises we're not anywhere close to done. We kiss for minutes as I explore his muscular back and his smooth, thick hair. My nails scrape lightly against his skin, and he groans. He trails kisses along my neck, and his teeth graze my earlobe.

"I want you." He breathes out warm air next to my ear, and it traverses my entire body. I want him, too. But my brain short-circuits from pleasure overload, and words don't form. He trails kisses over my breasts. The cool air teases each wet nipple as he takes his time worshipping me. Then he travels farther down. I miss his heat over my torso, and I twist my nipple, luxuriating in the sensation of my now sensitized skin.

He grips the edge of my panties and pajama bottoms and pulls. He almost pulls me right off the sofa.

"Oh shit," he mumbles. And I can't stop myself from laughing. But he kneels before me, his knees on the floor, and all laughter subsides when his attention falls to my most sensitive of places.

I whimper as his soft, warm tongue dips inside. Then his finger. *Oh, god. I remember this. He's really, really good at this.*

Sunlight pours through the open windows. I'm lying back on my sofa, naked, with a man kneeling before me on the ground and his head between my legs. The back of the sofa forces my neck into an uncomfortable arch. Anyone from across the street could see in.

I grip a chunk of his hair. *This is crazy. What am I doing?*

His teeth tease, and a burst of tingles pulse, and I squeeze my thighs and close my eyes. My toes curl as the muscles contract so hard it hurts. Everything contracts, and my back arches from the powerful sensation. He kisses my thighs, spreading my juices onto me. Attentive, studied eyes gaze up at me, and a slow grin spreads.

"Good?"

"Incredible."

He stands from the floor and shifts me onto the sofa. With a steady gaze, he throws a pack of condoms on the table, unbuttons his pants, and they fall to the floor.

"I need you." He crawls over me, and I spread my legs, welcoming him.

"God, I am so hard for you. It's painful."

I test his words, reaching between us, and he lets out a deep growl. He kisses me, and it's as if he's famished...for me. And focused. On me.

"I dream of you. Fantasize about you. I can't get you out of my head."

Our teeth clash, and as I stroke him, he tweaks my nipple, eliciting a sharp pain, and then I'm the one whimpering. And quivering for more. I move to venture down, and he stops me with his gaze and a quick shake of his head. He reaches for the condom pack, and I let him go, watching as he sheaths himself.

"I didn't come here for this." He says it to himself as he positions himself over me, and I lift my legs, making room.

"I want you." That's all it takes. Any hint of hesitation deleted. He positions himself right at my pussy, and we both watch as he slides in. He's slow, studying me, glancing between where we join and me.

"Okay?" he gasps.

"More." It's all I can get out.

We find our rhythm, me thrusting up as he drives down, and it's loud and hypnotic. My nails scrape his skin. I squeeze his muscular ass to pull him into me. Even though I just came, watching him, hearing us, the heady scent of sex, the slightly voyeuristic element, knowing anyone across the street on the building's roof could see us, it all combines to equal an exhilarating potency. And god, those dark eyes. So intent, laser-focused. My muscles strain. My core throbs with intense pleasure. He raises higher on one arm. With his free hand, he finds that little erogenous nub. He works it over and over. All those muscles tighten. My orgasm rips through me. I scream and moan like a porn star, uncontrolled. Uninhibited. His veins in his throat protrude, and his thrusts become erratic. His head falls beside mine as he quivers above me. He's out of control, out of focus, lost, and I'm completely taken in.

He crashes beside me, our bodies aligned and faces close. He gasps for air as his chest heaves. His arm wraps around my waist, and he tugs me closer, skin to skin.

"Fuck, that was better than I ever imagined." He kisses my forehead, then my nose, then my ear, then he nibbles on my lobe.

"So, you've imagined this?" I can't help but ask. I mean, I know I've imagined him. I can't look away from him when he works nearby. And I've thought a million times about our time in the kitchen. Hell,

I'll never sit on this sofa without remembering this. But I've never been sure if he had the same inclinations. Even after the kitchen, he seemed distant. Definitely not that into me.

"My friends?" His voice lilts up in a question.

I respond with a curious, "Yeah?"

"They say I'm obsessive."

"You are?" I rub his bare ass. Perspiration is evaporating, and goose-bumps are lighting across his skin. I kiss his neck and finger all the minuscule bumps on his lower back.

"I can be. And you?"

"Yes?" I press my lips to the little dip above his clavicle. "Obsessed might not be the right word. That can be negative. But I think of you all the time. A crush is what Kairi says. If she's right, then I'm crushed."

"Crushed? I'm not sure that sounds better than obsessed. But let me tell you a secret."

I playfully nibble along his jaw. Our hearts have stabilized, as has our breathing, and I feel this incredible need to place my lips on all his exposed skin. Little soft kisses along his throat, below his ear. He squeezes my hip.

"Secret?" he reminds me.

"I'm crushed, too."

# TEMPORARY (STOPGAP)

ERIK

"Hey, Vivi. While you were upstairs, a delivery arrived. I signed for it."
José gestures to an enormous brown cardboard box that's too big to
sit behind the counter, and he has it wedged in the hallway. The bath-
rooms are farther down, and the box partially blocks the passage.

Vivi bends over the box to read the label, and José sends a knowing
smirk in my direction. *Fuck. He heard us.*

"The guy wanted to bring it on down to the basement. But I didn't feel
right doing that. I'd have to either let him have free run down there or
leave the register open. We had customers in the store. He said it was
heavy. If you need me to carry it down, I can."

"Oh, it's okay," she tells him. I make a mental note to check the footage
and see if the same guy with the cheesy dragon tattoo is the one who
wanted back down in her basement.

"Well, I've closed out the register. I'm gonna be on my way." The clock
on the back wall reads five o'clock. I lost track of time, very unlike me.
But I just had the best afternoon of my life, so I will not obsess over it.

141

We napped on and off in between sessions involving me studying her body—closely. I don't think I've taken a nap since elementary school. And I've never spent an afternoon wrapped up in a woman.

Vivi rips at the packing tape, and her long, loose skirt swishes with her movement. I visualize with accuracy the curves beneath and remember how she felt bent over, my hands on her hips.

Vivi rips the tape off the seam of the cardboard box. José lifts his backpack over his shoulder and repeats, "I'm gonna head. See you in the morning."

That gets Vivi's attention.

"Oh, yeah. Thank you so much, José. You're a lifesaver. So, you really think it's worth staying open on Sunday?"

"Yes, I do. But, ah, you might want to consider some soundproofing options, you know, if you're going to be upstairs with customers downstairs."

The moment his comment registers, her cheeks flush. It's a sharp contrast between her white-blonde hair and those whisper-pale blue eyes. She's a siren.

She's frozen in place, one hand over her chest. I follow José to the door, and we exchange knowing grins. I could slap him for saying anything, but I'm on cloud nine, and I can't hold on to any annoyance or anger. I flip the sign to closed and twist the deadbolt.

"You want me to help you with that box. Then we can get out of here? I'm kind of hungry. Maybe we can stop for dinner on the way to my place? If you still want to go?"

"He heard us."

"Maybe." I'm still grinning. "We gave a good show." *You're loud, and I like it.*

"Oh, my god. I would've never."

"It's over and done with. Let's get this downstairs."

"I can't believe he heard us. How mortifying."

I bend to hoist and stop about a foot off the ground. I'm not a weak guy, but that box packs some weight that tugs on my lower back.

"What's in here?"

"Wine. I'm surprised they delivered on Sunday. But I guess they don't want to keep it in their possession any longer than necessary." She unlocks a lock on the basement door. It's a basic interior knob lock that can be undone with a bobby pin. She flips the light switch, and I follow her down, carefully feeling for the ledge of each step since the box hampers my vision.

Other boxes are stacked in corners. Refrigerators line one wall, only they aren't normal refrigerators. Wine bottles reflect light through the glass doors, and red digital displays show the temperature of each case. The walls are stone, and the air is damp. In one far end, there's a leather club chair, a blanket, and plastic candles in glass hurricanes surround the area. In the center of the room, there's a small high-top table with bar stools around it. Stacked crates cover the table and rest in groupings on the floor. It's a mess. There is zero organization.

"You ready?" I ask after I set the box on another box, under her direction.

"Wait just one minute." She reads a letter from inside the package and searches through the contents. It's all bottles, but they're in interior packing to protect them. She reads the labels on the bottles, one by one.

"Here we go," she says. She lifts two bottles with matching labels and opens one refrigerator, and sets them inside. All the refrigerators hold rows of wine bottles. She has enough wine to host a banquet and then some.

"You like wine?" Call me Captain Obvious.

"I'm a collector." For a time as a kid, I collected stamps. It's chilly down here, so I climb the stairs seeking the warmer air. She follows me back into the daylight.

She turns the knob, locking the room. I should tell her the knob is pointless, but it's inside her store, which now has security cameras, so rather than sound like the paranoid guy Kairi and Trevor are always telling me I am, I don't mention it. Besides, what's the worst that could happen? Someone drinks a bottle of wine that she'd never, ever miss.

We have dinner at a little hole-in-the-wall Vietnamese restaurant that's off the square, then set out for my new house.

I've never walked with a girl and held hands. Another first. My phone vibrates, and I don't want to let her hand go, so I don't answer it. Her hand fits perfectly in mine. She has her hair in one thick braid. Earlier, I watched her nimbly fold the strands, mesmerized. And now I'm looking forward to removing the band on the end and loosening her thick locks. They're long enough that when loose, the ends brush the tops of her breasts.

The phone vibrates once more. It's brief, which means whoever called probably texted next.

"Do you need to get that?" I don't want to, but I run a security company. I have to. I pull the phone out of my pocket and read a text from Wolf.

*W: Call me.*

Out of habit, I don't call him back in front of Vivi. He didn't say it was urgent. When we arrive at my ranch rental, she's full of compliments as I give her the tour.

"I like the style of this place."

"It was furnished." It's fine if you like mid-century modern. It's not exactly like a scene out of *Mad Men*, but it's not too far off either. All I cared about was the location. I'd be closer to Vivi if I could, but two miles was as close as I could find. This is a three-month rental with an option to extend. "There's the pool." I point to the window. She takes the bait and heads through the sliding glass doors. I hold up my phone.

"I'm gonna call this person back. I'll be right out. You want anything to drink?"

"Do you have wine?"

"I'm not sure." I doubt it. "Let me check."

"If not, water is fine."

I dial Wolf as I enter the kitchen and begin opening cupboards.

"Hey. So, you were right."

I pause and look out the window. I halt breathing until I get a visual lock on Vivi. She's sitting on a lounge chair beside the pool.

"About?"

"Those guys are definitely scoping out her place. But they're not after either of you."

"How do you know?"

"He watched you leave and didn't follow. Instead, he looked through the glass front door. Then he went around behind back and tested the backdoor lock. He's seen the front door camera, not the cameras hidden over the back door."

"That's all he did? Twist the knobs?"

"That's all. He caught my attention when he was peering through the glass again. We're going over prior footage, checking if there's something else. He's not there right now. If he's planning on breaking in, he could be waiting until later when it's dark. Is there artwork or something in there?"

"A local guy's paintings. Books."

"First edition? Anything of value?"

"I don't think so. Nothing's in a glass case. I'll ask. So, you don't think this is Kane?"

"No. This guy's tag traces back to Marin County. But I suppose it's possible his assignment is to bug the place. Maybe he didn't do it because he didn't have the equipment. But he's been hovering for, what, two to three weeks?"

"Same guy as before?"

"No. Different car. Different plates."

"Fuck. This is not a high-crime area. It has to have something to do with us. You're not going to have two unrelated people scoping her store."

"Well, he's gone now. Want me to assign a guy?"

"Yes."

"To her or to the store?"

My sister's wrath impedes my thoughts. She'd never been angrier with me than when I placed cameras in her home and didn't tell her. For surveillance, I like cameras. They're also great warning mechanisms. Assigning a security detail is intrusive and works best when the person being protected is aware. I can't do more without talking to Vivi.

"The store. For now."

# COUNTER QUESTION

VIVI

"Hey, sis." My lounge chair and the view of his rectangular aquamarine pool are divine.

"Hold on," Celeste says. The water sparkles, and the fresh-cut grass surrounding the gray stone pool perimeter lends a hotel quality to the backyard. It's a small space, but well done. Over to the side of the pool are two comfortable chairs beside a round fire table. He's renting, so I wonder if the owners removed the gas tank.

"Sorry about that. I'm so glad you called." Her voice cracks.

"Oh, no."

"I'm going to lose it." Celeste sounds like she actually might.

"What's going on?" I envision fights over how much he's walking.

"He's hammered. And he's falling down everywhere. He's going to injure himself. And he's mean as a snake. I can't take it." This is not expected.

"He's drunk?" Our grandfather knows how to hold his alcohol. We make alcohol for crying out loud.

"Henry O'Doul got some new scotch, and they went to taste it. Only the men because you know they're all fucktards and wanted to smoke cigars and compare dick size. I don't know what happened. Like if they opened whole bottles and chugged them...but when they came back, Henry and Granddad were clinging to each other. Laughing. And could barely stand."

"That's..." It's kind of funny, but I'm not laughing because of the strain of painful emotion in her words. I hold my breath for the bad part.

"The entire way home, he laid into me about how I'd never find a man. That I might as well be a man. Get a sex change. I'm too hard. Too bitchy. Too controlling. Need to lose weight. My thighs are too thick. No man wants to be upstaged. I'm too intimidating." The tirade ends, and I'm pretty sure I hear her sobbing in the distance, as if she moved the phone away from her mouth.

"Hey, hey, hey," I repeat softly, unsure she can hear me. I find my sandals and shove my feet into them. The back patio overhead light shines down, creating a gleam over the glass, and it acts as a mirror. "I'm coming over there," I tell her.

"No, you don't want to. He's not like you've ever seen. You don't want to see him like this. Trust me."

"What's Max doing?"

"Manhandling him if he tries to move. Picking him up off the floor. He's letting Max have it too. Telling him he needs to work harder. Berating him for our bottom line. Not figuring out a better export structure. The fact we had to pay that ransom years ago. Says he let Max handle our site and our intranet, and he should've never done so. It's like he's held on to a list of grievances, and now they're pouring out. Only I haven't heard him tell Max he needs to lose weight."

"I'm coming." I don't disconnect the call but press it against my chest. Erik's stern expression greets me when I slide the sliding glass door open and enter the den. He's behind the kitchen counter with a phone pressed to his ear.

"I've got to go," I mouth.

"Wolf, I'll call you back." He places his phone on the counter. "What's wrong?"

"Family stuff. I need to head back."

"I'll drive you. Will give me a chance to meet your family."

"Tonight's not the night. Thank you."

I am out the front door and raising the phone back to my ear when he touches my shoulder. I'm frazzled. My sister's on the line, and I need to get home. Concerned, kind eyes slow my departure.

"It's okay," I reassure him. "It's just my grandfather." I hope that's enough explanation. "I'll see you tomorrow?"

"Let me drive you," he says. But I'm already out the door. Celeste hung up on me while I had the phone pressed to my chest. But it doesn't matter. I just need to get home. Max and Celeste shouldn't have to endure this on their own. Only those two miles feel a lot farther when in a rush.

A charcoal gray car sidles up next to me, and the passenger side window rolls down.

"Vivi. Get in. At least let me take you to your car." *Oh, thank god.*

I get in, and we zoom forward.

"You got your Tesla." I think he mentioned it came in, but this is the first I've seen it.

"Did he fall again?"

"No. Nothing like that." Unless you count falling down drunk. He's a big man. They should've let him drink until he passed out.

"Well, I'd feel better if I could drive you. How far away is your family?"

149

"Far. Over an hour's drive. And I'll spend the night." I don't have to pack. I have extra of everything in my bedroom. All I need is to run in and get my keys.

"I'd like to meet your family." It's the second time he's said that. I like him, but what's the obsession with my family? What guy presses to meet a family? Unless he wants an in. But he works in security. He wouldn't benefit from making connections with a vineyard.

He pulls up into the back alley behind my store, and I hop out.

"Thank you!" I shout, then open the back door gate without a look back. Keys, then to the car.

By the time my wheels crunch the gravel behind the old farmhouse, it's pitch black out. Bright white dots scatter across the sky. I strain to hear any signs of discord, such as yelling or loud bangs, but the only sounds are the familiar lull of crickets and toads.

The back screen door creaks, and I kick off my sandals. The main floor is dark. I climb the stairs. Light seeps under Celeste's bedroom door.

I lightly rap as I push her door open.

She's on her bed, fully clothed. Her cheeks aren't red, but they look slightly swollen. She's wearing her favorite Bruins sweatpants and one of Max's long-sleeved fraternity shirts.

"You didn't have to come all the way out here," she says. But of course I did. I didn't want to go into business with my family, but that doesn't mean I'm not a part of our family. I crawl onto the bed beside her.

"Where is everyone?"

"Granddad finally passed out. He's on the sofa in the living room. We put a blanket on him and left him there. Max headed out. He called an Uber. He's meeting up with friends at some brewery."

"Is he as beaten up as you?" If yes, he'd come home in rare form. Our family knows how to hold its liquor, but when emotions climb, so does our intake. But, thanks to my parents, we never, ever drink and drive.

"I know he was drunk." She falls back on her pillow. I lie down beside her on my side. "It hurt. Because you and I both know that what's said while drunk is what's thought while sober."

"Granddad loves you. I don't believe he really thinks any of that."

"Yeah, right. He says all that stuff when he's sober, just kinder."

"He's old-fashioned. He wants us to be married, and he's frustrated he can't just force us to do what he wants."

"You always take his side."

"I am not taking sides. Or actually, I am. I think he was way out of line. But I also think—"

"See? Sides."

"No. I also think what we are seeing is an old man who is scared. What he said to you and Max had nothing to do with you and everything to do with him. Chloe's mom kind of went through this with her grandmother. It's hard. He slipped on a tractor, Celeste. He's been getting on that tractor for decades. Like, what, seventy years? Didn't he start driving that thing when he was ten? Chloe's grandmother freaked out when they tried to take the keys to her car. And I remember Chloe talking about how hard it must be to give up independence. Do you remember how happy we all were when we got our keys? When we could finally go out on our own?"

"I really don't need to hear about what he's going through right now. If you could have seen him — he was a bastard. Mean." Her lips contort.

"He thinks he needs to lose weight."

"He does," she's quick to point out.

"And he feels like he's not working enough."

"He can't work as much as he used to."

"Yeah, but weren't those both things he attacked you and Max for?"

"Are you trying to tell me he secretly wants to get married?" I laugh, more at her incredulous expression than anything else.

"No. That part might have been him homing in on an Achilles heel."

"I'm not looking for a husband." Venom accompanies her retort.

We lie there in silence for several minutes.

"You're probably right." She reaches for the remote. "Want to watch something?"

I agree, and she flips through channels. We stack pillows against the headboard and get under the covers, just like we used to do as teens. I'm hoping she picks something from our youth, something heart-warming like *The Gilmore Girls*, but she picks a grotesque vampire show. I don't really care, but I'm also not into the show, so I pull out my phone and click over to the Zeitgeist app.

Firefly: Well, I've got one for the record books.

I scroll through our prior correspondence. Something I just do. Probably a habit I created because this little channel we have is a slow communication zone. It's surprising when a response comes through. I think we've been on at the same time, maybe a handful of times since we quit playing the game.

Phoenix: Do tell.

Firefly: My granddad got fall down drunk. Nice, right?

Phoenix: All okay now?

Firefly: Yes. He said horrible things to my siblings.

Phoenix: And you?

Firefly: No. I wasn't home. I feel guilty. Like I should
   have been.


Phoenix: You can't always be there. You think tomorrow
   will be a better day?

Firefly: Not for him. I know what a hangover is like at
   my age. I wouldn't want to have that at 79.

Phoenix: lol. Everything else okay in your universe?

Firefly: I'm seeing someone.


I hold my breath after hitting send. We never, ever talk about our
dating lives. On the television screen, the character turns into a were-
wolf and eats through a whole crowd of people on the streets. It's like
the 1800s or something. Celeste is captivated. The scene is gross.


Phoenix: Do you like him?

Firefly: I do. It's new.

Phoenix: Potential?

Firefly: Yes.

"Who are you texting?" There's a commercial running. Celeste is leaning over to read my screen.

"An old friend."

"Have you gone out on a date with that guy?" she asks. I have no desire to tell her about Erik. There's no reason to give her one more thing to hound me about. I shake my head, implying no, and return my attention to the conversation in my hand. He hasn't said more. Short, swift conversations are the cornerstone of our decade-long online friendship, but I've been curious for so long. He could be married by now. We just don't talk about it.

Firefly: Are you seeing anyone?

My gaze flits between a dark, haunted house-like mansion with torches as the characters hunt down special creatures that can hide in walls and the text dialogue on the screen in my hand. Each time the screensaver interrupts my view, I swipe and angle it to my face.

Phoenix: I am.

Well, there it is. He's dating someone. If he was married, he'd probably say that. So, he's dating someone. He could live with her. In all these years, we've never asked about each other's love lives. It's bizarre. He's a good friend. But he's a virtual friend. There are lines that don't need to be crossed. Information neither of us needs. It's all good.

My phone rings and Erik's name lights up on the screen. The call breaks Celeste's fixation on the *Penny Dreadful* episode, and I tell Erik to hold on and quickly exit the bedroom.

"Hey, what're you doing?" He rarely calls me. He's a texter.

"Just calling to check-in. Are you back home?"

"No, I'm staying out here with my sister. I'll be back in the morning. José isn't opening, so I need to."

"Did you lock everything up when you left? Do you want me to double-check?"

"That's sweet of you to offer. But no, I'm pretty sure..." I pause. Did I lock the back door? I'm attempting to visualize it, and now I'm not one hundred percent. If he hadn't asked, I wouldn't wonder.

"I'll check for you."

"You don't need to. I'm pretty sure I did. If I left a door open, it would be the back door, and no one will break in there."

"I'm close by. I'm walking through the square. You all locked up and safe in your family home? You guys lock the doors, right?"

"Yes, we do." We actually hardly ever do, but Erik seems like the type who would worry. He's never seen my family home. We're off the beaten path, and there's a big-ass iron gate that closes after the tasting room closes. Seattle must not be that safe of a city, or he grew up in a bad neighborhood because he cares a lot about locked doors. "So, you're just out and about walking? Is it completely dead?"

"It's peaceful." There's a lull in the conversation. I enter my bedroom and open drawers, searching for a nightgown. "I'm glad things are okay with your family. I understand what it's like to worry about your sister."

"You worry about your sister?"

"All the time."

"Why?" He takes a long time to answer, and I sit on the edge of the bed, expecting I'm about to unlock a piece of Erik rising.

"I don't get to see her often." I process his words, and before I can formulate a counter question, he says, "Get a good night's sleep. See you tomorrow."

# THE BEST OF ALL WORLDS (AKA OPTIMUM OUTCOME)

ERIK

The sign on The Bookery flips open as I approach. I check the time. She's punctual. Most of the parallel parking spaces along the street are vacant. By lunch, free parking will be scarce.

The bell jingles as I enter, scanning the store for a mass of white hair and those blue eyes I see even when I close my eyelids. She's gotten under my skin in a way I can't explain. I'm not one to believe in supernatural crap, but I swear I sense her. She's in the room, and I step forward as kinetic energy pulls me into her vortex. The soles of my shoes thud across the weathered wooden floor.

She rises from behind the counter, and the corners of her lips turn up into a smile. She's wearing a white tank top that fits snugly against all her curves. At her waist, a colorful floral skirt hangs loose, and the fabric drifts around her. I can't see her feet, but I expect she's in her Birkenstocks.

"Morning," she says.

I stand before her as a mix of relief and, dare I say it, happiness purges my chest. It's been less than twelve hours since I saw her last, but I didn't like seeing her unsettled last night. I didn't like having to let her go to deal with whatever was brewing all on her own. Last night, she sounded better on the phone, but her smile has a leveling effect. My breathing normalizes and tension eases.

"I'll have my normal." That had to have been the worst possible greeting. I've never had a girlfriend. In high school, I didn't see the need. In college, I dated here and there. More group dates and hook-ups. In Europe and Asia, I discovered clubs where like-minded individuals could meet each other and have sex. Minimal conversation was the expectation. Repetitive occurrence was rare.

This is new to me. I don't know how to act. Did she expect me to greet her with a kiss? Would that be normal? She shows no visible signs of annoyance as she brings me my coffee and water without ice.

"I'm glad everything's okay." I told her that last night, but I need to say something to fill the space between us and let her know I'm not a total ass. Texting is easier. You can read it and think about it before you hit send. The door chimes and we both check the entrance. Two older men enter, and one of them immediately heads to the table with a large sign that reads "Area Maps."

She's wearing a thick, shiny lip gloss, and when a polite smile forms, those light blue eyes shimmer. My breathing cinches and I can't look away. In my peripheral vision, the cursor blinks, awaiting my completed commands for my morning systems report. I watch her skirt swish as she returns to the counter. She's wrapped up her thick hair and looped it into a low-lying bun with loose strands curving out from the sides. With her hair captive, the lines of her shoulders are exposed. I'd like to kiss her along those lines, to feel her shudder as I blow on the sensitive skin below her ear.

My phone vibrates. Wolf's number shows.

"Hey," I answer.

Her eyes find mine from across the room. The skin on her chest, just above her tank, flushes. It is unfortunate that I'm so taken by this woman, but I like that I'm not alone in this whirl of chemicals. Yes, I am intelligent enough to know this little crush is nothing more than pheromones that will settle down with time.

"Did you see my text?" Wolf's urgent tone takes me to task.

"No. I'm setting up now."

"You responded to those Santa Barbara emails earlier this morning." Is he questioning me? I responded to those group emails about office space from my phone this morning before running through my jiu-jitsu routine.

"What's up?" I'm clicking around on my laptop, getting to the messaging app, but he has me on the phone. Reading his text would be inane.

"Ascension Media's CEO received a ransomware notice. They want five hundred thousand."

"The ransom amounts seem to be rising, don't they?" Sometimes it feels like these blackmailers pull amounts out of the sky. Ransomware has become a multi-billion-dollar industry. "What've they got?"

"They claim they'll leak credit card numbers."

"Do they have a lot of them?" Consumers in the United States have credit cards exposed all the time.

"They own a slew of cable companies across the country, so yes. But they claim to also have memos and contracts."

"Let me guess. Those contracts show varying deal terms?"

"That's what I'm guessing. The CEO wants me to meet with him in person, so there might be more to it."

"Oh. Like something personal?"

"Maybe." Wolf didn't sound impressed. We didn't care what it was they held over his head. From our corner of the world, the FBI aimed to weaken the burgeoning ransomware market. The US government —hell, all governments—urge businesses to refuse to pay. Each time a company pays a ransom, it encourages more incidents. But, at the same time, the government is slow to help. Often companies can't afford to take the risk that data will be released before the FBI can shut down the threat.

Sony Corporation stands out as a warning to all corporations weighing threats. They ignored threats from North Korean hackers, and the emails shared ended up costing business relationships millions of dollars, generated bad publicity, and cost the president her job.

"Is the CEO coming to us, or is this one the FBI has asked us to manage?"

"CEO wants to hire us. FBI hasn't mentioned this case."

This is where we find ourselves in murky waters. The way we are structured, the US government is one client. We are allowed to take additional clients. But the FBI, Homeland Security, and other groups see us as a team member.

"You want to take it?" I ask. Wolf called me. A phone call constitutes noticeable interest.

"Maybe. It's the pathway into their server that's interesting to me. I could swear I've seen these breadcrumbs before. Can you take a look?"

Hours later, I call Wolf back. A chicken salad croissant and pickled carrots and onions are sitting beyond my laptop. Starved, I pick up the sandwich and take a giant bite. Behind the counter, José bends over his laptop. I don't see sky blue eyes anywhere.

Wolf answers my call with a direct, to the point, "Did you see what I'm talking about?"

"Yep. It's a similar style used by the Russian group Black Plague. We can check in with NSA and see if they've got any leads. They'll want to be updated."

"I'm flying out to Arizona in the morning. We're meeting in the desert. He's paranoid."

"The guy's company has been hacked and is being held hostage, and you think he's paranoid? I'd say he's received one hell of a wake-up call, and now he's going to heed his IT team's request for upgrades."

"I guarantee you he's going to pay. They always do. I think that's why he wants me to meet him. I think he wants me to hold his hand and walk him through how to pay with cryptocurrency."

"If that's what he wants to do. He'd hardly be the first executive who paid up."

"He wants us to handle his security moving forward."

"Did you tell him we based the company out of Santa Barbara?"

"I'm trying to find an office manager. And HR to help with logistics."

Jingles capture my attention. Sunlight through the glass in the front door highlights her white-blonde strands, and she smiles, speaking to José. The cash register drawer is open, and stacks of pennies stretch along the marble countertop.

"What're your thoughts on moving?" he asks as light blue eyes find mine and a light pink spreads across her pale skin. She doesn't clink when she moves, but with all those bracelets, one would expect a tingling sound. She returns her attention to José. He waves as he heads out for the day. "Erik. You still there?"

"Yeah. I'll stay here for now. That was always the plan, right? Physical security with you, cybersecurity operations up here with us."

"Is that what Kairi and Trevor want?" Frustration stirs. The guy was probably sitting a stone's throw away from them, and he's asking me.

"I believe so. We can do our work anywhere. If they want to move, they can."

"Might be good for us to all be in the same place."

"You're sounding prototypical 2019." He chuckles, and I take it as my cue to end the call.

"Did you finally eat?" Her skirts sway as she approaches, as do her hips. The light above glimmers on her lip gloss. She smiles.

"You look happy." She lifts the plate with my half-eaten sandwich. "Is your Granddad okay?"

"He is. He said some things he shouldn't have to Celeste, but he's full of remorse today."

"And Max?" She told Phoenix, not me, he'd been drunk. But they both lived with him. It wasn't a stretch to suspect he'd been awful to both of them. It was a good thing Vivi hadn't been around to take his verbal lashing.

"He left first thing this morning, way before Granddad made it out of bed. But I've talked to him. Max is tough. A few beers, and he's fine. What were you working on this afternoon? You were in your blackout zone."

"My what?"

"Your focus. I've never seen anything like it. I left a sandwich and drink for you, and it's like you didn't even see me."

"I probably didn't." From a security perspective, not the best trait to have. It's one reason I need to work in a secure zone. "Thanks for bringing me food. Can I return the favor? Get you dinner?"

"It's chilly outside." Her gaze falls to the front door. The sign on the door still announces the store as open, and she moves to flip it. The limbs on the skinny trees planted in squares along the sidewalk twist in the wind.

"I can order take out," I suggest. I could have her back to my place, but there's a coziness to Vivi's. The exposed brick walls and beaten wood flooring offer a warmth my modern rental doesn't.

"I have an idea." She discards the remnants of my sandwich in the trash and runs water over the plate. Her skirt leaves all her curves to the imagination, but I remember. The pads of my fingers itch to reach for her. She dries her hands on the cloth as I contemplate location. Right here out in the open, anyone could see, but if I could get her upstairs, I could bend her over her sofa...

"If you go pick up take out, I'll set us up downstairs for a private cellar dinner. Have you ever eaten dinner in a cellar?"

"No." In the basement, the air is chilly. In her thin cotton tank, her nipples would respond to the cool air.

"What are you in the mood for?"

*You.* "Anything you want."

"I'm thinking American. If I call in an order, will you go pick it up? Did you drive over or walk? Maybe I should—"

"I walked. I can take your car if needed."

"That's right. You can."

She calls in an order while I pack up my workstation. She holds out a set of keys for me, and I grip her wrist and pull her close, claiming the curves of her hips. The thin, flimsy fabric of her skirt bunches beneath my hands. She laces her finger behind my neck. I kiss her softly. The weight of the day subsides. My hands cup the globes of her firm ass, and she rocks her hips against me. Those soft lips press against my neck, and I suppress a groan.

I've heard others talk about when something felt right. I've seen other couples cling to each other. But I've never needed to hold another human being close. So close, her heartbeat pulses through me. So close, her scent fills my nostrils, and the fine hairs all over my body stand at attention. My nose rubs over hers, my cheek presses to hers, and her fingers roam my back. I've wanted to do this all day. I just hadn't realized how badly I wanted her until just this moment.

"You'd better go. The food will be ready." Her breath tickles my ear. I don't want food. "Go on. I'll be waiting." Those sky blue eyes hold a tempting promise. I kiss her one more time, deep and demanding, relaying a promise of my own.

The guy at the restaurant she selected alternates between scrolling on his phone, laughing, and walking around showing other people something I could only guess is an idiotic, pointless video, answering the restaurant phone, and doing every single thing other than checking on our order. When the chef finally brings out a brown bag, the top bent over and stapled closed, the kid asks if I want him to double-check the order. I say no, pay, and can't help but wonder if I'd been that dimwitted and slow when I was a teenager.

Back at Vivi's, I walk from the alley where she parks, through her backyard, and rap lightly on the back door. I turn the knob, and it twists. Unlocked. I enter, lock the blasted door, and call out, "Vivi."

The store lights are off. Underneath the coffee counter, string lighting remains permanently on, and it lends a soft glow in the darkest corners. Darkness enshrines the rows of book stacks. The chairs rest upside down on the tables, a sign she's swept the floor. My shoes thump against the wood. I climb the stairs up to her apartment, but three stairs up, I see a dim light below the door in the hall downstairs.

"Vivi," I call out again. Up the stairs, on the landing, her apartment door remains closed, and no light shows beneath the doorjamb.

I return to the hallway and twist the knob. Flickering yellows and golds illuminate the stone wall along the stairwell.

"Vivi?"

"Down here." I breathe out a sigh of relief and pound down the narrow stairs. I pause at the landing in awe. Everywhere I look, candles flicker. The messy space has been transformed. All along the edges, in clusters on crates, in nooks and crannies in the wall, orange and gold fire flickers. The effect is mesmerizing.

Vivi's skirt swishes as she approaches. She holds her arm out, and her tank rises, exposing a smooth line of flesh.

"What do you think?"

"It's...stunning."

"It is, isn't it? I love it down here. I've had Chloe down here a couple of times, but I've never gone all out with the candles for her. They're all battery-operated. I'd love to have real candles, but it's not worth the risk of fire."

Yeah, if these were all real, it would definitely be a risk. Some of the stacked crates are made of a brittle, dry, thin board that I imagine would catch fire easily. I am not positive about the flammability of wine, but it is alcohol, so, theoretically..."Good idea."

She leads me to a small table with a white tablecloth and high stools. She's set out a place setting for both of us. I have the strangest sensation of being in a scene from our game. As if our characters had entered the dungeon, and now villains will leap out from behind the walls, and she and I will join forces to slay the enemy. I visualize the scoreboard floating to the right, displaying our remaining lives, the strength scores, and our available weapons.

She lifts the brown bag and sets it on the stool. Her white-blonde hair holds an ethereal quality in the firelight. I've never seen anyone so beautiful, so elegant, natural, and at ease. She turns, and her loose, flowing tendrils spill over her shoulder, curving over her breast.

"Are you hungry?"

"Famished." But I'm not talking about food.

"Well, let's get you fed." The bag rips as she pulls at the sides. I step up behind her and trail kisses from her ear down her long, delicate neck.

I tease her hip bone and the curve of her waist. A finger slips beneath the band of her skirt. Smooth, luscious skin greets me. She twists in my arms, and her movement teases my groin, almost cruelly. *Fuck, I want her.*

"Or if you want, we could talk first. Eat a little later." The tease in her voice is unmistakable. My dick thickens. In the quiet room, I hear myself swallow.

"I like that plan." Her glossy lips turn up, and her fingers intertwine with mine. She leads me to the back of the room into a dark corner, surrounded by clusters of candles of all shapes and sizes. The candles ensconce a large leather club chair. A fur throw drapes the chair, and a worn paperback book rests on the small table to the side. A bare-chested man graces the cover of the book, and there's a sword hanging off his belt.

"Is this where you like to read?" I like the vision forming. Her, sitting down here in the dark, white hair glowing, reading smut, getting off among the candles.

"It is. I like this room."

"And that's why you buy so much wine?"

"It doesn't have the same effect if the wine racks are empty." With a gentle push on my shoulder, she directs me down into the chair.

Her pale, creamy skin gleams under the candlelight. She lifts the edge of her tank and pulls it over her head, exposing a simple white lace bra beneath. Her tooth drags over her lower lip, tempting me as she reaches behind her. The bra falls to the floor. I grip the armrests to prevent myself from reaching up and touching.

Her perfect, full breasts sway with her movement, and her nipples beg for my mouth. The curve of her waist and her flat stomach are mesmerizing. She is sensory overload. Her hips sway as she fidgets with her skirt band. The colorful fabric falls to the floor. Her thumbs hook the sides of white lace panties, and she shimmies her hips and thighs, and the scrap of material joins the skirt in a pool at her feet.

My cock strains painfully beneath my zipper. She places her hands over mine. I spread my legs, and she stands between them, her legs bumping the front of the chair. She bends, and her glimmering strands fall forward, the tips skimming my shirt. Those blue eyes and lips hover temptingly close.

"You doing okay, there?" she teases.

I swallow and once again hear the muscles in my pharynx squeeze together. My throat is painfully tight. "You're fucking gorgeous."

"And what would you like to do to me?"

I regain presence of mind. "Oh, no. What would you like to do to me? This is your fantasy." I am not naïve enough to think she created this setup without a vision of how she saw the scene playing out. My girl is a gamer. We enter rooms with a plan.

Her tongue slips out over her bottom lip, and I yearn to bite that lip. To rip my pants off and pull her down on me. For her to ride my cock. For her breasts to bounce as she does so. But this is her scene.

One by one, she unbuttons the buttons on my shirt. Goosebumps dot her arms. She kisses me, soft and teasing, as her fingers reach my belt buckle. I long to touch her. She tugs on my waistband, and I lift my hips. She yanks on my pants. I take mercy on her and help them down. I move to stand, to kick them off, but she shoves me back down.

My pants remain gathered at my ankles, but I forget all about them as her breast comes within reach of my mouth. She pushes my shoulders back against the chair. I swirl my tongue around the darker skin, tasting her luscious nipple. She whimpers, and all too soon, she lowers herself onto her knees before me.

She massages my thighs. Her gaze locks on mine, and she bends further. Her tongue flicks across my tip. The brush of her soft warmth sets me off. I feel her touch in the base of my spine and deep in my groin. My toes curl, and my eyes roll back as she lowers her head, taking me deep. Fuck. I love a good blowjob, but this...the fire, her bent on her knees, the damp chill air that envelops my cock each time her head rises. But more than any of this, it is her. Firefly. My fantasy come to life. I fist her silky strands, urging her for more, yet so fucking careful not to push too hard.

She brings me right to the edge, then replaces her mouth with her tight grip. Her tongue traces my balls, then she sucks, and I almost come out of the chair.

"Fuck, baby. I don't want to come like this."

"Where would you like to come?" She cocks her head to the side and offers a hint of a smile, light flickering against a teasing, sexy, confident-as-hell woman.

"In you. Buried in you."

She raises up, lining up one thigh beside mine, lifting her bare pussy over me.

"Wait. Condom." Her core glistens in the firelight, and I grip her hips, directing her to my mouth. With one of her legs planted on the ground and one to the side, I seize the chance to taste. And I love the way she tastes. She is wet, as turned on as I am. She trembles and moans and quakes. I find her tender little nub and circle my tongue, then graze my teeth. I use my fingers until her back curls over and her one standing leg bends, unable to hold her weight. Her belly rests over my head, and her hands clutch my back as her glossy strands tickle. Her gasps for air echo through the stone-walled room.

As she catches her breath, I awkwardly reach, fumbling for my pants and a condom. I have never been the guy to carry condoms around, but Vivi changed that. She hears the crinkle and raises slightly, a smile crossing her lips as she watches me cloak myself.

And then she takes my cue, one leg on each side, and slides down, taking me inch by inch. Her legs slide deeper into the folds of the chair, and I tilt my hips up to meet her, gripping her hips, guiding her.

*Fucking hell. Never has anything been this good. This right. Magic. A potion of epic proportions.*

In our games, Firefly had been an enchantress. She could slay the mightiest beast, kill the strongest warrior. Her character had been legendary. And yes, somehow, the physical incarnation of Firefly blasts away the virtual.

She rides me, taking me in, using me to fulfill her needs. Watching her ride me, her hair flailing wildly as she rocks my world, her breasts bouncing is a living fantasy. She squirms as I find her sensitive clit and send her over another edge. She pulses around me as her muscles spasm. Her lips open, and she tilts her head back. She's gorgeous and wild and mine. Her hips still, and my hips thrust up, hard and urgent. The familiar pull at the base of my spine wins out, and I release as she collapses onto my chest. Her soft breasts press against me, and I gasp for air as I pulse deep inside her. The moment ranks as perfection. Unforgettable. Earth-stopping. Mind-numbing. Wild. Magic.

She stills over me. My hands grip her hips, keeping her flat against me, as close physically as two people can be. *I love this. I love her.*

The notion chills my skin. She lifts up, and I fall out of her. She snuggles against my side, and I tug the heavy fur throw over us as our breathing settles. She presses kisses to my chest, and I lift her hair, wrapping the thick locks around my knuckles. I need to take care of the condom, but I don't have the energy. I want to hold her.

*Love?* No, Kairi hit it on the head. I have a crush. A crush unlike anything I've ever felt. Scientists proved the sensations and emotions can be attributed to chemicals. Of course, she is also a friend. A friend I have held close to the vest for almost fifteen years. We are friends, and I let loose and crushed. I have never been through this before, but I have seen it with others. Trevor, for example. Wolf. They'd be into someone for about a week or two. And the chemicals would simmer down.

Our crush will follow suit. But she and I, we can ride this out. Enjoy our natural high. All the while, I can keep her safe from the lowlifes circling. I kiss her forehead and luxuriate in the sensation of her naked skin against mine. When this passes, our friendship will remain safely ensconced in a virtual realm. It is the best of all worlds.

# SIGNING THE CHECK

VIVI

*Chloe: Dinner tonight?*

Chloe's text shoots a dagger of guilt. She must feel like I've abandoned her. That's an awful emotion for a friend to invoke and not my intention.

But, undeniably, I have been absent for the past week. Between visits back home to check on Celeste and Granddad and spending every evening with Erik, I haven't made it over to Chloe's once.

Erik and I have fallen into an easy routine. He works in the shop and wraps up as I close, and then we discuss dinner, which leads to us being at one of our homes…and naked. The last few nights, we've ended up at his place. He has more room and a gorgeous pool. We have yet to go swimming in it. The heater isn't working, but I love sitting by it at night.

*Me: Can't. Having dinner with Erik.*

I read the text and imagine how she will feel receiving it. Chloe and I have been best friends since kindergarten. We do not neglect our friendship. I need to hear about her latest dating adventures. And I need to download with my girl. Things are good with Erik, but I sense he's holding back. If I'm honest, maybe I am, too. Erik and I are alike in that opening up is scary, and I haven't pushed because I don't want to be pushed. I need a good girl night to sift through my percolating mental journey. But Erik has reservations tonight, so I can't bail on him.

*Me: Want to join us?*

The phone vibrates, and Chloe's name flashes. I pick it up off the counter but don't answer. Erik remains intent on his computer screen. José sits at a table a couple of feet away with a stack of books. He uses the slow times to enter more books into the system for resale. I catch his attention and mime that I have a phone call and will take it outside.

We don't need to keep the store library quiet. But with Erik working nearby, I mind the noise.

"Hey," I answer as the back door creaks.

"Is it just the two of you?"

"Yes. Right now. But we can ask his friend Trevor if you want."

An extended silence falls across the line.

"Is he cute?" Nutsedge grows in my flower bed along my fence, and I bend down to pluck the weeds.

"Yeah. He's…" I pause, trying to think how to best describe Trevor. He is ordinary. A normal guy. The kind of guy we were friends with in college. "Wait, you've seen him. Remember that day you loudly pushed me to ask Erik out on a date? He was the friend with him. If you don't like him, then there's the other guy. The big guy. They call him Wolf."

"I think it might feel weird. Like you're bringing both sides to meet each other. Go out and let me know how it goes. Then maybe I'll join in later." Chloe turning down the chance to meet any potentially available man falls outside the normal zone, but I won't push her. Instead, we make plans for a girl's night.

At five, I flip the sign to closed and lock the door. The click of keys as Erik types away filters through the now vacant store. I graze my fingers through his hair, and he loops an arm around my waist. He presses his lips to my belly.

"Ready to call it a day?" We have at least thirty minutes before we need to leave. He could continue working if he wants while I go upstairs and change.

"I need to wrap this up." He caresses my thigh through my skirt. I like how comfortable we've become with each other. I like how he feels free to touch me wherever he wants. I may not know all his childhood stories yet, but we share physical intimacy. And we have time. There's no rush.

"What should I wear? I'll go up and get ready." He made a point of telling me he wanted to take me out. It's not necessary, but I am growing tired of take-out. I should probably cook for him, but I don't usually cook for myself.

"You look perfect. I love your long, flowing skirts. I love how your form-fitting tops fit on you." He wiggles his eyebrows. Then his playful expression transitions as his gaze falls on my protruding Birkenstock. "I know nothing about the restaurant."

I do. I will change my shoes.

I kiss him. A simple press of my lips to his, but it lights a yearning. We could push this chair back, and I could climb in his lap...but he pats my rear and dismisses me, returning his focus to his laptop. The focused businessman routine turns me on, but should it? Whether it should or shouldn't, it does. I like that he has his own life, his own business, and it consumes him. It makes the moments when I am at the center of his focus more thrilling.

At the thirty-minute mark, I return downstairs. He continues typing away. My platform espadrilles clomp down the last of the stairs with extra intent. The noise does the trick, and he looks up. I've put on a new skirt with a high slit and a white tank with a built-in bra that boosts my breasts and fills them out. He closes the laptop lid. Mission accomplished.

---

Catelli's is a high-end Italian restaurant and one I love. I expect I will see a few people I know, and I'm okay with it. Unlike on our first date, he knows I am a Rossi. It hasn't changed his opinion of me in the slightest. I like him, and I am prepared to introduce him to friends and family. I think. We approach the hostess stand, and Erik gives his name.

She smiles and says, "Yes, Mr. Yeung. It's now a party of four, right?"

Erik's brow scrunches, and he shakes his head.

"Really? I took the call." The young girl—she might be eighteen, but I'd bet she's closer to sixteen—flushes. She touches the pad in front of her. "But someone called—"

The doors open, and in walks Trevor and a familiar-looking woman.

"We're here," she says.

Erik glares at the two of them. The woman beams back, chin out, almost daring him to deny them joining our table. Trevor leans toward me and brushes his lips across my cheek.

"Good to see you, Vivi." He offers a small smile and avoids looking at Erik.

"Hey. Good to see you, too."

The hostess holds four thick leather menus and beams at us.

"Right this way, please." She takes off to the back of the restaurant. She's either completely unaware of the awkwardness between Erik and his friends, or she's fully aware and getting the heck out of Dodge.

We all follow, with Erik and me taking up the back.

"Is that Kairi Morrigan?" I ask under my breath. Erik nods.

That's why she is familiar. She's Max's age. Her high school boyfriend, David, used to be close friends with Max. She has changed since high school...as one would expect. From what I recall, in high school, she was skinny, a little taller than me, maybe even waif-ish. Now she has strong, enviable arms, like she's an avid yogi. Still feminine, but clearly strong. Her stick-straight, dirty blonde hair has a blunt cut edge and falls midway down her back. There's a toughness to her I don't recall. But when she smiles, she softens. Chloe had mentioned someone saw her in a grocery store. But how does she know Erik?

"Sorry for invading your dinner, but I had to see this for myself," Kairi says. There's a noticeable frost between her and Erik.

Her statement increases my discomfort level. Erik studies the menu, disregarding her, but I'm pretty sure his expression is one of annoyance. Trevor sips water and doesn't seem overly concerned. Something is up, but I am not picking up any vibes that say she's a scorned lover or she's jealous. But there's definitely something there.

Since he doesn't respond, I bite the bait. "What did you need to see?"

"Erik in a relationship. Dating someone." The waitperson fills her glass with water and keeps his gaze down. I reach for Erik's hand beneath the table. There is an undercurrent of indignation. I glance to Trevor, and he's fiddling with the napkin. I am confused.

"It's new," I say.

"So, Kairi and Vivi, you know each other." We both smile, and I unfold the napkin onto my lap. Erik's tone reminds me of a parent giving guidance to a table of children.

"Yes." Kairi maintains her forced, fake smile. She tucks the menu flat against her. "How is Max doing? I haven't seen him in, god, it must be, I don't know, ten years? I saw him once right before I graduated from college. He's running Rossi Vineyards now, right?"

"Well, he's working with my sister, Celeste, and my grandfather." She grew up here. She's familiar with vineyards and family businesses. Who's running the show can be a contentious matter. "He'd love to hear from you," I offer.

"I should really drive over there and see him. Who all does he still keep in touch with?"

And then we fall into a disjointed, uncomfortable conversation with her naming a name of someone four years older than me, and me answering to the best of my ability their current whereabouts and life status. It occurs to me about midway through dinner, Kairi must not maintain a social profile, or else she'd know all of this, the same way I do, from Facebook or Instagram.

"You planning on moving your dog? Or is he ours now?" Trevor asks at a break in the conversation when it seems there's no one left to ask about.

"You have a dog?" I can't believe he has a dog, and I didn't know.

"We can talk about it later." The two guys lock gazes, and I am officially uncomfortable. It's possible his rental doesn't allow pets, but what kind of person leaves his dog behind and doesn't plan who is taking care of it? Kairi is unreadable. No, that's not true. She's distraught. She's frowning, and I sense concern.

"And, Trevor, where are you from?" I ask because I don't want to continue playing where-are-they-now with Kairi, and because it's painfully obvious there's an undercurrent of dissension my gut is telling me to avoid. Trevor lifts his napkin to his lips and dabs. I follow his gaze to Erik.

"Washington," he says. *Oh, like Erik.*

"Did you two know each other?" I ask. They both frown.

"Oh, good god. You two are driving me crazy," Kairi spits out. They all glare at each other, and I sip my water, lost. Any question for a diversion tactic might set them off further. How do you know each other? What kind of work do you do? How long have you worked together? Any question that pops in my head risks dialing up the agitation, so I do the next best thing and excuse myself to go to the restroom. I have a list of questions a mile long for Erik, but I have no desire to cause a scene in public.

When I return to the table, it's obvious the threesome worked things out. The tension has evaporated, and Erik is signing the check.

Erik turns up the volume on a song in the car as we drive away. It's an older song I don't hear often, and I like the beat. As I tap my foot to the Foo Fighters, the dark night passes in a blur, bright headlights and red brake lights diminishing the farther we travel. Erik could set the car to drive itself, that handy dandy feature he showed me back when we first met. But he chooses to drive, hands on the wheel in a responsible ten-two position, his gaze mechanical, checking the rear view and side view periodically.

He pays me no mind. He's lost in his own thoughts and the road. I really don't know the man driving the car. He asks questions about me, he pries into my life, but he offers few insights into his. And tonight, with his friends, was just plain weird. It's possible I read the situation incorrectly. But I do not believe Kairi was happy about Erik and me. And in my experience, if a woman is jealous, it's because she has feelings for the guy. They were short with each other. If they don't like each other, why bomb our date? Is Kairi Erik's ex? But if that was the case, what kind of person would invite herself to dinner? And bring Trevor. It doesn't add up. Did they all go to sex clubs together? Does she miss him? Does she miss him in the way Chloe misses me, or is there more there?

The only thing people really talked about regarding Kairi Morrigan was that she'd become a lesbian. Changing teams had shocked the valley. Not that we aren't open-minded here. The west coast is an open-minded locale. But she'd spent all of high school as David James' girlfriend. They'd been prom king and queen. Voted most likely to get married. Just goes to show how much things can change.

The music is too loud to ask my questions, and I am certain that it is on purpose. Erik's jaw muscles flex as he drives as if he's replaying conversations from tonight. His grip on the steering wheel is tight. The food from dinner is unsettled in my belly. My nerves are frayed. I can't make sense of what happened, and a sense of dread builds.

# GREY

ERIK

We exit the highway and turn into the neighborhood streets. Yellow lights pour from windows, mixed with the occasional dark opening with a haze of blue. The yards are empty, and there's a quiet lull. Tonight, there is no wind, and the tree limbs and bushes are still.

The moment Vivi left our table, I lit into Kairi.

"What the hell do you think you're doing?"

"Keeping you from doing something you regret. You may be telling yourself it's just sex. I know that's your modus operandi with women. But it's different with her. You care about her. Do you really want to bring her into our world?"

Trevor piped in. "Kare, you've got to chill. Both of you. In the military, we talk about challenges assimilating after coming home from war. That's what we're going through. All of us. He's doing the right thing. He's building a life. You can't hide forever."

The garage door opens automatically as we approach my house. I haven't yet decided what I'm going to do. But I did drive her home. She's silent. Those light blue eyes track my every movement. She must have a million questions.

The loud music halts with the closure of the car doors. Our footsteps on concrete, then wood, replace the blaring alternative music mash.

"Tonight was interesting." She's poised. She's waiting. And I don't know what to say. Kairi is correct. She's more than sex. The last thing I want is for her to end up like Lara. But Trevor is also correct. Life goes on.

In my world, there's safety with a first name basis. Or with an alias. Safe in that she can't locate me. But if we're practically living with each other…

"You have to tell her. Give her the choice." Kairi's words replay as I scratch my scalp.

"Erik?" Vivi stands two feet in front of me. Waiting.

"I know you have questions." I pinch the bridge of my nose. Kairi did this on purpose. She gave me no choice. I wanted to believe I was keeping her safe by keeping her in the dark. I tried that defense with Kairi and Trevor tonight, and Trevor all but mocked me.

"Come here." I take her hand and lead her outside, through the sliding glass door, to the lounge chair by the pool. "There's a lot I need to tell you."

"Did you date Kairi?" *What the...?*

"No." Her thought processes ramble through wild scenarios; I know this about her. But wow. That's a bizarre conclusion to arrive at.

"But you lived with them? And work with them?"

"They're business partners. And I can promise you. There's nothing between Kairi and me."

"What was Kairi so pissed about?"

180

"She doesn't think I should date you." Vivi's head cocks to the side. She's confused, and I'm probably not making sense. "Tonight, she said if I'm going to date you, you deserve to know everything." Restless energy propels me forward.

"What the frick is going on?" Frick. Fuck, she's cute.

"Can you give me some time to think about this? I need to work through the possible outcomes." It's something Firefly and Phoenix used to do when we encountered a new level and found ourselves exhausting our resources. I watch her closely for any spark of recognition.

"Kairi is not your ex?" Why is she hung up on that?

"No." I shake my head as I say it. "I don't have any exes, actually."

Surprise flickers across her face.

"Dating isn't my thing. You can probably tell I'm not good at it."

"So, we're dating." She smiles. A heavy weight bears down. All because of Kairi. Pushing.

"Obviously," I answer.

"We're in a relationship?" She's still smiling. Why isn't she asking me the hard questions? She has an inquisitive mind.

"Yes. Right?" We're in the crush phase. That's what we said. You don't spend every day and night with someone, like we have for the last week, unless you're dating. She reaches for my pinky and tugs. I sit beside her on the lounge chair.

"I think so," she answers, and her head presses against the side of my arm.

"I didn't mean for it…" I stop because that line of thought doesn't lead anywhere good. The whole 'I only meant to fuck you' line of reasoning is one that even someone as socially inept as I am can recognize is a gnarly path. I remove my glasses and pinch the bridge of my nose.

"I need to come clean. Open up to you. You need to know everything, and then you can decide if you are still okay with seeing me. Kairi is right. You might not want to ever see me again. I need to give you the choice."

"What do you mean?" She sits up from her reclining position, tension evident, smile gone.

"It's gonna sound mysterious, and it's…it's not. It's just…Okay. I don't want your imagination to go haywire. My security company?"

"Yeah." She threads her fingers through mine.

Once I share everything with her, there's no going back. There are no antidotes that delete data from the human brain. But the only people I'm protecting by keeping her in the dark want me to tell her. And if we are ever found and have to relocate, it'll be much easier for her to understand if I let her in. Those light blue eyes are curious. And with an exhale, I test her empathy.

"It's new. Before we returned to the States and created it, I was a part of an expansive organization. Scattered all over the world, but linked. I liked to think of us as hacktivists…you know, white hats with a cause. But, unfortunately, funding the good causes requires some black hat maneuvers."

# BUT I GO

VIVI

"Illegal?" I watch him closely. I toy with hacking, for fun, but this isn't the time to share hobbies. My fingers tingle with an awareness he's about to say something important.

"Yes." He answers and watches. Waiting for my reaction.

"And now?" I prompt.

"Various US government entities are our clients. The government condones everything we do." He rubs his eyes vigorously. "In theory," he adds.

"And I assume you gained immunity or something like it for past crimes?"

"Something like it. They offered to put us into a witness protection program, but as hackers, we'd cultivated so many aliases, our real identities would be as effective as anything they'd come up with. And we didn't want to be in their database. Too many people want to hack that."

"Are people looking for you?"

"I have a former partner who...I believe...will come after us. Trevor and Wolf are less certain. They believe he's on to bigger projects—"

"But you don't buy that?"

"I don't. But Trevor and Kairi always tell me I'm paranoid. And maybe I am." He shakes his head. His forearms rest on his legs. Doubt shrouds him. "I've spent years on the run. Eluding governments. Causing havoc from the shadows. It's possible my mind plays tricks. Sees danger where it doesn't exist. But I don't want to take risks. I've told you more than I should, but how can I not? How can I bring you into this without telling you? Without giving you a choice?" His fingers tug at his hair. "Kairi is right about that. That's what she was angry about. She didn't want me, or us, to continue down this path without giving you a choice."

"What choice?" I stumble upon that word. What does he mean?

"To be in my life. And risk being attacked. Kidnapped for ransom, or...worse." I raise an eyebrow at the drama. "I know. It sounds crazy. I get it. And I guess that's the other option. That it's all in my head. You'd be dating someone with paranoid tendencies. I'm sure a psychologist would have a field day with me."

"Have you seen a therapist?" I believe everyone on the planet could benefit from a good soul lifting therapy session. But I don't see the man before me as the therapy type. He paces before me, head bent.

"It's not paranoia when it's real. Sitting out here poolside, in the middle of nowhere, it feels safe. But...no one will convince me it's safe. Kane, that's my old partner, he'll wait until we least suspect it, and he'll strike."

"Why do you say that?"

"Because that's what Sun Tzu preaches."

With a gentle touch, I lure him to the lounge chair. He sits back, and I snuggle against his side. His arm wraps around me, and his eyelids close. The shadows have always unnerved me. I wouldn't say they scare me, but I definitely flip on light switches quickly, or scurry to my car in a shadowy parking lot. To know that there really is someone out there, I couldn't imagine how jumpy I'd be. How on edge.

"In the games I used to play, the bad guys always jumped out from the dark, or from far away corners, off-screen." I press a kiss to his throat. "The shadows are scary because of the unknown. Game designers know this. Horror movie directors know this." He caresses my hip, and I stretch to press a kiss on the tender spot below his ear. "But we plow through. We don't turn off the game or stop the movie."

"Years ago, we didn't believe we were in any real danger." He removes his glasses and closes his eyelids. I brace myself, girding for him to share something I don't want to hear. "I can't tell you everything, as some of the information is classified, but a small group of us decided to splinter from our parent company. We expected there would be fallout. But we were focused on attacks on our servers. We hunted for viruses or surveillance." His jaw muscles flex. When he opens his eyes, they are dark and haunted. "He hired an assassin. Kairi's girlfriend, she died." He looks me in the eye. "It's not me being paranoid. And Kairi's right. I shouldn't bring you into this. I should put distance between us. I don't know what I've been thinking. I think I rationalized you needed me to keep you safe. From thieves or...But she's right." His eyes glisten. Emotion seeps through his skin, through the thumping of his heartbeat.

"She expects you to, what...not date for the rest of your life?"

"Not until we know it's safe." He exhales and brushes his palm over his face. "She's right."

"Hey, don't I get a say?"

"You probably shouldn't. And it is hard. On one hand, it feels like it's history. On the other hand, I don't know. We underestimated him once. Right now, Kane doesn't know where we are. But, at any given time, we could work on a project where someone out there would like to find our true identity. We take all the precautions, route through servers around the world. For years, I only used burner phones. It's only recently I agreed to use a phone provided by the government. I like to think we are all diligent. But all it takes is one slip-up. For someone to figure out our general vicinity, and then to visit, asking questions. Searching for a recluse who works from home, or maybe from the library. If someone figures out who I am, they could come in and ask harmless sounding questions to learn the true identities of the others. Where we live. If you notice, I don't have an Alexa. Once a week, I open up my laptops and inspect the boards and all elements for anything that looks out of place."

"You live on edge." I whisper the words softly into his ear. He rolls over onto me, resting the bulk of his weight on his forearm. Those astute brown eyes harbor secrets, aliases, and identities.

"Wait. What's your real name?"

"Erik." I study him. He's not avoiding my gaze, but he swallows, and I raise an eyebrow. I want his honesty. "Lai. My last name is Lai. Not Yeung."

"So, what I found out about you online? That was…" There were photographs.

"I created it all." My mouth opens in wonder. I hack into accounts, but I don't create them. "When I realized you were researching me. But almost everything in there is real. I tried to be as honest as I could. I really am from Seattle. I attended the University of Washington. I have a sister I don't see often. You are my first girlfriend. Ever."

He kisses me. Warmth implodes from within. My brain clings to a strain of questions, but his kiss vaporizes those thoughts. He tastes like peppermint. His hand rides up my thigh. I tug on his shirt, and he lifts up long enough to allow me to pull it over his shoulders. I trace the smooth skin of his chest. The hard ridge of his erection presses against my thigh. We're all lips and hands. His lips tease the tender skin along my throat and down, over my heart. With a firm pull, my breast glows under the moonlight, exposed to the brisk night air. The fence around his backyard isn't that high, but I can't see any neighbors' windows, so I assume they can't see me. His tongue claims mine, and once again, thoughts evaporate.

His warm mouth sucks on my nipple, and I arch. Vibrations filter up my spine, and I roll my hips. He palms my crotch over the skirt, and I shift to give him better access. The vibrations halt. The hem of my skirt rises up my legs. And once again, he warms my core with his hand.

Vibrations beneath me resume. The vibration enhances the pleasure. He slides my panties to the side, and I whimper. Eager. *Does he have a vibrator? Or a cock ring?*

"Fuck," he growls. He lifts off me, and I reach for his belt buckle. The cushion vibrates. He reaches behind him for his phone. It was in his back pocket. He reads the screen.

"It can wait," I half plead, half question. He tosses it on the side table and covers my body with his.

Humming intrudes as his phone vibrates against the glass tabletop. His breath tickles my ear, and I wrap my leg around him.

"I've got to check this. He's calling too many times." His tone is apologetic.

"Okay. Get it." But I cling to him, not wanting him to leave the chair. I'm half undressed, with my skirt above my waist and my shirt below my boobs.

"Hey." He sits straight up. I pull my top over my breasts and readjust my bra. "Are you sure?"

His urgent tone catches my attention. He's up on his feet. He picks his shirt up off the ground and balls it in his fist.

"Viv." His startled expression sprouts goosebumps all along my arms. "Someone's breaking into your store."

"The Bookery?" But why? I have less than fifty dollars cash in the drawer. Unless…those startled dark eyes. "Do you think it's because you've been working from there? You don't keep a computer there." But he's already pacing away from me, phone to his ear, conversing with whoever is on the other end. *How does this person know?*

"I'll go." His words snap me to attention. *He'll go where?*

He ends the call and drops the phone in his pocket.

"Stay here."

I jump off the lounge chair, rushing behind him.

"Where are you going?" Even as I ask, I know the answer. "Wait." He doesn't. I have to break out into a run as he tears down the hall to his car.

"Stay," he shouts. Like I'm a dog.

I run around the car and am halfway in the passenger seat, door open, when he punches reverse. He slams on the brakes.

"Out. I'm not bringing you into my shit." Cold fury pours out. "Out. Now. I'll call you."

I close the car door. The Tesla silently whips down the driveway in reverse then speeds off. *I should call the cops.*

Only my pocketbook is still in his car. I never brought it inside. Someone should call the cops. Maybe they're on the way there.

It's two miles from his house to my store. I take off down the sidewalk, racing past tranquil houses. My heartrate ricochets. Running out of shape while being scared out of my mind and frantic is not a good combination. Sweat forms below my breasts, and on my brow, and in my armpits. My sides cramp, and I chug in the dry night air. My sandals are flat, but they're also high espadrilles, and are not made for running.

If this Kane guy is after him, what could he want with my store? Do they think he's there? Are they there to kill him? Is it a hired assassin? There's a rustling sound. Someone is near. My heart rate skyrockets.

*Ruff, ruff, ruff!*

"Holy shit, you just scared me," I tell the dog.

It continues barking until a voice from the house shouts, "Here, boy."

I continue and round the corner. My store is dark. I creep along the sides. He told me to stay. But this is the valley. My hometown. I feel like the dumb girl in the horror movie, the one you scream at to not go there. The silence unnerves me. Are they inside? Is Erik? The tips of my fingers tingle. He told me to stay. Possibly a smart directive. But I go.

# BACKDOOR ACCESSIBILITY

ERIK

A white van with a Lightning Fast Shipping logo sits in the alley. I peek inside. A coffee cup sits in one cup holder and a water bottle in the other. Possibly two intruders.

They could work for Kane. Setting up audio and video tracking? Although audio and video tracking isn't exactly Kane's style. He'd want access to my computer. Or phone.

My fingers hover over the handle on the back door of the van, but I change my mind. If they're inside, I'd rather catch them. I can explore the van later.

The back gate creaks, and I peek through. The backyard is still. The back door, however, is ajar. I text Wolf.

*E: Empty van in back. Going in.*

*W: They're still downstairs.*

Provocative. What's downstairs? Her breakers? Phone lines? Cable? Ideas pinball. If they're techies, they probably won't be good at combat. Maybe that's why there are two. I press against the back wall of the house, in the shadows, and inch toward the door. Trapping them in the basement is one option, but getting them out of there could be dangerous. If I wait, I can attack as they exit and gain the element of surprise.

*W: Cops on the way.*

"Careful."

"Ow. Fuck. Watch it."

Bang. The screen door slams against the back wall.

Under the cover of the shadows, two men, both wearing baseball caps pulled down low over their foreheads, carry a large packing crate. Each man carries one side of the crate. Both are dressed in dark colors. One is wearing jeans, and one is wearing shorts.

I don't have a gun. My weapons are the element of surprise and my body. *Don't fight your opponent. Fight his moves.* My coach's words come to me.

A wheeled metal carrying contraption lies on the ground, and the two men slowly lower the crate onto the device. They rub their palms. Whatever is in the box is heavy.

"All right. I'll unload. You double-check behind us. Make sure we didn't knock anything over. Lights out. All that shit." With a bowed head, the guy in shorts steps to the back door. The other guy bends to lift the handle on the trolley.

These are not hired assassins. These are simple-minded thieves. Unbelievable. Are they stealing books? No. The basement. *Wine.*

*Whir. Whir. Whir.*

The sound is distant, but both men freeze.

"You said there was no alarm."

"There isn't."

The siren grows louder.

"We gotta get out of here," the jeans guy shouts.

"What about the wine?"

I step forward, out of the shadows, silent. The shorts guy sees me first.

"Who the fuck are you?"

The jeans guy takes off running. I lunge forward, catching him by his collar and pulling him backward, hard and fast. The sirens are loud.

I kick out a leg, tripping the guy, and knee him in the back, pushing him forward on the ground. He squirms. He's not a fighter.

"Who are you?" The female voice shreds my focus. Vivi. *Where the fuck did she come from?*

I watch the shorts guy warily. It's dark, and I can't see his facial features. He's trapped. Cops will come through that back door any minute. I scan his waistline. No gun. I zero in on the uncontrolled man. If he steps to Vivi…

"Ow." The guy below me complains, and I fist his hair and smack his head into the ground, all the while watching Vivi and the perp in shorts.

He flips open the crate. Each second slows. An image of a crate of guns flashes. Hand grenades.

Light glints off a bottle of wine as he holds it high in the air.

"Don't," Vivi exclaims.

"Let him up. Or I throw this." The man says this with the confidence of a man holding a loaded weapon.

"Throw it," I taunt.

At the same time Vivi shouts, "No."

Her hands are out, and she's inching toward him.

"Stay. Back." I tell her through gritted teeth.

"Police." An officer with a gun pointed exits the back door. Another with a flashlight follows. Both men process the scene before them.

"Stop. Everyone. Just let us leave, and I don't throw this."

The cop's gun remains pointed at the guy. I lean forward, completely confused. *Throw the wine, asswipe.*

"Ow. Man, that fucking hurts." I shift my weight, remembering I'm pressing the guy below my knee into hard gravel. The cop's gun swings my direction. I hold my palms up.

"This guy broke in. With that guy."

"Just put the bottle down." Vivi's voice is calm. You'd think his finger is on a trigger.

His shoulders sag, and he lowers the bottle as he realizes no one's going to let him escape because of his threat to hurl a bottle.

The cop with the flashlight approaches, takes the bottle, and directs him to stand against the fence. He checks him out for weapons. The other cop radios back.

"Two suspects detained. Robbery halted. Backup requested."

The cop holsters his gun and takes out his flashlight. The bright white light blinds me. I get up off the guy, and he mutters expletives.

"Thank you, officer." He shines a light on Vivi. "This is my place. Thank you."

"You know this guy?" he asks. White light flashes over me.

"Yes."

"What about these other two?"

"Never seen them before." But then she squints and steps closer to the other cop and the guy standing by the fence. "Wait. I do know him. He's a carrier."

Sure enough, there's the dragon tattoo. The man in jeans isn't familiar. He's wearing a different baseball cap than the one that has taunted me on camera. The guy we'd seen on camera wore a solid black cap. Tonight, he's wearing a Mets cap. He's leaner than I expected, but maybe it's added camera weight? He's definitely not the guy in the sedan watching The Bookery, but maybe that guy really was just waiting for someone.

The cop flashes his light over the packaged bottles in the crate.

"These yours?" he asks Vivi. She inspects the contents. Wine bottles.

"Yes." One by one, she unwraps and unfolds them.

"So, you boys out stealing wine?" one cop asks.

"You think these are the same guys who stole from French Laundry last month?" the cop by the fence asks.

"They know how to pack the wine." He turns to Vivi and asks, "How much would you estimate this crate's worth?" She's still going through the wine, as if searching for a particular bottle.

"I don't know. Maybe half a million." She says it nonchalantly. Like she's playing a *Price Is Right* board game, and she's saying, 'Oh, maybe a gallon of milk is five dollars.'

The other cop directs the one on the ground to get up and he checks him out. As they read them their Miranda rights, I circle the crate, peering inside for the first time, expecting to see bottles encased in gold.

"I don't understand." My breathing has regulated, but my mind remains at a standstill. It can't compute. It's not Kane. I got that. They were stealing from her. Wine. Wine that you can get from a grocery store. Half a million?

"Well, it's about four cases of wine in this crate, I'm guessing. But it's this bottle he was holding up. And this other one. One is a graduation gift from my grandfather. Other one is a birthday gift for him. I had them in a special wine refrigerator." She pauses and looks to the men. "He must've checked out the cellar at some point when I wasn't down there."

"Did you ever leave him downstairs on his own?"

"Maybe when the phone was ringing."

I'm doing the math in my head, and it's not adding up. Four cases, forty-eight bottles. "How much are these worth?"

"On average, I'd guess six thousand? But that one he was threatening to throw?" She casually points at it. "Similar bottles auction for close to one-fifty."

"One fifty?" I ask. I need clarification because none of this computes.

"One hundred and fifty. But my grandfather bought it for less. Domaine de la Romanee-Conti." She's thoughtful. Her lips pucker.

"And you drink this?" I can't grasp it.

"Only on special occasions." Special. Her skirt swishes as she maneuvers around the crate. "But like I said, most aren't nearly that expensive."

"So, the wine we drank?" It was good, but six K good? She smiles.

"No, I didn't bring out the good stuff for us. That was maybe a few hundred. Really, a lot of this I just buy for investment purposes. Or to trade. This bottle here is one I recently acquired. It's for my grandfather's eightieth."

"On his eightieth birthday, he's going to drink a hundred-thousand-dollar bottle of wine?"

"Probably not. It's for his collection."

Sirens approach. I sit down. I rub the bridge of my nose. A dull ache forms behind my eyes. Ridiculous wealth. Obscene. It's the thing that first tipped me off to concerns about Kane. But Vivi doesn't match. She's wearing clothes that don't flaunt brand names. Her jewelry is mostly beads or silver. Cheap. She lives above her shop in a rather small apartment. Her Range Rover is old as fuck. She makes no money. Kairi's comments come back to me. *The Rossi girl.* I took it as a reference to her last name. Her family owns a vineyard. She's never introduced me to her family.

I spent over half a year on Kairi's vineyard, and it's nothing more than lines of grapevines on a hillside. Kairi said that someone oversees the vines and harvests them, and they pay her mom. But she made it sound like it covered the taxes on the land.

A couple more cops enter the yard.

"How can wine cost that much?" I ask no one in particular. It's not the most pressing question, but it's the one I can't let go of.

A low chuckle nearby alerts me to a cop standing at my shoulder.

"Not from around here, are you?"

"No."

"It's insane what some people will pay for wine. Me, I prefer a good microbrew. So, you mind if I ask you some questions?"

"Yeah. Sure." I stand because I don't like looking up at the man in uniform. As I do, the weight in my pocket reminds me of Wolf. "Just a minute," I say to the cop.

*E: All clear.*

Of course, Wolf would've seen the cops from the cameras. My brain is fogged.

# OUT

VIVI

"What is your name?" The nearby cop holds a notepad and pen, taking notes as he interrogates Erik.

Neighbors peek through the back gate. The loud, nerve-wracking sirens are off, but the yard is anything but silent. Red lights flash in a whir, casting uneven shadows on the trees lining the sidewalk, the fence, and the side of the building. Multiple cops are standing around like they own the place. A couple of uniformed police officers surround the two intruders. I would guess the two men are in their twenties or thirties. Their entire lives thrown away because they concocted a clever get-rich-quick scheme.

Those two men have families. People who love them who are going to find out in the morning they're going to be spending a long time in prison. It'll play out in the papers. Wine theft gets excessive media attention in the valley. One guy I read about who stole wine from a restaurant got fifteen months in prison. But then, after that, it's an existence as a felon. And would these two even know how to sell my caliber of wine? You don't sell this on eBay. A sadness envelops me because all I can think as I watch the cops circling these two guys is that they upended their lives, all because they believed they discovered a pot of gold.

"And your relationship with Ms. Rossi?" The question draws my attention. "How do you know her?" the cop clarifies for Erik.

"She's my girlfriend." Our eyes meet, and a flush of warmth heats my exposed skin. I like hearing him call me his girlfriend. "Can you take me through what happened tonight?"

"I got an alert that someone was breaking in. I came down to investigate." He goes through, telling him what he saw, what he did, and I listen, a bystander amongst a whir of action.

"Ah, hold on. You mentioned an alert. Is there a protection system?"

"On the camera. There are security cameras in the front of the store, in the backyard, and in front of the register." *What?* Stunned, I continue listening to the police officer interrogate Erik. I didn't install cameras. I put a lock on the basement door to comply with insurance requirements, but I hung the key on a hook below the counter, which the guy with his head in his hands, the guy who helped so many times carrying my wine down the stairs, saw me use to unlock the door.

"Any of this wine yours?"

"No. None of it."

"Do you know when she came into possession of it?"

"You'd need to ask her." Erik looks to me as if to say *she's standing right there.*

"Right," the cop says. He flips through notes on his notepad. "I think I've got everything I need from you. Thank you, Mr. Yeung. Ah, Ms. Rossi."

"Yes."

"Are you feeling okay? Can you answer some questions for me?"

"It's my place. I would've thought you would start with me." It's a petty response. But I'm the proprietor. Yes, the oenophile club includes women. I am not invisible.

"Right," he says and scribbles something on his notepad. "And your name is?"

"Vivianne Rossi."

"And you own this store?"

"Yes. And I live above it."

"And this wine? Are you insured?"

"Yes."

"Do you know these men?" I'm pretty sure I already answered this question, but this time someone's taking notes, so I go with it. I answer all his questions. He guides me over to the wine. Someone is using a camera to photograph the area...the crime scene. Then, one by one, each bottle is photographed.

My phone rings, and I see it's Max calling.

"Hi."

"Ronnie told me that there was a burglary at your place. You okay?"

"Who's Ronnie?"

"Friend of a friend. Wife's a cop."

"Right."

"Were you there?"

"No."

"Should I come down?"

"No, I'm fine. I have a friend with me."

"Chloe?"

"No. Someone else."

"Who?"

"Why does it matter? I'm fine." The cop is observing me, and the weight of his observation unnerves me. I wiggle my foot as if it's asleep. It's not, but I want to see if he watches the movement. He does.

"Was it a wine heist? Ronnie said it might be the same thugs who took wine from the Laundry."

"I have no idea. They're questioning them away from me."

"You sure you're okay? I can come down."

"It's after midnight. You wouldn't get here until one. I'm fine. I'm ready to go to bed."

"And they just wanted wine?"

"You remember I told you I got Granddad's birthday gift from us?"

"Not really."

"Well, they got that. Plus some of my collection. It was the delivery guy."

"Ohhh." He draws it out as he connects the dots. "Well, get some sleep. I'm coming down tomorrow. I want to check out your cellar. We might want to reconsider storage options." The proverbial *we* bothers me. There is no we. I moved out of our family's home. This is me. But I'm not about to argue with Mr. Observer hovering.

Trevor arrives and leaves while I'm being interrogated. Erik alternates between talking on his phone, texting, and answering questions. The heat of his concerned gaze chafes me. He's not doing anything wrong, per se, but it bothers me to no end that more cops have talked to him than to me. I shouldn't be overly sensitive, though. He is the one who saved the day.

While overseeing the photographing of the wine bottles, one of the cops has Erik re-enact how he overtook the one thief and manhandled him onto the ground, knee in his spine. I doubt the reenactment serves the gathering of data for justice. The testosterone level in my backyard is quite high. The reenactment offers fine spectator enjoyment.

By the time the strong men carry the crate down into my cellar, and I'm given more than one lecture about not storing my key out in the open, and I receive recommendations to sign up with a security service that automatically alerts the police, and another cop pats me on the shoulder and tells me how lucky I am to have a man like Erik in my life, I'm simmering. If I were in a game, I'd be the round bomb with a little string sticking out and the yellow flame getting closer and closer to the nefarious ball. Yes, my emotions are nearing the explosion point.

*Tick. Tick. Tick.*

"I've checked everything out. No one else is here. I've locked up the front. Do you want to stay here or at my place tonight?" I'm in the hall. My back door, behind me, is unlocked. Because I don't know the answer to his question. I have yet to decide.

"I have questions," I inform him. He leans a shoulder against a wall and rubs his nose. His glasses rise above his eyebrows as he does so.

"Okay."

"Who texted you that my place was being broken into?" It all happened so quickly. I didn't think about that earlier.

"Wolf. You met him."

"The large, tattooed guy." I mutter it, not as a question, but he nods in the affirmative, anyway. "And how did he know?"

"We set the cameras to alert for movement. He knew it was late, so he checked it out."

And now for the million-dollar question. "What cameras?"

"Do you want to see them?" He shoves his hands in his front pockets. A surge of frenetic energy vibrates within.

"Why are there cameras?" I want to know where, but that's not the most urgent question.

"For your safety." He says it like it's obvious.

"You installed them. Without my knowledge?"

"I didn't know if you'd be okay..." Right there. That's when it hits him he's walking in a minefield.

"Tread carefully, Mr. Lai." I raise a single eyebrow, and I'm pretty sure I get the look right this time, because fear registers in his expression.

"I wanted you safe."

"Because you thought what, exactly?"

"Actually, because I didn't trust that guy. He seemed off."

"You act like you know nothing about wine. But yet you put cameras up in my place. You didn't tell me your real name." Kairi didn't want me dating him. He has an outlandish story.

"Vivi."

"What's your game?"

"Huh?"

"Did you know who I was before you ever walked into my store?" It's something I've worried about. It's something I always worry about. That I'm a target. That someone out there wants to use me, and they'll feign liking me — all for money. Anything for money. He pointed out all the ways someone could find my name. But he didn't tell me his name.

"Vivi. Be real."

"Answer me. Did you know me—"

"You need to calm down." *Wrong answer.*

"I am fucking calm," I scream. "Get out. I need you to get out. Right. Now."

"Veev…come on, now. Let me explain."

"No. No. I'm too tired. I need to sleep. I need food. I need coffee. And I…need you to get out." I press my back against the wall and point at my back door. "Out."

"Let me—"

"No. I'm too tired. I don't trust myself to think through whatever bull-shit you spout. Get. Out."

"What do you think—"

"Out. Now."

"Just so you know, I didn't put any cameras in your personal areas. I learned my lesson on that. I respected your privacy."

I have no idea what the frick he is going on about. He's done this before? The bomb explodes.

"Oouuut!" I scream.

# PLAUSIBLE DENIABILITY

ERIK

*Fuck.* How'd we get to this?

Everything blurs through the haze of headlights. My garage door opens automatically on approach. The slam of my car door bears a surreal quality. Like I'm trapped in a game room.

Only it's not a game. Soldiers will not appear. I won't be able to select my most powerful weapon and blast away the opponents. How I wish I had a stick in my hand with the sole goal of rising to the next level. If only real life allowed you to reload saves after making a mistake.

The anger. She'd been an inferno. Those pale cheeks flushed. And not with pleasure. Rage. An inferno of rage.

Fuck. Cali had been pissed, too, but she'd listened to reason. She understood. And I did nothing wrong. Most people have a camera over a register. I thought someone was watching her. Someone *was* watching her! Jesus. It wasn't me being paranoid.

I crash down on the sofa, and my head bangs against the hard armrest. *Fuck*.

This could be for the best. Kairi believes I shouldn't bring her into our fold. And technically, I haven't. I can walk away, and she'll be better off. She knows my last name, but if someone comes around asking questions, she'll use my alias. I trust her.

Even if she never forgives me as Erik, I still have her friendship. She doesn't know I'm Phoenix.

The problem is, now that we've had a tangible relationship, now that I've held her and made love to her and stared into those sky blue eyes, I don't want to go back to a virtual friendship. The idea of returning to a couple of texts a week hammers away at my ribcage. I want to tap the ground in surrender. Let me up. I don't know how to twist out of this.

My phone lies beside me. The phone Wolf insists I carry. I pick it up and tap on the Zeitgeist link. I scroll through exchange after exchange. I hover over the exchange we had the night of my mother's death.

*I'd been on a plane miles above, but I had connectivity. The cabin lights were low, and almost everyone, including my father, snoozed. Grief wrapped around and split my insides in two. Beneath my rib cage, the ache was unbearable, crushing, the agony so intense my brain didn't function. Not like normal. My Mom. Memories flashed like photos on my phone. Pressing my face into her belly as she hugged me. Clinging to her leg, tugging on her skirt, wanting to be picked up. Moments in time I hadn't thought about in decades. I needed the tortuous slideshow stopped. I flicked on the app icon. On my real phone. Possibly not smart, should anyone be tracking me...but a part of me didn't care. Giving up, turning myself in...sounded pretty damn good to me after learning Mom died in surgery at the hands of a surgeon I handpicked and flew to Seattle.*

*Phoenix: yt?*

*I didn't expect an answer. But one came.*

*Firefly: hi! Can't sleep. U?*

*Phoenix: my mom died*

*A lone tear escaped from the corner of my eye. Typing it out hurt like a mother. I couldn't imagine saying it out loud. Thank fuck I hadn't had to tell Cali. A stranger did. The fucking surgeon I flew out. Ranked as one of the best in the world. He told her. Fuck, I could've never been the one to tell my sister. Devastated. That's the only way I could describe her reaction.*

*Firefly: Omg. I'm so sorry.*

*Firefly: But...I know there's nothing I can say. Words won't help.
What happened?*
*Firefly: Or if you don't want to tell me, that's fine. I hated telling people about my parents. As you probably remember.*

*Firefly: So, here's the thing. There's nothing I can say that will make it better. But I can promise you. It will get better. That pain you feel right now? It's not going to always be so intense. You're in for a roller-coaster. Horrible days. Better days. Shit days. But one day? It'll be a better day.*

*Phoenix: I loved her so much.*

*Firefly: I know.*

*Firefly: She's in your heart. Always.*

*Firefly: I still hear my parents. Their voices. They never leave. Always a part of you.*

*Phoenix: I couldn't save her.*

*Firefly: ?*

*Phoenix: I researched doctors. Found the best. Ran numbers. Surgical success rates. None of it mattered.*

*Firefly: She knows you loved her. It's not your fault.*

*My throat tightened, and I had to look away. I couldn't breathe. I held the phone tight against my chest for god knows how long.*
*The lights on the plane turned on. Morning service began. I lifted my phone.*

*Firefly: Some things are beyond our control.*

*Firefly: Do you remember the time you hacked into the game code, and we were allowed to play level forty-nine over again? I do. Unfortunately, life isn't a game. We don't have that kind of control. But what you do have is a childhood and adolescence with her by your side. All the memories. She's a part of you.*

*Firefly: At the end of the day, those are the things that got me through.*

*Firefly: This sucks.*

*Firefly: Tomorrow a better day.*

Tomorrow a better day.

Our refrain. It started in reference to level thirty-three when we'd lost most of our weapons and stash. We'd made a bad strategy call, and gnarly wolves had killed us both multiple times. We'd resolved to read the groups and figure out how to destroy the varmints. Tomorrow a better day. She'd written...or I had.

But that became our refrain that got us through getting stomped more than once. Later, when we'd outgrown the game...when shit happened, we'd toss out the phrase. When her parents got sideswiped in an intersection, I didn't say it immediately. I'd had no idea what to say. But I did eventually type it, and kept typing it, uncertain it was true at all...but I'd hoped for her sake.

Tomorrow, maybe she'll be calmer. More rational. Less emotional.

———

Bright light cascades through the sliding glass doors. The sprinkler system spreads water over the patch of lawn in the backyard beyond the pool. The cloudless blue sky combined with the green lawn forecasts an optimistic outlook.

Will she be rational today? What will be the best plan of action? Giving her time? Showing up with coffee?

She hasn't called. She hasn't texted. Should I reach out to her? Or is she still an irrational, raging inferno?

I study code. I write code. Code either works, or it doesn't. Relationships. Women. They are non-binary. Illogical. I don't have a group of experts to go and consult with. No boards on how to navigate this issue. But I do have a sister.

"Erik?" She answers hesitantly, her tone tinged with disbelief.

"Yep."

"Calling from your real phone? This is the number in my address book."

"Yeah." I've been taking fewer and fewer precautions lately. Burner phones were a hassle.

"Is everything okay?"

"Yes." And no. "How're you guys?"

"Good. We're really good. It's so great to hear from you. Like, actually hear your voice and not another update from Logan or Dad." Ah, shit. She's right. I owe her conversation.

"Tell me about Dylan." My nephew is the most important person in the world to her, so ten minutes later when she's wrapping up telling me all the ways he's like our mother and he's also showing signs of being extremely advanced, I know I said the right thing.

"I can't wait for you to meet him."

"One day soon," I promise. There's a lull. She knows there's no clear definition to my *soon.* "So, I need some advice."

"Okay."

"Do you remember the cameras? At your house. At the beach."

"Sure."

"You understand now why I did that, right?"

"Understand? Yes. Agree? No."

"Huh. So, okay. Back then, when you were really pissed. What would've been the best thing for me to say to get you to calm down and understand? To get you to be rational?"

"To get...Erik, what have you done?"

# STRUGGLES WITH MORE

VIVI

"What you doing out here?" Granddad grunts as he pushes off the back porch swing, stabilizing himself with his temporary cane.

"What're you doing up so early?" I'd hoped to sneak in without being noticed.

"Been getting up this early for decades." He says it like it is a justifiable reason for getting up this early in his theoretical retirement.

"Max already up?"

"Yeah. I'm gonna meet him up at the Larchmont patch a little later."

My eyes burn, and my balance falters. Lack of sleep attacks me under the stillness of the early morning chill.

"Don't get all pissy. I'm allowed to drive the four-wheeler around. I'm being careful."

"Huh? No, I'm—go. I'm going up to bed."

"Bed? You okay?"

"Just tired."

"At five-thirty in the morning?" He settles back in the porch swing and kicks at the ground to rock the bench. For a moment, I am taken back to my college years, when he'd sit out here like a sentry. Max used to say he was looking for signs we'd been out partying too hard. Our parents were killed by someone who had been partying too hard. The kicker had been my father's alcohol level showed he'd also been driving impaired. Wine country brings that out in people, and back then folks around here weren't so concerned with drinking and driving. Still, because of our experience, the Rossi kids would never drink and drive. I always equated it to the kids of smokers. Most of them grew up hating cigarettes.

"When you see Max, ask him. My place was broken into. Everything's okay. I'm fine. Just sleepy. Wanted to come home." He lowers his chin, and his bottom lip protrudes. One hand rests on his belly. I escape inside before he asks questions.

In Celeste's darkened room, I kick off my shoes, squeeze between her bed and the wall, and climb into the vacant side. The burning sensation on my eyes dims, and my sister's soft snores coax me to sleep.

Rich, roasted aroma surrounds me in warmth. The ground underneath me drops, and I roll, then blink in confusion. Bright light streams through open windows. Celeste sits next to me on the bed. The feather top mattress dips down from her weight. On her thigh rests one of our grandmother's coffee mugs. The handles on her handcrafted mugs boast a signature wonkiness, and the one on her thigh is no exception.

She holds it up. "Coffee?"

"Why are you waking me up?" I whine.

"Because I'm guessing you need to talk, and I've only got about an hour before I need to get going. I've got meetings in Sausalito today."

"I don't need to talk. Go." I pull a pillow over my head.

"You were out drinking and driving—"

"No." She knows better. I would never.

"So, you want me to believe you decided at some ungodly hour to get in the car and come crawl in my bed for no reason at all?"

"Yes."

"Veev." A hard jab strikes my ribs.

"Ow," I screech. "Stop it." I hold my arm out and heave my thighs around to face her, prepared to push her butt onto the floor.

"Something is up. Tell me."

I glare at her, but what I see is Erik's face from last night, and my confusion returns full-force. I gather pillows to stack against the headboard and reach for the mug of coffee.

Flavorful, rich, and full-bodied warmth. I close my eyes to appreciate the wonder. *God, I love coffee.* A heavy exhale from the other side of the bed warns me of the patience seeping from my sister.

"Fine," I grumble. "Last night, some weird shit happened. And...I don't know what to think about it."

"Max said some guys got caught trying to steal wine. Did you know them?"

"No. I told you I'm seeing someone, right?"

"No."

"Well, I am. Or I have been."

"Shit." Her voice drops, and her hand clutches her chest. "It was the guy you were dating? He set it up?"

"No. No. Nothing like that." She chews on her lip, and I can tell her worries are flying far out in front of us. Or maybe not so far out in front of us. And that is my biggest worry.

"Well, talk. I don't have all morning," she reminds me, impatient as ever.

"Last night, I discovered he put security cameras around The Bookery. Is that not weird?"

"Ew. It is. He didn't tell you?"

"No. He didn't."

"Why?"

"I don't know. I can't figure it out. He was worried someone would break in…"

"And then someone did." She sips on her coffee. I can see the wheels turning, just like mine. "That is suspicious. But has he done anything else that's weird?"

"He works from my store. All day, absorbed in his laptop. His friends that I've met are nice. Kairi Morrigan."

"Oh, really? How's she—never mind. Do you want me to call Kairi? Find out about him?"

"No. I'll research him." My heart believes he's trustworthy, but if this were Chloe, I'd be forcing her to stay away from him until I did thorough due diligence.

"What does this guy do?"

"He's in security. But, like, internet security. Servers, websites."

"Well, then, it makes sense he'd want to secure your business. But why not tell you?"

"I don't know." It's unsettling. Our family's business is enormous. I want to believe he just did it out of concern for me, but there's always the possibility he has a bigger game up his sleeve. But no matter how I play it out in my head, watching my shop doesn't gain him access to Rossi Vineyards. And he can't be behind the wine heist. He wouldn't be the one to bust it.

"How long have you been seeing him?"

"A while." I shrug. "It's still new."

"He's not from around here, is he?"

"No."

"You haven't mentioned him. Or brought him around. You are always reluctant to bring men around here." There's an unstated accusation, and my defenses rile up.

"Can you blame me? This isn't a regular home, Celeste. This is an estate. A billion-dollar company. No one looks at me the same, or you, or Max, once they connect us with this place. We don't have a yard, Celeste. We have grounds."

"I hear you. But let's be honest. Most of this land is open to the public and for business purposes. Our family home is nothing more than a large farmhouse. You may not work with us, but this is still your home, and you're still a Rossi. You always will be. Bringing someone home is hard for you because it requires opening up, sharing who you are, and trusting someone to still like you for you. Believing they'd like you without the Rossi name."

"I know that. And we're not there yet." The big sister expression she's giving me challenges me for the truth. "I'm not there yet. And this whole thing...cameras. There's more to it, too." I'm not sure how much I want to share with Celeste.

"What was his reason for not telling you about the cameras?"

I think back. "I didn't really give him a chance to explain."

"Well, maybe start there. Look, I'm all for being cautious. But I think we Rossis are slow to open when we come around people who don't already know who we are. I'm not saying you need to bring him around, or move the relationship along faster than you're comfortable, but give him a chance to explain. I'm curious. And I think I will call Kairi to get her take. If he's some sort of stalker, then that's a whole different issue to handle."

"He's not a stalker." That's ridiculous. Isn't it? We've been dating. What I've felt with him…it's not…I'm not stupid. I think of the married guy who came on to Chloe. There are bad men out there. Could sex be clouding my judgement?

"How did he explain himself?"

"I didn't completely let him. But he's in security." He told me someone could be after him. Maybe those cameras had nothing to do with me at all. Did he believe he needed cameras to sit in my shop?

"Do you like this guy?"

"Yeah." She squeezes my calf. We are a touchy family.

"Look. I know that shit with Max freaked you out. But not everyone is like that. And that was some Hollywood-level drama. At least listen to his story."

Victoria faked a pregnancy. All to get married. It didn't come out until Granddad handed her the pre-nup and said she'd either sign it or Max would be cut from the family business.

Celeste stands and stretches down to the floor to touch her feet. "Don't you need to be opening the store?"

"Nah. I'm closed for the day. The police are coming back, and I'm going to call the insurance agent. Apparently, I'm not up to date on my insurance paperwork."

"Holy shit. Can you imagine Granddad if that theft happened, and you weren't insured?"

"I have homeowner's." I doubt it would cover me, but I don't share that detail. I feel dumb enough.

"Lucky," she sing-songs as she heads into the bathroom.

"Let me know what Kairi says, okay?"

She nods. There's pity in her expression. I am not easily susceptible. Am I? I research people. I am more aware of traps out there than ninety-nine percent of the population.

I pull out my phone and text Phoenix in the app.

*Firefly: How do you know if you can trust someone?*

It's an open-ended question that's going to bring about him asking me questions. But there's something about having a long-distance friend with a slow response chat line. The chat line, at times, becomes a journal. And that question is what weighs most heavily.

After Celeste showers, I follow her in to take my shower.

"Why don't you use your bathroom?"

"Because I like yours better." I smile wide, teasing her. Really, I do like hers better. Besides, since I don't come around that often, none of the stuff I need is ever in my bathroom. Her room and bathroom feel like she never left home. It feels like we never left home.

As I dry my hair brusquely with a towel, a hard rap pounds on the bathroom door before swinging open.

"He's here." Celeste's eyes are wide.

"Who?"

"Your lover boy."

"Huh?"

"Mr. Cameras. He's downstairs. Talking to Granddad."

"What?" My mouth drops open. "Shit. Celeste…that means—"

"It means nothing." She shakes her head, and I can only stare at her, heart taking off on a rapid run, brain lagging behind. "Hey. Look at me." She stands in her business attire, arms crossed, looking the part of a businesswoman and not my sister. "He knows your first and last name, right? And you said he's a computer guy? Google, hun. And you said he works with Kairi?"

*Right. Right.*

"I don't see a Victoria situation here. Can't hurt to hear him out." She looks far too mature.

"He's with Granddad?"

She smiles. "Yep. I gotta run. Otherwise, I'd totally stick around to see this."

———

As I round the corner, following the deep rumbles of conversation into the family den, I pause, taking in the sight before me. Granddad has assumed his corner of the sofa, where he sits each night to read a stack of local papers from all over the valley, scanning the obits. Erik perches on the edge of a nearby chair, running shoes flat on the floor, back erect, his black shorts pulled up high. He looks more like a teenager than a thirty-something adult.

"Come on in, Vivi. I've been entertaining your friend here. Erik." He nods, pointing at Erik as if I can't see him. "Not much of a wine guy." He licks his lower lip. He mutters something...Most likely a disparaging comment. "Well, I need to head down to the reception center. Viv, can you walk me out to the porch? She'll be right back to you, Mr....?"

"Yeung."

"Aha. Right. Yeung."

Granddad leads the way down the hall to the wide front door. I dutifully follow, uncertain what kind of reprimand I might be about to receive. Showing up in the early morning? Having an unexpected gentleman caller? Or has he learned I had valuable wine in my home in a barely locked cellar? There are a few paths this conversation could take.

He steps onto the porch, stiff and slow. He pulls the door closed behind me, and his scrutinizing gaze zeroes in on my face.

"You dating this guy?" He clutches the top of his cane, and his hand trembles slightly. The cane's slight circular pattern catches my attention.

"I don't know." He squints, giving me the same look he gave me when I told him the wine coolers in the grocery bag weren't mine shortly after I'd turned sixteen. "I mean, yes. We've been...dating." That tongue protrudes over his bottom lip. "But I don't know if we will be moving forward."

"He's not from around here." He says it with prejudice.

"No, he's not."

"Seattle." Again, a negative statement.

"Yep." There really isn't much I can say. Granddad prefers locals. Locals are good people.

He lets out a loud sigh and waves his hand. He waddles over to the four-wheeler parked on the circular drive. His gait is off-kilter due to the gnarled cane in his right hand.

When the engine roars to life, I open the door.

"Does he not like me?" Erik sits forward, elbows on his knees, hands clasped.

"We didn't talk about it." I fold my arms across my stomach and lean against the doorframe. "What're you doing here? How'd you find me?"

"Kairi had a feeling you'd be here. She called Max. Spoke to him."

"And Max told you to come out here?" Max isn't the most protective brother, but inviting a stranger out to the farmhouse is out of character.

"He didn't invite me. Just confirmed you were here. Kairi gave me directions." His eyes narrow. "Do you not want me here? I came to talk. To check on you. If you want me to leave..." He stands and shoves his hands in his pockets. *Hear him out.* Celeste's words come back to me. *Not a Victoria situation.*

"Well, you're here. You want coffee?" With a solemn shake of the head, he declines. "Want to go for a walk?"

"Sure."

"Well, let me get a to-go cup."

"Is José opening today?"

"No. Cops said they'll probably be back this afternoon. I figure it's better to have the store closed. Let them get all their questions out of the way. Close up the crime scene. Keep it from being a spectacle." He follows me to our kitchen as I wordlessly prepare my coffee.

"It's crazy."

"What is?" I hold the back screen door open for him while gripping my coffee thermos in the other hand.

"Those guys from last night. So much work to steal a beverage. If you're going to choose a life of crime, it's an odd choice, that's all."

"What would you choose?"

"Well, for a heist? Ideally, something light. Something without a complicated resale. Low risk and high reward. They stole a beverage. Something people can buy from the neighborhood grocery."

"People have placed a high value on fermented grapes for centuries. Since the Greeks and Romans."

"Yeah, but back then if someone stole it, they did it to drink it. It's mind blowing. If they weren't going to prison, I'd be tempted to sit down with them and offer advice."

I kick a rock and give him a half laugh as his meaning hits me. "And what crime would you recommend?"

"Data." Erik isn't one to utter the word "duh," but the unstated emotive rings in the air. "Don't need to resale it. Just threaten to do something with it, and you can make millions. And you can do it all from an undisclosed country through untraceable servers routed through multiple countries. So much smarter. Or...there are plenty of other options. But taking your work van and physically stealing an item. It's a twentieth-century crime. The domain of unsophisticated thugs."

"Erik, did those two guys strike you as the type of guys..." My words trail. *Stay on topic.* "You said you came to talk. About those guys?"

"No." He dips his head, hands in his pockets, matching my speed. "I wanted to talk to you about last night. I wanted to explain. And apologize."

"For?" I prompt.

"I should've told you about the cameras." Yes, he should've. And what did he say last night, he'd done it before? "Where are we going?"

I lead him down a narrow dirt path between two rows of grapevines.

"Lilac hill. There's a place to sit up here."

"All this is your family's?" Wonder laces his question.

"Technically, it's a part of a trust. But yes, it's family land."

"It's beautiful out here. Similar to Kairi's family place." Our vineyard is at least ten times the size of Morrigan Farms.

The grade increases, and we hike up the slope in a single-file line, legs bent. When we reach the plateau, Erik circles, wide-eyed, taking in the expansive view. Grapevines, rolling hills, as far as the eye can see. The sun shines high above a clear sky.

He points. "What's that?"

My throat tightens, choking down a mix of nerves and uncertainty. He's oblivious, taking in the scenery. Was this an act, or did he really not know? The stone mansion he points to reminds me of a castle tucked in an Italian hillside. Close up, the building is far more impressive, boasting twenty-five-foot-tall oak entrance doors. We use the downstairs for our tastings and the surrounding areas for weddings and private parties. To accommodate the crowds, we built a large parking lot over to the side. From this angle, you can't see the parking lot, but the expansive area with pavers and the circular fountain add to the stately aura...or so I think. Erik has already moved on, and now he stares off in the other direction at a storage shed nestled in a dip in the valley.

"You grew up here?" he asks conversationally, as if making small talk. As if he doesn't have a ton of explaining to do, and as if I don't have to use my best judgment to determine if I can trust anything he says.

"Erik, let's sit."

Up here on this spot, the highest point on our property, we created a lunch area for those working. It's a haven, with a weathered wooden picnic table and two matching benches.

"Be careful. Splinters," I warn.

We sit on the same bench, backs to the edge of the table. I suck in air, my chin tucks against my throat, and a fit of sneezes has me covering my nose and tears peeking from the corners of my eyes. I forgot my allergy medicine.

"Bless you." He's relaxed, like everything's fine. He's given a half-assed apology. But I'm not certain I can trust him. I still don't understand.

"I'm guessing that the security cameras in my business...in my home...stem from the paranoia you mentioned."

"Not in your home." I open my mouth to argue, and he intercepts, "Not upstairs. I considered it, but I remembered how angry Cali got... so I didn't. And yes, some say it's paranoia."

"Okay. Okay." I'm calm but somehow also agitated. I pace back and forth. The dry, rocky soil crunches beneath my shoes. I don't want to be a fool. I don't want to be deceived. "Let's take it apart step by step. Cali is your sister?"

"My twin."

"I didn't know you had a twin." He nods, and I have an urge to ask him all about life as a twin, but that's so off-topic. I shut my eyes to focus. The anger from last night has mostly disappeared. It's hard to stay firm without my temper on hand.

"And you put cameras in her home?"

"I did."

"To protect her?"

"I feared she was being targeted."

"Why?"

"I undermined a complex hack job. It was a hack on the utilities in a small country...but the way they did it, they'd suspect the Russians. It could've had extremely negative international consequences. When I scratched the job, Kane was pissed." His lips have fallen into a flat, straight line, and I suspect he's not seeing what's in front of him, but instead, he's reliving the past. "Kane and I used to have long philo-sophical discussions surrounding Sun Tzu. *The Art of War?*" He peers at me, questioning if I know the book.

"Yeah."

"One of the tenets is that if a soldier defies an order, or acts without orders, then he should be beheaded. Obviously, this day in age, no one takes that literally. It's more a point that you can't successfully fight an enemy if you can't trust everyone within your ranks. You need to be aligned. Except, Kane...he hired an assassin."

"To kill your sister?"

He sighs loudly as his hands grip the edge of the bench. "The assassin came after us. There were several of us working from the same rented condo. He didn't come in with guns. Kane wanted to make a statement. The attacker sliced the throat...not a true beheading, but the implication was clear. Kairi..."

"She was the one—"

"No." He jumps in, hearing my alarm and what I assumed. "He didn't attack Kairi. It was Lara, her girlfriend. It's what I started to tell you last night. We didn't know if it was a mistake or if the order was to go after our loved ones. We fled. Then Cali's apartment in Seattle got ransacked. It became clear he was targeting our significant others. Which made sense in a sick, twisted way...because if he kills us, we don't suffer. If he goes after who we love, we do."

"So, you put security cameras in?"

"I relocated her, so no one could find her. And set her up with a high degree of security. And we set about working to dismantle the company. We began sabotaging their initiatives."

"And?"

"He eventually located us. And hired an assassin."

"Seriously?"

"Unfortunately. It's why Kairi isn't wrong when she tells me I shouldn't date you. He found us once."

"But you're in the United States. Can he—"

"You can hire someone to do anything, anywhere. You just have to know where to look. And he does."

"Holy shit." He's talking about the Dark Web. I've dabbled, but I've never come across anything like this. Assassins? No wonder he doesn't care about wine theft. "You really don't care at all about..." But wait, if he needs money.... "How are you financed? How do you make money?"

"Well, like I told you. Security. The United States government is our largest client. I'm still focused on stopping Spectre. And other crime syndicates like it. The only difference is now we get paid in US dollars instead of bitcoin."

"Why not tell me about the security cameras?"

"I barely knew you. I mean, you have a cash register, and it irked me you didn't have security." I sense he has more to say on this subject by the way he grits his teeth, but he goes on. "I had this feeling you'd say no, and then I'd do it anyway, and that's worse."

"Erik…your logic. It's faulty."

"No. It's accurate."

I breathe out exasperation. Am I still angry? No. Can I trust him? This story is too wild to be something he would fabricate.

"You really don't care about the Rossi estate at all, do you?" I study his reaction. He squints into the sun which is now high overhead.

"You kept your financial situation hidden because you thought I'd care about money more than you?"

"What do you know about my financial situation?"

"Only that it must be positive if you can afford half a million dollars in wine. And you don't flaunt your wealth. It's almost as if you didn't want me to know."

"Well, our family has had incidences. It's made me cautious."

"Someone hurt you?"

"Not me. Max."

"We're quite a pair, huh? I'm paranoid hired assassins will attack, and you're paranoid the only people who want to get close do so because of your money."

"I'm not paranoid. I just don't want to be stupid."

"Was Max stupid?" The question throws me.

"No. But that's the scary part, right? If someone like Max can fall for an act, then I'm a prime target."

"Well, I can assure you, I like you for you. I don't care about the Rossi estate, or overpriced beverages that will one day turn to vinegar, at all." The breeze picks up, and I let out a litany of loud, uncontrollable sneezes. He holds out a tissue.

"Thank you." I blow my nose with a loud, unladylike honk. A small bird flutters nearby then flies away. "So, tell me about your sister."

"She's a linguist. She's brilliant. She had her first son a few months ago."

"You're an uncle."

"An absentee one." He frowns.

"You can go visit."

"Maybe."

"You know, I think it's time that we both let go of the idea of someone lurking in the shadows."

"Do you, now?"

"I do."

"Unfortunately, I disagree. I came back here to talk because I don't want you to be angry at me. But Kairi and I talked more this morning, and…" He rests his forehead on his hand. I join him on the bench. "It's hard because I do have this known enemy out there. Maybe he won't find us, maybe he will. I believe my sister's safe. She's married to an agent. But if he wants to hurt me, that only leaves you."

"And let me guess…Sun Tzu doesn't recommend letting bygones be bygones?"

"No."

He runs a finger over the scroll on my arm. The light touch raises the hairs on my arms. It's as if his touch conveys an electrical current, and it must, because a warmth fills my chest. His expression is pensive. I trace the lines of his jaw. The outside world, the nearby vines, twisted on the rails, fade to black, and all I see is him. He has more to say. And he's struggling with it. He's not sure he can open up to me. Or maybe he's planning on listening to Kairi and ending us now.

"Erik?"

# WHAT THE EVER-LOVING F*CK?

ERIK

Those trusting, whisper-light blue irises suck me in. The words on the tip of my tongue vaporize, replaced by a message of higher priority.

"I love you." I grit my teeth. Hold my breath. I think I've known it since I first caught her in a visual. The day the bell over the door jingled, casting a spell, and the distant friend morphed from avatar to flesh.

Her gaze falls, and she pats my chest. Pats it. Inside, there's a crash. All systems down. She doesn't feel the same way. But how could she? She's known me for a fraction of time. Would it matter if she knew she tattooed one of my avatar names onto her arm? Our virtual connection has never been romantic. Purely platonic. If I tell her, am I grasping for a similar response? Is that what I'd expect? Would it be too strange to tell her now?

"That would mean a lot more to me if you didn't tell me that on the same day you saw all of this."

I snap out of my downward spiral. "What?" But she's already returning down the path. "Vivi," I call. "Vivianne. Stop."

She doesn't.

"Vivianne. You can't really—"

"No. I don't. Logically, I know. It's just poor timing on your part. You don't fully understand. I can't expect you to."

I grip her wrist and tug, forcing her to face me.

"Vivianne." It's the first time I've ever said her full name. The long, formal word sticks in my throat. Those light blue eyes resuscitate me. With determination, I continue. "Vivi. Let me make a few things clear. Farm life isn't for me. I don't give a damn about these twisted vines. Or the land. Or your bank account. You've never asked me, and for that matter, I've never asked you. But I suspect I have more money than you. And mine isn't tied up in land. When I told you I've never cared about money, not only was it the truth, but it's easy for me to feel that way because I get paid well. I also got in on bitcoin way back when most people couldn't understand what it was. I don't have to work. I work..." I stop, pinching the bridge of my nose. I just need her to understand. "I work because I helped build a monster. And I need to dismantle it. I work because I understand it's the wild, wild west reloaded, and the bad guys are carrying the equivalent of machine guns and rocket launchers. And we need people out there working to maintain a semblance of safety. Not for money." I growl out the word. It's something I'm growing to hate because greed is the fuel that is behind so much of the bullshit we're experiencing in what should be nirvana. The Internet holds tremendous promise, and ultimately, at the bottom of all the convoluted bullshit, it's greed that threatens to rip it to shreds.

"I love you. And yes, it's early. It's fast. I didn't want to fall for you. But I couldn't stop myself. In here," I pound my fist on my chest, "we have a connection. I sense you in a room. I'm drawn to you in a way I can't even explain. I love that you're a dreamer. An optimist. You're always looking for more in yourself, but you don't push for more in your friends or family. You're as beautiful on the inside as you are on the outside." I point at my brain. "I can't get you out. You are an addiction. And it's frustrating as hell because you'd be much better off without me. I don't need you to say it back to me. I just need you to understand that this...what's going on here, and in here," again, I thrust my index finger at my temple, "has nothing at all to do with the Rossi estate, or your bank account, or whatever bullshit reason you have convinced yourself someone out there might fake caring about you."

She stares blankly at me, void of emotion. The absence of a response speaks volumes. She doesn't feel the same way. Therefore, she doesn't know how to respond. This reckless pursuit of her was pointless. I put her in danger for nothing. I should've just listened to Kairi. I tear off down the path, back to my car.

It doesn't matter. It's a good thing. I don't have any business being here. My hands ball into fists, and anger surges. Anger at myself for ever walking into her store. For letting curiosity win. For spending time with her. For allowing myself to get close to her when all I did was bring her into my fucked-up world, and why? To force her to come up with words to push me away? To come up with bullshit excuses for building a wall? Did I really think I'd come clean, tell her everything, tell her I had money sitting in offshore bank accounts, and then she'd fall into my arms and we'd make out? So fucking foolish. Nonsensical. Illogical.

"Wait. Stop." Her voice sounds distant. My feet slip on the pebbles ground into the path. But I catch myself and rush on.

"Erik. Wait." She sounds closer. Heavy breaths float in the wind.

Her light touch wraps around my wrist. She tugs.

"What?" I grit, spinning to face her.

"Where are you going?" She's flushed. Those light blue eyes infiltrate, and I can't take it.

"Why did you get so angry?"

*Because you don't love me. And you shouldn't love me.* "I'm not angry."

"Why did you..." She steps closer, and her palm lightly presses against my chest. She gazes up at me, tilting her chin, her mouth inches from mine.

On her tiptoes, she offers herself up. Her silky threads tangle in my fingers as I pull her closer. She wants this. She wants me. I misunderstood. Overreacted.

For a split second, our eyes lock. *I'm sorry. I care. I want you.*

My lips fall to hers. There is nothing gentle, nothing soft in our kiss. All the anger, hurt, and confusion pours out of me. She whimpers and moans. I caress the curve of her ass over her long skirt, pulling her up against me, using her body to rub against mine. Blind with need, I reach under the waistband, beneath her panties, to her bare skin, hoisting her up.

I stumble and she giggles. The kiss broken, our noses rub, and I breathe her in, light effervescence.

"We can't. Not out here." I blink, taking in our surroundings. There's nothing but vines. To our right, to our left...grapes. The dirt below us is sparsely covered in blades of grass and weeds. But I don't care. I need her.

"No one's out here." I squeeze her buttock and reach as far as I can and allow my longest finger to pry into her warmth. I nuzzle her neck.

She places her arms over my shoulders and tempts me with kisses along my jaw.

"We're not alone," she whispers.

"What do you mean?" I stand straighter and higher but still hold her against me.

"At any given time, there could be over a hundred employees on the grounds."

"Inside?" I ask, hopeful. We can't be that far away from the house where I parked. She places a soft, wet kiss below my earlobe, and my wicked hard erection strains in my jeans. "How far is it?"

She takes my hand. Glossy strands catch the sun's rays, seemingly floating behind her as we rush down the path. She giggles as our speed picks up. It's a light, carefree sound, and I grin like a fool. A fool...but there's something about the whole situation. It's new and different, and it's a sensation I don't entirely recognize. But under the blue sky with twisted vines all around us...I recognize it. Happiness. I am happy.

The white farmhouse comes into view, along with the large, paved backyard area where my car is parked. There's a tractor that wasn't here before. Vivi leads me to my car. She rests her back against my car door and reaches for me, pulling me down for a delicious, teasing kiss.

"My granddad's inside. And I'd bet Max is too. Maybe we should just go back to your place?"

My place is a minimum of forty-five minutes away, but I'm also sporting a stiff erection. Therefore, not in the mood at all to meet her older brother. I groan into her neck and rock my hips against her. She giggles again.

"All right. Let's go. Do you need anything here?"

"Yeah. I need to run in and grab a few things. You want to wait out here? Or come inside?"

"What will be fastest?" She gets it. I know this because the way she presses up against me tells me she's fully aware of what she's done to me, and she needs friction, too.

"I drove here," she reminds me.

"I'll follow you. Go get your stuff." She kisses me, and it's doing nothing at all to quell my need. I'd love nothing more than to lift her skirt and drive into her up against my car, but I'd never do that to her. Not in a place someone could walk up on us. Where she would be mortified in front of her grandfather or brother. I break our kiss. "Go."

She hustles across the pavers to the back door. A sun halo on her bright hair forms before she slips inside.

Out of habit, I pull out the phone Wolf provided. It's an iPhone. I prefer BlackBerry, but I like that my iPhone can charge when I drive my Tesla. I loaded this phone with my favorite apps and news sources. I have a box of burner phones in my trunk. But they suck. I keep them in case I fear someone might be listening. Or tracking.

I've been using this new phone for the delivery service app and the weather. I connected one of my oldest Twitter accounts to this phone, and now, to bide the time, I scroll through the feed. Only Trevor, Kairi, my sister, and Wolf have this number. And Vivi. If anyone connects the two of us via this phone, then they've already connected too much.

But maybe Vivi's right. Maybe it's time for me to stop looking over my shoulder. Maybe Trevor and Wolf are right. We shouldn't spend so much time looking backward. Instead, we should focus on the future. Maybe my sister and all those close to me are right, and I've grown too paranoid. Too worried. There's a cloudless blue sky, and the temperature is a perfect seventy-two. Birds chirp in the distance like I'm on the set of a kid's movie.

My Twitter feed is random. Most of the gamers I followed back in the day no longer tweet. There's a tweet about one politician going to jail, and I click on the replies. Some happy, some pissed, some funny memes. There's a news story about a ransomware attack on a big box retailer. I hover my thumb to click, and the screen goes black.

The iPhone powers down.

All areas of my peripheral vision go black.

Did I not charge it? No, and it charged the entire drive here. *Fuck!*

The phone is charged, but I throw open the car door and place it on the charging rest in my car.

A large white Apple logo and multi-lingual welcome screen appears. My skin, my blood, my bones—all go cold.

The screen door slams closed. Vivi smiles. There's a bag over her shoulder and a bounce in her step. I jump out of the car and pop open the trunk.

I open my laptop. A message pops up. The Gmail password is incorrect. Please enter your four-digit password.

"Fuck!" I scream.

"What's wrong?" She glances at my screen. "Do you not remember?"

"Fuck, fuck, fuck, fuck, fuck," I chant. The box of burner phones sits before me, and I grab one, quickly dialing Kairi's number.

"What's wrong?" Vivi asks again, still chipper.

"I didn't set up a four-digit number," I grit out. This is beyond bad. This is fucked.

"Hey," Kairi answers.

"Check everything. We're under attack. I'm on my way."

I slam the trunk closed, and a second later, a car door closes. I lean into my car and stare at Vivi.

"What are you doing?"

"I'm going with you." She pulls the loop on her seatbelt over her, snapping it in place.

"Like hell you are."

"No, I am. Or you can leave, and I'll follow."

"You don't know where I'd go."

"You'd go to Kairi's vineyard, right? That's who you just called. Do you want me in your car or following you?"

Memories of the last attack surface. The gun, the knife, the blood. Tiny black dots appear. I can't.

A mechanical snap sounds. She directs me. Hands on my arms. She pushes me down into a seat. The passenger seat. The door shuts. She's in the driver's seat. The seat moves forward, then up. She adjusts the rearview mirror.

"Lean forward. Put your head between your legs." What is Vivi saying? "I spoke to Kairi. She says to bring you. She hasn't found anything yet, but she's looking. She and Trevor are on the lookout. She doesn't see anything yet. Here's your phone if you want to call her."

"Wait...what?" Small businesses pass through the window. The blue sky, mailboxes awkwardly lined up along a busy country road.

"Kairi says I don't need to call the cops. But we can call nine-one-one. Do you think we should?"

"No. No. The attack could all be..." The thundering in my head eases. "No. This attack is virtual. If it was physical, they wouldn't tip me off by hijacking my phone. They shut everything down. But Kairi..." I lift the burner phone, redialing.

Vivi grips the steering wheel with both hands. She sounds calm. Her attention is on the road. But, Jesus, if he hurts her, I'll kill him in the vilest manner conceivable.

"Erik?" Kairi questions through the phone line. "Are you okay? Vivi said—"

"I'm fine. I had a moment. Just...what are you seeing?"

"Nothing. Everything's normal." Concern colors Kairi's tone.

"My phone powered down. It's hijacked. It's my personal one. Tied to my real name." Everything Kairi is monitoring is blanketed with aliases and untraceable accounts. "My laptop's hijacked too. You're monitoring the security cameras, right?"

"Trevor's on that."

"Wolf's still in SB. Right?" I ask for confirmation.

"Yes."

Shit. Maybe he's been watching. Maybe he knows we're down our strongest defense player.

"He's on his way back. Which number got hijacked?" The clatter of keystrokes sounds through the phone, the sound oddly soothing and calming. My palms are sweaty, and I wipe them one by one on my jeans.

"My personal." I tell her the number in case she doesn't have it memorized. "Do you think he's just fucking with us? Letting me know he's traced us?"

"I don't know. Just get here. It might not be him. I'm not seeing anything right now."

"No unusual error reports?"

"No." She sounds annoyed. "Are you tweeting right now?"

"No." My face twists in frustration at Kairi's asinine question. *Focus, woman.*

"Should we fear hackers? Intention is at the heart of the discussion."

"What?" *Has she lost her mind?*

"Your account just tweeted that."

*What the ever-loving fuck?*

I grab Vivi's phone. I need to see this bullshit for myself. She's got every app open. Her interface is a colossal, disorganized mess. I click, click, click. Give up. Pull down for search, type in Twitter, locate the app, and track down my accounts.

# MAKE IT HAPPEN

VIVI

My heart rate spikes in a way it's never, ever spiked. The pads of my fingers tingle, and it's not sexual. It's nerve-wracking. It's a stomach twisted in knots, touching a live wire and jumping back, shocked and in pain kind of tingle.

Erik seems to have recovered from his panic attack, but he's pale, and he's wiping his palms flat out on his jeans over and over. This is insanity.

"Why don't you call the police?" I practically screamed at Kairi. Seeing Erik bent over, barely able to breathe, scared the living daylights out of me. Whatever he fears…it's bad. It's really, really, really bad.

Kairi said they're basically the police. But do the police have panic attacks? I can't imagine Erik ever holding a gun. He doesn't look like the type. Kairi said they are the ones to call when this happens.

"Just get him here." That's what she ended with. So, I'm driving like a lunatic in Erik's Tesla, and that's when the alert lights the screen in the middle of the car that he has twenty miles left before we need to recharge.

The address to Kairi's is already entered. I know how to go there, but I entered it to double-check myself. If there's a wreck or something, I want to be rerouted. And she's fifteen miles away.

"We're fine. We'll make it. Just don't use the auto drive." Erik says.

I nod, and he picks my phone up and dials, presumably to call someone other than Kairi, because she basically kicked him off the phone. How he remembers so many phone numbers is mind-boggling. If my phone powered down, I could call no one. That's how many numbers I have memorized other than my own. Or, well, I suppose I remember the farmhouse landline phone number. I grew up in that house and had to learn it for school.

As I turn right onto the gravel drive that winds through Kairi's family property, Erik is dialing yet another number. I've noticed he has alter- nated between using my phone and the temporary burner phone he had in the back of his car. For some reason, it doesn't bother me at all that the guy I'm seeing, the guy who just told me he loves me, carries a box of burner phones around like a common drug dealer. Or, at least, I've never met a drug dealer, but I've heard they use burner phones. I asked Erik why he did that, and he mumbled to himself, not to me, an answer. I suspect he can't decide what's safer.

And that right there is what has me on edge. When I park beside an old, rusted pickup truck, I don't know what awaits us. If an assassin dressed in all black with a face mask is on the way, or if some thug with an AK-47 is going to pull up and blast through the back of the house. Either scenario feels conceivable.

Erik jumps out of the car, dashing toward the back door, his laptop and phone clutched to his side. I am slower getting out of the car. For one, I'm not even sure how to turn this car off. I'm looking for a button or lever.

"Come on," Erik shouts.

"How do I—"

"Just get out of the car. It turns off on its own." *Weird.*

He waits for me as I round the car. His expression is cold. But he's not mad. His brain is off in another stratosphere. He's physically present in the driveway, but ninety-five percent of his thought processes are in an alternative plane. I've seen it before from The Bookery. His focus is otherworldly. But, right now, what I'm seeing isn't healthy. Not being able to breathe, what I saw back there, which I am positive was a panic attack, isn't healthy.

He presses against my back and pushes me forward, rushing me into the house. I see him scan the sky as if he expects to see a helicopter or a drone. The door slams behind us, and Erik is off. I've never been inside this house before. It isn't Kairi's family home. I think it's just a house on the property. Lots of vineyards have these random houses sprinkled about. Maybe at one time family members or someone on staff lived in them, or maybe they were built with the exclusive purpose of garnering additional income as a rental. There are no photographs. The art hanging on the wall is faded and in cheap frames. It's the kind of art one buys in Home Goods or Bed, Bath & Beyond. The walls are painted beige. It's a drab color people around here liked around 2005 to 2010. The place needs a fresh coat of paint and some TLC.

Controlled shouting floats up the stairs. The layered emotion reminds me that if someone is about to storm the building with machine guns, then the color on the walls is immaterial.

I follow the shouts down a narrow stairwell into a basement. The carpet is a short shag in an off-putting brown. It's a depressing color combination.

Peals of laughter echo through the fake wood paneled hallway.

"Dumbass!" Trevor shouts.

Kairi is laughing so hard she's bent over, holding her sides as if she's cramping. I guess this means no one is going to storm the building, but I say nothing. Erik has one hand over his eyes, his glasses raised on his forehead, and a half-grimace, half-smile across his lips.

"What's going on?" Laughter has to be a good sign.

"It's not Kane," Trevor tells me as he paces the room, smiling. "Your lover boy, Mr. Cautious, used an ancient Twitter account to tweet his dissatisfaction about a restaurant delivery."

This is so over my head, but I don't want to come across as the dumbest person in the room. "And so they hacked his phone?"

"No. Well, not the restaurant people. He has a three-digit Twitter account."

Erik stares out the window. He's gripping a chunk of his hair. I don't get it. At all.

"There's a group of hackers out there who covet three-digit Twitter accounts. And guess what this schmuck's account was?" I don't bother guessing...there's no point. "OG1."

*Okay.*

"It stands for original gangster one." Kairi explains it like I'm five. She should maybe shoot for three. "He hasn't used it in ages, but he has a shit ton of followers. So, when he unleashed his annoyance at Slap-Jack's for getting his order wrong, it was like awakening a monster. They knew he'd just ordered from SlapJack's. And he'd ordered online, so they located his food order. From there, so easy."

I rock back on my heels as I piece it together. Now both of Erik's hands are on his head.

"All you need is a billing address and the last four digits of a credit card number to change your Apple password. They just locked him out of his phone and computer to disable him so they could hijack his Twitter account. It's probably some twenty-something yokel. But he'll be able to sell that Twitter handle for...what do you say?" Trevor directs his question to Kairi. "Ten K? Fifteen?"

"I have no idea." She falls back against the sofa cushions. Then she snaps her fingers. "Wolf. We've got to tell him. He's gonna be wheels up any minute."

Slowly, I move through the living space, stepping over wires and bypassing an empty pizza box to join Kairi on the sofa.

"So…if this guy located Erik, does that mean this other guy can locate him?"

Erik spins around and answers. "No. That Twitter account pre-dates college. He wouldn't connect it. It's from, like, 2006. I didn't even think about what name or account I tied it to. It's an unbelievably stupid mistake."

Trevor and Kairi may find it humorous, but I can tell Erik does not. He's shaken, still pale. I approach him with caution and wrap my arms around him. Pressure from his chin falls on the top of my head. Worry leaks out of him, ever so slowly, like icing from a piping bag.

"Dude, it was nothing. She's fine. There was never any danger." Trevor sounds exasperated. But I witnessed the panic attack. I sensed the extreme fear. Trevor might think this is funny, but I don't see the humor. Not when there's a tremor vibrating through Erik.

Erik pulls himself together, and he and Trevor go into an adjacent room to talk with Wolf. I follow Kairi up to the kitchen to get us all something to drink. I have an idea that's been percolating, and it occurs to me that not only does Erik need this, but she's the one who can help me make it happen.

# I AM PHOENIX

VIVI

Erik frowns when I insist on taking the Range Rover. It's a gas guzzler, and he prefers his car. But I plan on driving, and I don't want to deal with finding charging stations. The only thing I've told him is that I'm taking him away for a holiday and it's a surprise.

"I don't like surprises," he grumbles, but that's all he does. And that's one reason I know he needs to get away. He needs a break. No one can live on the run forever. Eventually, your legs give out.

He says nothing as I pack my clothes. Even more worrisome, he says nothing as I pack his clothes. He sits in a chair by the pool, hands crossed over his chest, still. Every time I glance out the window, he's in the same position.

It's all the things he's not saying, all the questions he's not asking, that gnaw away at me. When I went over my plan with Kairi and then Trevor, they asked plenty of questions.

"Will it be remote?"

"How are you getting there?"

"Does it have Internet access?"

Kairi verged on ecstatic as she helped me pull this off. After I discovered some dear friends were out of town, and I could stay at their home in Newport Ranch, everything fell into place at warp speed. While I schemed, Erik located the pissant hacker—his words. He'd confirmed that, yes, the guy did not know who he was. He held "no heat" against him. Erik and Trevor considered a counterattack.

"We could nuke him," Trevor flippantly says as I join them in Kairi's living room. Upon seeing me, he offers an explanation. "Nuke his accounts. Wipe his computers clean. Erase everything."

"Oh." I'd searched Erik's expression for a hint of amusement, entertainment, something. If he felt anything, he hid it beneath layers of frustration that he'd slipped up. Trevor and Kairi didn't see his reaction. But I had...and when I told Kairi, she agreed he needed a break.

"We've been at this nonstop for so long. Did he tell you?"

"Tell me what?"

"About the attack. About..." Emotion choked her words. I'd reached for Kairi, touched her, letting her know she didn't need to go on.

"He told me some."

"We've been nonstop since. And then he found us, and we came here, and..."

"You're still scared?"

"I don't want to be. I want to believe we're safe. I want to believe you are safe if you stay with Erik."

I want to believe it, too. Safe or not, I plan on staying with Erik. When I believed the absolute worst might happen, my instinct wasn't to run away. It was to stay by Erik, to support him.

Trevor cleared the Newport Ranch location. The home we will be staying in is a part of the resort, but it's isolated. We shouldn't have any reason to leave the resort. Twenty miles of hiking trails, astounding ocean views, and a place to decompress. Erik needs to decompress.

Really, they all do, although for some reason Kairi and Trevor seem to take it better than Erik. Or maybe I just don't know them as well. Maybe one has to know someone well to identify his fault lines.

José had been more than willing to take over The Bookery. It was funny...I'd gone so long being the only employee. And José had come along and hired multiple sales assistants in a matter of weeks. This would be my first vacation since opening the shop. Erik and I both need this getaway.

Headlights from an oncoming car flash from the transition of high beam to low. Erik stirs beside me. He has been asleep since I merged onto the 101. And silent before that. I wonder if panic attacks wipe someone out...maybe they wipe someone out in a similar way that someone can wipe a computer. His unnerving silence certainly makes me think so.

His seat raises. He wipes his eyes, shifting his heavy frames up to his brow.

"Where are we?"

"Close to our destination."

"Still not going to tell me where we're going?"

"Nope." I grin. It's good he's talking. He's awake and interacting.

"Did I ever tell you I don't like surprises?"

"Huh. Maybe once or twice. But that can't be true. Everyone likes surprises."

He gives me a look that both disagrees and conveys his opinion that my idea is lunacy. Fine, whatever.

Minutes later, a light ahead shines on the wood carved sign for The Inn at Newport Ranch.

"California?" he asks. I nod. "Nice."

"Have you been here before?" I doubt it. I wonder where he thought I'd be taking him. We're in a car. The reasonable options are limited.

"Newport Ranch? No."

"It's technically Fort Bragg. This is a resort. Friends own it. We don't have to see any of the other guests if that's your preference. We're staying in a house away from everything else."

"A house? For us?" I purposefully turn my head to minimize the risk of giving anything else away. Yes, he said he doesn't like surprises. But I can't resist keeping the best surprise from him. I am literally giddy.

I park the car and hop out onto the pavement. From the back here, the house doesn't look like much. Or, rather, it looks like a jigsaw one-story home covered in faded driftwood. He carries our tote bags in over one shoulder, and I hunt for the lights. This home isn't technically a part of the resort, but when my friends are out of town, they'll rent it out. The eucalyptus aroma that greets us lets me know they've had their staff go through and give the place the guest treatment. It smells like a spa, and I'm not surprised at all to see they set the kitchen up for guests. Coffee and tea options are laid out, and a basket of fruit, nuts, crackers, and cookies. I'll have to tell Lesedi she's outdone herself.

Erik stands before the oversized window, one of many that overlook the expanse of the Pacific. He can't see it all at night, but this coastline will remind him of Washington State. Black rocks rise above the ocean in stunning formations. Through the glass, the roar of the ocean seeps through in a rhythmic, subtle pattern.

I lead him to our bedroom. The foot of the queen-size bed is a couple of feet from another large window. I love this room. It's not the master, but sleeping in this bed is like sleeping in a dry, comfortable boat that's landlocked. The sounds of the oceans drift through all night, but the cozy bed doesn't rock. Bright yellow stars scatter across the sky. It's an otherworldly experience.

We silently prepare for bed. He pulls back the thick white comforter and the spartan white sheets. His glasses are still on, and he puts his hands behind his head. The weight of his gaze caresses me. I brush my teeth and wash my face with the bathroom door open. My backside tingles. I set the hairband on the shelf near the sink and untwist the braid, letting the unruly strands fall around me because he likes it loose and free.

I enter the narrow bedroom and stand at the foot of the bed. I stand in the moonlight and meet his gaze. I undo the tiny buttons on my blouse, one by one. On a normal day, I'd pull it over my head. But removing it this way feels more alluring. I'm not wearing a bra, so when my top hits the floor, cool air circles my nipples. My fingers are warm against my skin. I clasp the band on my long skirt and shimmy it over my hips, and the fabric falls in a pool at my feet, taking my panties with it.

The bare wood floor is smooth beneath my feet. Sliding between the crisp sheets completely nude feels luxurious. The experience is scintillating, made more so by his steady watchfulness. His skin is warm. I align my body next to his, our thighs touching. My breasts rub across the firm planes of his chest as I lift, covering his body with mine, skin to skin, to kiss him goodnight.

When our lips touch, he comes alive. He flips me onto my back. His smooth, bare erection strokes my thigh, and I smile as his lips and tongue find the most sensitive spot below my ear. My body twists and squirms. I remove his glasses, setting them on the bedside table. He takes advantage of my stretched position, leaning across the bed, and fondles my breast, teasing the sensitized nipples.

"Vivi." He breathes out the word. It sounds like a prayer. After the day he's had, he needs comfort. Extra care and attention. I push him onto his back, my thigh between his, careful pressure against his groin, as I kiss my way down his throat, and down his firm chest, with a playful bite to his nipple that earns me a quick, hot slap to my ass, and then farther down. With my thumb, I rub the precum around his tip. He watches, eyes dark and ravenous. As my lips surround him, he lets out a low groan.

He guides me as I work him over. In my mouth, he expands, his girth widening, and I know he's close. He pulls me off him, flips me onto my stomach, and enters me. I gasp for air, and he grips my hips, lifting me slightly, positioning me to use my body as he needs, and it's hot as fuck.

His skin slaps against mine, over and over. His hands are everywhere. On my breasts, twisting my nipples, on my clit, rubbing, and I'm right there, on the edge, so close, and he drives me down on the bed. The headboard slams against the wall. *Thump. Thump. Thump.*

With each slam into me, I slide forward. I reach out and grip the sheets and push back against him. I'm spiraling higher and higher. He grips my hips, lifting me, angling me again, and his thumb grinds against my clit, and I scream. The orgasm rips through me so hard my toes curl tight as the muscles spasm, and he collapses over me, his weight heavy and warm.

Eventually, he raises up on his forearm, and I roll onto my side. He lies back, and I drape my body partially over his.

"God, I needed that," he breathes out into the room, like it's an admission. "I need you, Vivi." There's emotion in his words, and they wrap around my heart. If I doubted it before this, I don't doubt it now. He owns me. I'm in love with this man.

"I need you, too." I'm not scared. He's not playing me. I trust this man with everything. He's complicated, but in his core, in his soul, he's good. And all these feelings and sensations flowing through me, it's as if sparks of electricity are flowing through my veins. It's as if I am a firefly, lit up from the inside. This is what love feels like, and I'm in awe.

Side by side, we gaze at each other, our heads sharing the same pillow, our breathing synchronized. Every now and then, he touches me. My hair, my cheek, my shoulder. It's as if he's confirming I'm present, that I'm not a concoction from a dream. He lifts my hand and kisses the knuckles, gently turns it and presses a kiss to my palm, then over my tattoo. The warmth of his breath skirting my skin sends goosebumps along my arms.

"I have to tell you something, Viv." I place a kiss against his throat, inching closer, eliminating the inches between our naked bodies. *I love you, too.*

"Yeah," I urge, tempting him to share his thoughts. Hope builds. I want to hear him say it once more. Then I'll follow.

Our bodies are aligned, and the beats of his heart in his chest pump against me. I press my lips to his throat as he swallows.

"I don't want there to be secrets between us. I am tired of letting fear rule my life."

"Good." His fingers interlace with mine, and he raises my hand. His lips caress the tender skin over my wrist, over the blood vessels, and down to the script.

His words are strangled, yet loaded.

"I am Phoenix."

# INTRUSION DETECTION

ERIK

Bright, blinding light cascades over the bed. I shield my eyes. Struggle to gather my bearings. A fluffy white comforter covers me. I'm in bed. Alone. *Shit. That's right.*

"What did you say?" Shock reverberated through her words. I stilled, instantly regretting ever telling her. What the hell was I thinking?

"You're...?" She pulled the sheet over her breasts, covering herself, as she backed away. Confusion etched on her face.

"It's not bad, is it? We've been friends since you were a kid. That's all it is. You were my best sorceress. We climbed the catacombs together." Inside, I smiled at the memory. We'd fucking crushed that level. Outside, I didn't smile, because her reaction freaked me out.

"Cata...so...why not tell me? When you first came into the store, why not tell me?"

"I didn't plan it. I just wanted to see what you looked like."

"How did you find me?"

"You didn't really try to hide yourself. You don't do anything to hide your VPN source. It wasn't hard to triangulate your location." She nodded slowly. Too slowly. We promised not to locate each other… but that was, like, ten years ago. A promise like that, doesn't it expire? "All I planned on doing was seeing if you were really female. You were so damn good at fighting, I half expected you to be an overweight middle-aged man. I was just curious. And bored."

"Bored." She reiterated the word like it was ugly.

"And then I saw you. And I got to know you."

"But you already knew me, didn't you?"

"Yes, but—"

"Why wait until now to tell me? We've been texting in the game. I told you I was seeing someone." Her tone climbed in octaves, becoming more shrill, and I shrank back. "When you told me your real name, why not tell me then?"

"Don't be mad." Yeah, that was a mistake. Darkness cloaked the room, and I detected rising rage. So I rushed to fix it. "I didn't want to risk losing what we had. I love our friendship. And my life is so fucked…I figured if dating you didn't work out, if I screwed it up, I'd still have our friendship. The only reason I told you now is that I don't want any secrets between us. I love you."

Her warm touch on my shoulder gave me hope.

"I need space. We can talk in the morning." She got out of bed. The white of her nightgown fluttered under the moonlight as she dropped it over her shoulders. Powerless, I watched as she left our bedroom.

"Tomorrow a better day?" I called out to the dimly lit hall. But she didn't answer…

I leap off the bed and rush to get dressed. Would she leave me here? No. She has to be here. In the driveway, I spy her ancient Range Rover, and my pulse slows. She's here. The faint sounds of waves crashing call to me. There's a narrow path along the side of the house, and I follow it in the direction of the ocean.

Boulders rise out of the swirling Pacific like beasts rising from the underworld. The rocky coastline reminds me of some beaches my family used to go to in Oregon. Stunning and gorgeous boulders against the vast sea. A gray fog clouds the horizon, and an orange sun peeks through high above. It's late in the day. I slept late, after struggling for hours to sleep alone.

There's coffee in a glass pot on the kitchen counter, and I pour myself a mug. It's lukewarm, so I nuke it in the microwave and head outside to find Vivi. Our beach access is a private walking path that curves down onto a narrow beach. Judging from the sand, I would guess it's close to low tide. I scan up and down the beach. Human outlines off in the distance are to the north, and I head in that direction.

As I get closer, the shapes become clearer. It's a middle-aged couple walking the beach. I don't see Vivi, and I didn't bring a phone. I decide to head back in the direction of the house. I'll call her.

She could still be angry. She may need time alone to think through everything I told her. But I'm still the same person she grew to know. If anything, our relationship should be stronger now that she's aware we've been virtual friends for ages. Or maybe she's rethinking a relationship with me. A bird squawks overhead before diving into the cold waters.

I couldn't blame her. We have no idea how long we'll be living under a shroud of uncertainty and fear. It's an exhausting life.

Headlights cut through the fog on the road leading to the house on the overlook. The house we're staying in. I climb the hill, wary. My nerves burn.

It's probably nothing. She probably ordered delivery. Or room service travels to this outpost house in vehicles.

I reach the house, and a shrill cry pierces the air. I halt. Listening. It's a baby's cry.

There's a black SUV in the driveway. The car doors are all open.

"Cali?" My twin sister steps away from the open side door, holding a baby.

Logan, her husband, comes around from the back of the car holding bags. *What? How?*

"It's okay. We took every precaution. Private plane. Whole nine yards." He's grinning and holding out a hand. I take it on reflex.

My sister is holding an enormous baby. It has tears running out of the corner of its eyes, and there's a giant plastic thing wedged in its mouth. She holds it out and smiles.

"Do you want to meet your nephew?" He looks about as happy as I feel.

"What's wrong with him?" The plastic thing bobs up and down, and I guess he's sucking on it — hard.

"Oh, I think the plane bothered his ears." The child has an enormous head. He's wrapped in a blanket, but his head dwarfs his body. Drool leaks out the side of his mouth and down his chin.

"He looks like Logan." He doesn't, actually, but that giant head has to come from his side.

"Do you want to hold him?"

"No." Cali laughs. I look to Logan. "Are you sure this is safe?"

"Yes. I emailed work telling them we won a trip to an exclusive spa in Maine, so the information at work about our whereabouts is incorrect."

"Where is Vivianne? I'm so excited to meet her in person. When she called, I couldn't believe it." My attention falls on my sister, and her question detangles.

"Vivianne set this up?"

"Yes. Didn't she tell you? Where is she?" Cali scans the driveway and the path to the front door.

"I'm not sure. She has to be around." Vivi's Range Rover sits twenty feet away. "Let's go inside. I've been out walking on the beach."

I help Logan with the bags. It's amazing how much crap they travel with. It's like my sister has forgotten how to pack now that she's married. The driver of the vehicle comes around and closes the tailgate.

"It's nice to meet you." He says to me, hand out. He's not in uniform. I don't take his hand because I can't figure him out. He's not armed that I can see, but he's muscular. He lets his rejected hand fall to his waist. The lilt of his lips shows he's more amused by my rebuff than anything. "I work for you."

"You do?" I hire people online all the time and do not know what they look like. But in return, they don't know what I look like. And they most assuredly would not be driving my sister.

"Based out of Santa Barbara." *Wolf.* Trevor and Wolf hired him. This guy works for us out of Wolf's security group. Got it.

"Erik," I say to him. "And you are?"

"Snipes." He looks to the remaining luggage on the ground. "You need any help?" Logan returns to the front and picks up some more bags.

"I think we're good," I tell him. "Sorry about that." I run my fingers through my hair. "I had…this was all a surprise."

"No worries. I'm scheduled to do pick-up. Trevor and Wolf have my number if you need anything. I'm staying close by."

I love my team. Wolf planned this, so we aren't without security.

"Great," I tell him. I don't need to know where, but my guess is he's probably on this property and will keep an eye out, just in case. I'll get his deets from Wolf.

Inside the house, the rooms are dark, and I hunt down light switches to flick them on. I haven't fully explored the house yet, but if Vivi planned this, I'm guessing there are extra rooms for Cali and Logan.

"This place is amazing." My sister is bouncing Dylan up and down as she stares out the large window overlooking the Pacific.

"Yeah. We just got in last night. Let me call Vivi, see if I can find her."

"She said there's a high chair here, and somewhere there's a crib. If we can get the crib set up, I'll see if I can get Dylan down for a nap. He didn't sleep well on the plane. I think he's overtired."

"Did you guys fly overnight?"

"Yeah. It would've been a great plan, given there was a bed in the plane Vivianne set up for us, except for this little guy here."

"You guys must be exhausted."

I leave them and locate my phone on my bedside table. Everything in the bedroom is just like I left it. The bed is unmade. Our clothes are on the floor where we dropped them last night. I call Vivi's number, and it goes straight to voicemail. I text her.

*E: Where are you? Cali and Logan are here.*

I am dazed. It's possible after everything I downloaded last night, Vivi isn't up to meeting my family. But she can't avoid them. They're here now. A loud wail punctures the quiet. They need a bedroom to get set up in.

I enter the large living area and duck my head into an adjoining bedroom. It's significantly larger than the one Cali and I are staying in.

"Is this room okay with you guys?"

Cali steps by me to check it out.

"It's perfect. Any idea where that crib is?"

"I don't. But this is a resort. I'll call the front desk. They can probably send one down."

"It's okay. I brought our Pack 'n Play. I wasn't certain if the hotel crib would be safe enough. It's fine. We'll use what I brought."

Logan enters the room with a cloth bag with straps. I watch as he unzips it and unfolds a portable crib device. The entire scene is surreal, mainly because I didn't have any idea my sister and her family would be arriving.

*Where is Vivi?*

I leave Cali and Logan to get settled in the bedroom. There's no response to my text. How angry is she?

Only a sliver of sand can be seen from the cliff we're perched on. If she's out there walking the beach, I wouldn't see. But she's surely aware of the time. She's the one who planned their flight.

Eventually, the bedroom door clicks open and shut. My sister joins me at the window. Her lips turn up in a knowing, kind smile. It's the smile she wears when she wants to tease me about something.

"So..." Cali's grin is contagious. I assume she's returned to her fourteen-year-old self, teasing me about a girl. "I can see why you like Vivianne."

"She is great. But...do you have any interest in going for a walk? I can't reach her on her phone."

"The signal isn't great out here. I noticed it on my phone." My twin gets me. She's always been the more levelheaded of the two of us.

"She must've lost track of time." Or she could have twisted her ankle when she was out walking this morning. That beach was pretty desolate, although not entirely void of human life.

"Come on. A walk will be great." Cali loops her arm in the crook of my elbow and leads me into the fresh air.

We fall into an easy tandem step down the trail to the beach. The air is warmer than earlier this morning, and the sky is bluer. The fog has burned off.

"You know, Vivianne orchestrated a Zoom call with Logan, Wolf, Kairi, Trevor, and me to plan this. She led the meeting. She's soft-spoken but forceful. I can see why you like her."

The vision of her pulling together everyone for this surprise—on a Zoom call, no less—distracts me. Wolf and Trevor will no doubt give me shit about it when we get back.

"And she's the spitting image of Mom."

That stops me in my tracks. "No." She's got similar hair color and eyes, but....

"She looks more like Mom's child than either of us ever did. You fell for someone who could be Mom's—"

"Don't say daughter." Disgusting.

"Okay. Well, twin. You fell for someone just like Mom. She even dresses like Mom." *She dresses like a woman. It's the way women dress.*

Cali shoves my ribcage the same way she did when we were ten. Ignoring her, I consider. Those blue eyes. She's always felt like coming home.

"It's okay. Lots of men fall for women who remind them of their mothers."

"I promise you I don't think of her like that."

"Oh, my god," Cali gushes. "I know that. I'm just saying it's easy to see what the draw was. Initially, that is."

"Do you remember that game we played back in high school and early college? Zeitgeist—"

"War? Battle? Yeah. I remember. It was the only thing you and I ever did together sometimes."

"Well, you liked to read, and you liked that boy…"

"Chris. Not that Dad let that go anywhere."

"Vivi was one of our teammates. Her avatar was Firefly."

"No way!" Cali's grin is expansive. She looks young and happy, and it's great to see. I haven't seen her this happy in years. All the stress I caused her, forcing her to uproot her life, it's all gone. She's wearing loose clothes, but they're different than Vivi's. She's in a monochrome outfit, whereas Vivi always wears patterns. "You know, I think I remember Firefly. She was a sorceress, right?"

"Yep."

"I think she saved me from a pack of zombies once."

"Yeah, well, she found out I was Phoenix last night."

"Oh." Her toe kicks a black rock and sends it clattering. "Wow." There are a few other beachcombers up ahead. The ocean waters are icy. No one is swimming. But it's an amazing day for a walk. "How'd she take that news?"

"When I woke up, she wasn't in the house. She didn't leave. Her car is here. But I'm guessing since she wasn't here to greet you, she's still processing it."

We're quiet for a few steps. "When she called and arranged this, she sounded concerned for you. It's why I stopped everything and packed. Why I flew in a plane overnight to get here."

"You didn't need to do that. I'm fine." Shit. My reaction yesterday must have scared Vivi more than I realized.

Cali studies me as we walk. I feel her gaze on me as I scan our surroundings, searching for Vivi. I recognize her sisterly concern that at one time annoyed me to no end. She tucks her hair behind her ears and then rubs her arm against me, shoving me a bit. Tactile, like always.

"I think you are fine. Now. Now that you aren't trying to do it all alone."

"I've never been all alone." I really haven't. I have a team. We work together.

"Maybe. But you shoulder a lot of worry all on your own. You can't do that forever. I think Vivi is exactly what you need."

The funny thing is…she's been there all along.

# EXPOSURE

ERIK

Cali and I cover the entire stretch of beach at the resort. There are a few rocky caverns, and I climb up and peer into the dark holes, on the off chance Vivi chose to investigate, and she slipped. I call out her name a few times, but Cali's amused smile shuts me up. She'll come home when she's ready. She's not a lost dog or cat. The idea that she's injured is silly. I get it. It's my paranoia or my anxiety acting up.

Logan texts Cali as we're returning up the embankment.

"He says he's starved. What're you guys planning for lunch?" It's close to two in the afternoon. I'm hungry, too, but I imagine these east coast guys are famished.

"Did he say if Vivi's back?" I ask.

She texts, but there's no need, because Logan's head appears up ahead on the path.

"The refrigerator is full of food. You guys okay with sandwiches?"

"Yeah. Is Vivi back?"

"No. I figured you guys had met up with her."

Cali and I exchange a glance. She's no longer looking at me like I'm a silly, paranoid guy. I step past Logan.

"You guys help yourself to anything in the fridge. I'm going to call Wolf."

He answers on the first ring.

"You're supposed to be on vacation," he says by way of greeting.

"I haven't seen Vivi since I woke up this morning. Can you ping her phone? See where she is?"

If he set us up to come here, he would've gotten the information so we could be tracked, just in case.

"Did you guys get in a fight?"

"Yes." He chuckles, or maybe it's an exhale. "Her car's here. I haven't seen her all morning. And she wasn't here to greet Cali and Logan. And I didn't even know they were coming." Out of the corner of my eye, I see Cali crawling around on the floor.

"Her phone's off. Last location looks like it's right where you guys are."

"Wolf, something's wrong. She might be mad at me, but she wouldn't just disappear."

"Last activity was at 8:28 a.m. Have you been searching for her?"

"Yes. I've walked everywhere."

"You know, that place you're staying has twenty miles of trails. Have you been searching those?"

"No, I've only been out on the beach."

"Okay. Let me get Snipe. He can find a dirt bike and check the trails."

"Do you think—"

260

"No. Don't go there." The line disconnects. Cali is on her forearms, searching beneath the sofa.

"What are you doing?" I ask.

She sits back on her heels and wipes her brow. "Searching for a note." She shrugs. "I keep thinking if she was mad at you, I could see her leaving and leaving you the car. But I can't see her disappearing without leaving a note."

Her logic is sound.

"Hey, you guys okay with ham and tomato sandwiches?" Logan asks. I have no appetite, but my phone buzzes, so I leave the two of them to deal with food.

Kairi's voice comes through the line. "Hey, there. Wolf filled us in. Do you happen to know the password to her phone?"

"No. Do you think you can hack it?" Kairi's hacking skills are improving, but it's not easy to hack an Apple phone. It's easier with an app with a backdoor or installed hardware.

"Do you have the phone in your possession?"

"No." I head into our bedroom. Forget looking for a note. I should be looking for that phone.

"If she was upset, who would she call?" Kairi is pragmatic. She's ticking off a list. First thing is to confirm she's actually missing.

"Her friend Chloe. You know her, right?"

"I can get her info. Anyone else?"

"Celeste? Maybe Max?"

"Okay. I'm calling them. I don't want to alarm them, but I'll find out if they've heard from her."

"Thanks, Kairi."

The bedside table on her side of the bed is empty, aside from two dangling earrings and a stack of bracelets. When she left this morning, she didn't get fully dressed, or at least, not dressed to Vivi's standards.

Logan swipes a napkin over his face, and a few crumbs fall from his beard.

"Here's a sandwich for you." He pushes a sandwich on a paper towel my way.

"Do you think we should call the police? Let them know she's missing? In case we need to do a search party."

His lower lip protrudes. He's considering the option. He worked for the Chicago PD, and he was head of police on the island I sent Cali to. Now he's NSA, but he's got both military and police experience.

"Cali said you guys got in a fight?"

I nod. Why does that matter?

"If we call the police, they're going to have a lot of questions for you. I'm not saying we shouldn't call them, but you need to be prepared. The boyfriend will be the primary suspect. You'll be caught up with them and won't be able to help find her." He shoves his hands in his slacks. "You were the last one who saw her."

Chills climb my skin. Chances are she's hurt on a trail. We could use a search party. But there's another chance that's out there, and Logan knows it.

A cry comes from the bedroom, and Cali takes off. My phone buzzes.

"Kairi," I answer.

"No one's heard from her. But Chloe knew her password, so I logged into iMessage."

"And?"

"Nothing there. But I discovered she has multiple accounts. Under different names. I called Chloe back and asked her about them. Get this." I pace the room. Kairi sounds giddy. I want to throw this burner phone against the wall. "She's a hacker. Low level."

I pull the phone away from my ear and stare at it.

"What?"

"Chloe says she used the multiple accounts to go after jerks online. You're dating a little white hat. Did you know that?"

"Noooo." I draw my answer out. On one hand, I'm not surprised she's more awesome than I knew. On the other hand…"How does this information help us?"

"Oh. It doesn't. Not really. I don't think. I'll let you know." The phone disconnects.

"The police are going to want to ask if there's any reason she would leave on her own. They'll want to know a lot about your fight. And they'll ask if there's anyone who might want to harm her."

"It wasn't a fight like that," I tell Logan. I'm pacing the room now. What kind of white hat hacking was Vivi doing?

Two hours later, my team packs the den in this beachside vacation getaway. Trevor, Kairi, and Wolf helicoptered over. One of the first things Kairi said to me when she entered was, "This isn't Kane's style." Yet everyone is here. And Kane isn't a country. He hires assassins. Maybe this is a more recent employee's style.

Snipes has been up and down the trails on a dirt bike he located. Laptops are out and open. We're no closer to finding her. At this point, I would estimate she's been missing for eight to ten hours. If someone did kidnap her, she could be anywhere by now.

Decision made, I turn to Logan. "We need to report this to the police."

Kairi looks up from her laptop. "I'm reviewing footage from the resort entrance. Two different video feeds. One is license plates. The other is a view of the driver and front passenger of vehicles exiting the property. I haven't seen her leave. I think she's still on the property."

"All the more reason to notify the police. We need to form a search party," I tell Logan.

"Kairi," Wolf's deep timbre overpowers the hum of activity, "can you check that feed for a specific tag?"

She nods, and he passes her a piece of paper.

"What've you got?"

"We've been checking out a few of the accounts she exposed in online forums. We've located most of the men, but this guy has multiple aliases, and there's a restraining order against him in Marin County. His wife filed it two weeks ago. I spoke to Chloe. It's a guy she met on Tinder."

"Okay. How would that guy know we are here?"

"I don't know. From what I can find online, I'd say he's pretty skilled. She might have nailed the wrong asshole."

"But we're not home. Like, you're running theory is he followed us for a three-hour drive." I tug at my hair. I slept for most of the drive, but that's…

"No. I'd say it's more likely if we had her phone, we'd realize she inadvertently clicked on something he sent her."

A flash of me clicking like a madman on her phone yesterday blinks before me. No, I couldn't have…

"I'll go down to the police station," Logan says. "Kairi, you and Trevor keep on the feeds. You all split up into groups and search the resort."

Cali straps my nephew into a contraption on her chest.

"What're you doing?" Logan and I ask at the same time.

"I'm going to help with the search."

"No." Yes, Vivi could simply be injured on a hike. But my gut is churning. Always trust your instincts.

"You're staying here," I command as Logan acquiesces and tells her she can ride to the station with him. They then debate driving down to the station versus calling, but Logan insists it's best to go into the station.

I stand above one of the large black cases Wolf carried inside when he arrived. I open it and lift a holster to fit around my waist. Then I select a gun.

# THINGS I SHOULD HAVE DONE DIFFERENTLY

VIVI

The hard edge of zip ties bite into my wrists and ankles. In television shows, when people are tied to chairs, they pull and tug, but I sit still. Any movement at all cuts into my skin. Moisture pools beneath the binding, and I can't see it, but I suspect it is my blood.

I remember one show where a woman, an agent, was tied just like I am. She somehow dislocated her shoulder, and that allowed her to get out of her bindings. I will not attempt such a feat. Although I do wish I watched a show or a movie that portrayed a more realistic method of performing a magic-worthy maneuver.

My full bladder aches. I almost wish Bradley would return. It's my fault he left. My big mouth. Instead of trying to befriend him, I challenged him.

There are many things I should have done differently. I woke up, and I should have crawled into bed with Erik. Waited for him to wake up so we could talk. But he was sleeping soundly, and I was wide awake.

Processing. If I'm honest, a part of me suspected, or hoped, Erik was Phoenix. After all, when he entered the shop and kept returning, there was an air of mystery about him. And Phoenix has always been my mystery.

If I hadn't gone outside to the car to get my laptop, I wouldn't be tied to this chair right now. There were so many warning signs, too. There I was, in the driveway, and he appeared out of nowhere. A warning sign for sure. Why would a random man, a vaguely familiar-looking man, appear out of nowhere?

I had seen him before. Had seen his photos under two different aliases. But it was my first time seeing him in person, and it took my pre-coffee brain a minute to compute.

"Vivianne Rossi?" he asked. He wore black slacks and a black crew-neck, and shiny dress shoes.

"Yes?" Mistake number one. Why did I confirm my identity? Why didn't I listen to my gut, which knew something was off? The whites of his eyes were too pronounced, his pupils too small. But I sensed these things; they weren't cognitive thought. It's only in hindsight I see it now. I should have run. Maybe he sensed I might run.

When he lifted the strange contraption, I hadn't ever seen one before. I stared at it.

"I need to speak to you," was what he said. But he didn't want to speak to me. He wanted to yell.

"Yes, sir?" Why on Earth did I say sir? *What the hell, Rossi?*

He scanned the area. He looked around the driveway, searching the grounds in the early morning fog. I could have run then. Or simply jumped in the car and locked the doors. I don't think it's easy to break the windows on a large SUV.

But no, what did I do? I closed the Range Rover door. Didn't even grab my laptop, the very reason I went outside. I left no breadcrumbs.

Of course, I can't be so hard on myself. I had no idea I was talking to a lunatic. The only thing I had to go on was that gut feeling, raising the hairs on my arms, the sense I should be wary.

Footfalls outside the room announce others are near. I scream with all my might, but all it serves is to burn my throat. My nose drips. The duct tape itches. I can't reach my shoulder to rub it, because when I move my shoulder, the wraps on my wrist cut.

If I can get out of this room, I'm home free. This guy doesn't normally do this. He hasn't thought everything through. As he told me. There are white remnants of the coke he snuffed on the table. He may not even remember where he left me. He's out of his mind high. I may be discovered by the cleaning service tomorrow morning. Assuming he didn't pay for multiple days, which I doubt he did. He seemed too frantic. His fingers trembled. An involuntary twitch curled his lip up to his right cheek every few seconds.

"You fucking bitch. This is all your fucking fault." That was what he said to me when he got me in the room. Which, why did I go with him? Another strategic error. I should have run. But that zapping thing he used hurt like a mother. I couldn't move my muscles at all for minutes. I didn't want him to zap me again. I was terrified he'd zap me again. I wasn't positive my muscles would move at any rate of speed. I knelt in the driveway. Immobile.

And then he put me in the trunk. I thought about kicking the back seat. I am pretty sure I've seen others do that on television. But it was pitch black, and the car was moving, and I wasn't sure what I would gain by kicking through. He'd probably zap me again. It's not like I would jump out of a moving car.

As I watched him pacing the hotel room, I lost my fear. Because I realized this guy didn't know what he was doing. And I got this idea that if I couldn't talk my way out of the room, I could overpower him.

He didn't even tie me up to start. I could have lunged for the door and screamed. Why didn't I? What was I thinking?

"What were you doing outside?" He'd been both angry and frantic. Sweat beaded on his forehead. His jaw was smooth, though. He shaved recently. I remember thinking he must have been calm this morning.

"Outside where?" I asked.

"Outside!" he bellowed. His skin reddened, and his crazy eyes bulged.

"I needed my laptop."

"You shouldn't have made me shoot you." He paced the room, speaking to himself. "All I wanted to do was locate you. I wanted to scare you. Hurt you. Like you hurt me."

I debated. Should I tell him I'm scared, or would he react like the crazies in the movies and feed off that? I'd seen shows where men became attracted to women in fear, so I only listened. Maybe I should have gone with a different approach.

"You look familiar. How do I know you?" That was the approach I went with, but by then, I had figured it out. Bradley Lilith. I outed him to his wife. And to everyone following his fake alias, Bruce Williams, on Tinder.

"You don't fucking know who I am? You destroyed my life, and you don't know who I am? That's why I needed to do this. You fucking cunt. You don't know anything about me, and you destroy my life. That bitch is taking everything. The house. My lawyer says our prenup is void. Thanks to you. My life fucking savings. You fucking bitch. You don't know what the fuck you've done. Who the fuck do you think you are?"

None of this was said to my face. It was said to the floor as he paced the room, head down. He was wild. Crazed. Not lucid.

"And then, you dumb bitch. You fell for my phishing attempt. Gave me your location. You wanted this. You wanted me to find you. You made it too fucking easy. You came out before I had a plan. Fucking cunt. Screwing everything up."

"I'll go. I won't say anything. I promise. We'll chalk it up as—"

"Shut the fuck up!" He held that gun thing in his hand and paced. He wasn't looking at me. All I had to do was make it across the room. He'd had me sit in a chair, and I was simply sitting there. Watching him. I should have picked up the lamp and thrown it at him. I should have screamed out my lungs.

Instead, I slowly rose out of the seat, watching him. I stood tall and lifted one foot.

"Sit the fuck down!" The black zapper butted my face. I sat down. And that was when he seemed to remember he had indeed planned something, because he had a plastic bag, and he pulled out zip ties. He tied my hands behind my back and each ankle to a leg of the chair.

I should have fought him. I should have kicked out. But I didn't. I watched him. It was as if that shock of that zapper fried my brain because I am smarter than that. What the fuck did I do?

"Why don't you have a real gun?" I don't know where that question came from. I don't know why I asked it. Maybe because that zapper hurt.

"Because they can trace bullets. My gun is registered." He returned to pacing. "I'll need to get you out of here. It's got to look natural. No reason to suspect foul play."

"My boyfriend will be looking for me. He'll figure this out. He's a hacker. He's smart, and he has SEAL friends." I actually have no idea if they are SEALs or not, but it's a word I knew that meant kick ass.

Then he placed a line of cocaine on the table. I sat silently, watching him snort up the powdery white substance. I realized he was high, which meant logic might not work.

"What do you want? What can I do?" I asked. "I promise. Let me go. I walk out of here, and I won't say a word. I owe you, anyway. Like you said. I should've never outed you."

"You destroyed my life." He gritted out the words and waved the black stun gun my way.

"I'm so sorry. Please let me go. I promise you—"

"Shut the fuck up!" He dropped the gun device on the bed. I thought maybe I could reason with him once the drugs took effect. But he lifted the duct tape from the bag. It was new, and he used his teeth to tear the plastic wrapping. If anyone ever found this room, his DNA would be on that plastic. Yes, that was what I thought as he tore the duct tape with his teeth. Another swab of DNA.

All those hours of crime television, and I could recognize where the DNA is, but I couldn't figure out how to get out.

"I'll be back."

That's the last thing he said to me. And it was hours ago. The tightness in my bladder is excruciating. My throat aches. I yearn for water. My arms tingle and my hands are cold.

Erik may have thought I was angry at him this morning. He may have assumed I needed space. It might have taken a while for him to figure out I'm missing. But by now, he's got to know. He has to know I wouldn't arrange for his sister to arrive and not be there to greet her. That would be making our issues public, something I would never do. He's got to be looking for me. But I don't have my phone. There's no way he can track me. I was transported here in a trunk. Unless there's a camera in the Motel 6 parking lot, there's no way to find me here. My best bet is the cleaning service, which won't come until morning.

Unless Bradley comes up with a plan for me. If he returns, it won't be good. I hope he paid for the room in cash. If he used a credit card, chances are he'll figure out the room will be traced back to him. Of course, who am I kidding? Me being alive is a risk to him. He's probably out buying supplies for whatever plan he devises to dispose of me. I don't see a way out of this. My best bet is a crazed man decides he can't go through with killing me, and he flees, leaving me here to be found. None of the options play out well.

There's one thing the television shows never really cover about people who are held captive. How do they go to the bathroom? It's gross, but I have no other option. I let it go, and warmth flows down my thighs.

# ORIGINAL GANGSTER

ERIK

"We got a match!" Kairi yells.

Logan has earbuds in and a laptop open as he converses with an FBI contact. Wolf has maps on the wall, and he's marking them, noting where his team has searched. He's also noted where there are cameras.

"Where?"

"At an intersection not far from here. License plate match for a vehicle leased by Bradley Lilith." She pulls up maps on her browser. "About two miles away. He's here. He has to be your guy."

Wolf pinpoints the location on the map on the wall.

"What kind of car?"

"Black Lexus sedan." Wolf taps on his phone, and Kairi clicks away on her laptop. My sister stands beside me, gently prodding my shoulder muscle. I've been online, perusing boards on the Dark Web. The least useful action item possible, but I figured some sickos like to post and brag.

"In the footage at the gate. I saw that car. More than once." Kairi's clicking away, and she points to the monitor. "This morning. He entered at 7:17 a.m." I can't see her screen from this angle, but I watch as her eyes scan back and forth. "And he exited at 8:59. But…hold on. I think I've seen this same car…" Wolf stands behind her, leaning for a better view. "There. He came back. Two. Oh. Four."

"Is anyone in the car with him?"

"You can't tell from the angle of these street cameras. They put them in with the intent of catching license plates, not passengers. Apparently, there is concern from patrons of hotels that they might be captured on film with lovers. Privacy." She wiggles her eyebrows and grins.

"Is he still here?" I ask. My skin itches. Kairi scans the monitor as she clicks. Wolf brought in two large black duffel bags, and I search for ammunition.

"What are you doing?" Wolf asks.

"I'm going after him."

"Wait. They just located him at another traffic light. Ten minutes ago. He's not in the resort. But he is in town."

"Get our team back here. We'll split up and head into town. It's not that big of a grid. We're going to locate him."

"I'm going to call area hotels. Maybe he's staying in one." Kairi picks up the phone.

"How is that going to help you? They aren't going to give out that kind of information over the phone. They don't even capture that data." I scan the area for the keys to the Range Rover. I can't locate them anywhere. As I'm lifting papers and cups, trying to think where Vivi might have left them, I hear Kairi on the phone.

"Hello. Yes, hi. My name is Katie. I'm calling with a request that is going to sound so strange. But I really need your help. I'm a little bit desperate."

I locate Vivi's pocketbook and dump out the contents. There are no keys. I re-enter the den. Kairi is still on the phone.

"I know. But has anyone ever cheated on you? I just need to know if he's there. With her."

My hand is on the door when I hear Kairi tell Wolf, "Drive by the Marriott. That receptionist wasn't helpful. I'm going to call Motel 7 next."

Wolf nods to her and points to me. "Come with me. You drive. I'm going to be busy relaying with the team."

I jump in his black SUV and press the accelerator, thankful for a scrap of information. Confirmation one of our suspects is in the area is huge. It can't be a coincidence. If he's hurt her, I'll kill him. Fuck it. I'm going to kill him either way.

Wolf gets a call. I only know because he speaks out into the air. "Kare. Update?"

"Motel 7. Good work. She wouldn't give you the room number? But she confirmed the vehicle. In the lot now?" While he's on the phone, he's tapping in the address, and I floor the accelerator.

"Update the police. My contact is Sergeant Reyes." Wolf texts as fast as I've ever seen him text.

The light at the intersection turns red, and I tap my fingers against the wheel.

"No room number?" I ask, confirming. "Do you have a badge to get them to tell us?"

"I doubt he used his real name to check in. We can knock on the doors. Ask people. I've got a photo of the guy on my phone. Just sent it to the team. They'll all have photos, too. Police are en route."

"She may not even be there." I voice my fear.

"We'll find her," Wolf says. It's the kind of thing one says, but one doesn't know.

I scan the parking lot as I pull in. There's no Lexus. It would stand out if there were one. This motel has seen better days. From the shadow behind the seven, it's clear this used to be a Motel 6. The new owners weren't particularly creative when they renamed it.

Trevor, Snipes, and others pull up in black SUVs and park beside us. It's late afternoon, and judging from the open parking lot, there are vacancies.

They split up, knocking on doors. I go to talk with the receptionist. Kairi is the one who is good at eliciting information. I am not. Unfortunately, it appears the receptionist watched all of us pull into the parking lot.

"Can I help you?" She peers over my shoulder, no doubt watching our men knock on doors.

"We're looking for someone."

"Same person that girl called about?"

"Yes, ma'am."

"You don't need to call me ma'am." The middle-aged woman is older than me. She's wearing jeans and a skintight top. "I don't think he's here. But his lady friend is. There's no reason to attack her. I'll call the cops on you."

"We're not here to hurt her. We're here to save her. Kairi...or Katie... told you that story to find out if he was here. You've got to believe me. It's my girlfriend in there. She's been kidnapped. The police are on the way. If you know what room she's in, you've got to tell me."

She points a long nail to a first-floor door.

I point my finger, and the guys all join me at the door with a brass number three. Wolf knocks. There's no sound.

"Did she give you a key?"

Fuck, I should've gotten one. I take a step back to ask the receptionist for a key. She's standing in the doorway, arms crossed, watching us with suspicion. There's a phone in her hand. No doubt she's prepared to dial 911. Wolf backs up and faces the door at a sideways angle.

"Wait," the receptionist calls. "I'll get you a key."

She unlocks the door, and Trevor pulls her aside, out of the way. We open it, and my insides simultaneously sink and explode.

Vivi is tied to a chair, and duct tape covers her mouth. Wolf and Trevor hold their guns in the air. Out of the corner of my eye, I see one of them enter the bathroom.

I run to Vivi. She's wearing the loose pajama pants she likes to lounge around in and a tank top. There are no signs of blood. I grab a corner of the silver tape and rip it off fast.

She gasps and leans forward. Tears leak out the corners of her eyes. I grab her shoulders, scanning her for injury.

"Are you okay?"

"My wrists."

Trace amounts of blood line Vivi's wrists.

"I need something to cut her free." The thick plastic ties have no give. If I pull on them, I'll hurt her.

Wolf joins me. His knife blade reflects light. In a flash, her wrists are free. She coddles them against her. Thin red lines mar her delicate skin. She's bent over her thighs.

Wolf kneels at her feet, slicing the binding. She's not wearing shoes, so once she's free, I pick her up and carry her.

Sirens loom outside, increasing in intensity.

"Did you call an ambulance?" I ask Wolf.

"I'm okay. I don't need one." Vivi protests.

Two cop cars with lights flashing pull into the parking lot, directly behind our fleet of black SUVs. Wolf leads the charge to talk to the officers.

I carry Vivi to Wolf's car. I set her down in the passenger seat and hover over her.

"I thought I'd lost you." My face is next to hers, and I clasp her trembling, cold hands in mine.

"No. I don't think he would have..." Her words trail off, frail and soft. She's uncertain. She doesn't know. And neither do I.

I have so many questions to ask her, but it's not important. A uniformed police officer stands at my side.

"Sir, is she okay?"

An ambulance pulls into the parking lot. The EMT opens the back doors to the vehicle. The police officer asks Vivi if they can check her out. He explains they also need photographs. An additional police car, lights on, no sirens, pulls into the parking lot.

I carry Vivi over to the ambulance. Her head rests against my shoulder, and I press my lips to her forehead. Emotions pour through me in waves. Relief. Concern. Worry. Her captor is still out there. I know what it's like to have an enemy lurking.

Wolf and Trevor are engaged with the police officers. Yellow tape now hangs along the section of the hotel room. White light flashes inside the room.

The EMT wraps thin white gauze around Vivi's ankle, and a cop edges me to the side as he proceeds to ask her questions.

I look off to the street. Cars are slowing down. Passengers and drivers alike are watching all of us. Traffic has backed up as drivers slow, taking in the scene.

A black sedan inches by. I recognize the driver. He's the same guy whose photo I uploaded on my phone. He's wearing sunglasses. Like every other passing car, he's taking in the scene.

My hand rests on the butt of my gun, and I step away from the ambulance and onto the sidewalk. There's no fucking way I'm letting him just drive away.

I raise my right arm to get Wolf's attention. I signal, pointing on the street. Wolf steps back from the police officer he's talking to. His gaze follows my finger.

The asshole sees us. He blasts his horn, and he guns his engine, swerving onto the sidewalk, attempting to pass the cars in the backlogged street. The car lurches forward, and I hold out my gun. Aim. Pull.

His back tire deflates. The car swerves off the sidewalk and into the bushes. The police officers take off, running. Two of the men in blue surround the car as he exits, hands in the air.

Another officer joins my side. "Sir, you fired that gun?"

# MINE

VIVI

The torn skin around my wrists and ankles burns. I slip on my pajamas and wrap a towel around my hair. The faint hum of crashing waves calms me. The thick white comforter calls to me, but voices carry through the bedroom door. And I am hungry.

I open the door, and a hush falls over the room. Then Erik is at my side, guiding my elbow.

"I'm okay," I tell him.

"Cali has soup ready for you." He guides me to the chair. "And I have the ointment from the EMT for your wrists and ankles. And gauze. After you eat, you'll sleep." He announces this last bit of information louder, and it's clear he's saying it for the rest of the room.

I sit at the head of the table, and six others join me.

"I'm okay." I offer a small smile. It's all I can force out. I am okay. It could have been so much worse. Hunger and exhaustion battle within me because while I want to eat, my eyelids are heavy.

The warm soup coats the back of my throat. With each swallow, more of myself returns. Erik pulls up a chair, inches from mine. His hand falls to my back, and he rubs gently, back and forth.

"I still think we should have taken you to the hospital." Cali sits a foot away, her dark eyes so much like her twin's.

"There was nothing for them to do." Every single person is watching me, and all of them are concerned. I sense it. "Really. I'm fine. If anything, I'm pissed at myself because I didn't use my head. Every woman knows you should never allow a captor to put you in the car. I should've fought harder." My memory of the moment is cloudy, but I didn't fight.

"Stun guns frazzle you. No one thinks straight. And you haven't been trained. Even if you had, he had those zip ties so tight, I don't think you could've escaped." Trevor's being friendly. He's relaxed, and there's a beer in his hand.

"What were you thinking, going after a stranger on the Internet?" Erik isn't relaxed. He's squinting. His head is at an angle. He wraps an arm around the back of my chair, and his other hand falls to my thigh. But it feels like he's touching me to assure himself I'm here, not to comfort me.

"I've been doing this for years." His eyes widen, and his mouth opens slightly. "Sometimes I get paid." Kairi hides a smile behind her beer bottle.

Logan leans forward, resting his weight on his elbows on the table. "You got lucky. It could've been a lot worse."

"I know," I tell him as Erik squeezes my thigh. He wants to say more, but he's like me. He won't say more in this sea of people.

"Did any of this make the news?" Erik asks the table. Wolf shakes his head.

"We're monitoring it. Obviously, there's footage of the cop cars at the motel. But so far, we haven't seen any footage with you or us. All the coverage right now has to do with Vivianne Rossi being kidnapped."

"Where is my phone? I've got to call my family."

"Police found it in his car. It's in evidence." Crap. My phone.

Kairi slides over her phone. "Use mine."

She has all the numbers I need. Celeste is emotional. Max is gruff. Granddad wants to drive to me, but I assure him I'm all right. And I will be. I am.

Erik holds me close, his arm around me, supporting my tired, aching body. Without him saying a word, I hear his frustration with what I've done. My lack of precautions. But he loves me. His love overrides all the negative. And yes, he's not perfect. But I trust him. I love him. And he's mine.

# HOLD

ERIK

Vivi is tucked next to me in bed, and we're bundled underneath the comforter. Outside the expansive window, morning dawns, and the soft sound of waves filters through.

Her head rests on my chest, and I curve my arm around her, holding her close. The light gauze wrapped around her wrist serves as a reminder of how differently everything might have played out.

She'd been playing a dangerous game. It was only a matter of time before she disrupted the wrong asshole's life. We were incredibly fortunate the guy didn't have the killer instinct. He'd wanted to scare her but was too drugged to formulate a solid plan. And there again, so lucky. The drug use could have easily gone the other way and helped him to cross the line to a complete psychotic break.

Footfalls and hushed whispers outside the room remind me we aren't alone. A screen door creaks and slaps shut with a bang. My sister and her family have probably decided to go for a walk along the beach so as not to disturb us.

Vivi's eyelids flutter open, and those light blue irises soothe my frazzled soul. She smiles. Then groans.

"We have guests. We need to get up."

"You don't need to do anything today except take it easy. And our guests are fine. They just went out for a walk on the beach. The refrigerator is stocked. They know where everything is. Your job today is to rest."

She stretches out beside me. One of her legs crosses over mine as she rolls onto her side. I love this. Waking up with her. And I came so close...

"What's that face for?" she asks.

"Vivi, do you understand how badly yesterday could have gone? Do you understand how lucky you are?"

She lays her head back down against my chest, and her fingers lightly graze over my pecs. I twist a long strand around a finger. I need for her to understand, but how? It's not my place to tell her what she can and can't do.

"I know it sounds strange, but I wasn't really scared yesterday."

"Someone kidnapped you and tied you to a chair, and you weren't scared?"

"I had this sense he wouldn't really hurt me. I mean, he had a stun gun. Not a knife. Not a pistol. He did have a wild eye. I did worry he was out of his mind, but I just never had the sense that he had it in him to actually kill." I disagree with her, but there's no point in arguing. She's telling me what she sensed. I can't argue with that. We'll never know if her sense was right or wrong.

"Maybe this time. But next time, you might not be so lucky. How did you even get into playing vigilante?"

"In a roundabout way, really. Our vineyard was hacked years ago. They accessed customer emails, credit cards. It was all pretty benign, but my grandfather feared, well, plenty, so he paid this ransom." The Rossi Vineyards hack. Spectre's work. Fuck me.

"Spectre is my old company. I wasn't a part of the Rossi attack. Not really. That was one of the hacks that made me start to suspect we were losing sight of our original mission." We set out to level the playing field. To take down the big, greedy corporations and share the funds freely. We set out to create a world where no one government or entity could be too strong. "I'm sorry. I didn't connect you, or, well, Firefly, to Rossi Vineyards. I had no idea you were related."

"In a way, it encouraged my grandfather to let the younger generation shoulder more weight. He felt so out of the loop with the technology. And it raised my interest in coding. I became curious." Ah, curiosity. I wouldn't be holding her right now if it weren't for curiosity.

"I found this Reddit group of coders. I'd take on a coding challenge. One day, the challenge was to hack into a fellow user's computer. Another day an Instagram account. Then someone mentioned you could make money doing it. And my first few jobs were for women who suspected their husbands were cheating. And every single time, those women were right. It pissed me off."

"So you began a one-woman campaign against cheaters?"

"I like to think of it as making online dating safer. It's just too easy for people to pretend to be someone they're not online. You know?"

"I do. But, Vivianne, look at me." I waited until she raised her head off my chest. "You are too important to me. I don't want you to take those risks."

"Aren't you taking risks?"

"Calculated risks, yes."

"You can, but I can't?"

"I don't know." I rub my hand over my eyes, and I see Kairi bathed in Lara's blood. "I've seen the worst. It's not an irrational fear." She fixes those baby blues on me.

"Sometimes fear is the enemy. Our worst case imagined scenarios are more terrible than are remotely realistic."

I wrap my fingers lightly around her wrist and shake it back and forth.

"You were just kidnapped yesterday. You had wine stolen in the same week. Are you listening to yourself?"

"All right." She grins. "Maybe I could stand to be more safety-conscious. I'm sure you'll point the way." She's right about that. I'm going to find us a house on a hilltop and have the most secure strong-hold money can buy.

"Why not go back to gaming?" I'd get her the best setup. Whatever she wanted. That's a safe hobby.

"Didn't I tell you back in the day? I reached a point where...it gets to me. The graphics are too visual. When I shoot someone and the blood splatters, I feel it. Like I'm injured. Like it's my blood. I throw a punch, and I feel it." I'd tell her she's being ridiculous, but again, her feelings are valid. And the gaming graphics only get more realistic with each upgrade.

"Did you ever sell your coins?"

"No." She lays her head back down. "I didn't get a good vibe."

"Good."

"Did you sell?"

"No. Bad vibes." I smile at her. She raises up and presses her lips to mine. Her soft breasts drag across my chest. This, talking with her, holding her...I can't give it up. I'm not strong enough. And she needs me around to keep her safe. I will do anything to keep her safe.

She lies back down. I pull the comforter up higher around her shoulders to cocoon her in warmth.

"I like your sister." Her comment warms me from within. Cali is my twin. It's important they like each other.

"I hoped you'd like her. Of everyone on the planet, she's the most like me."

"Hmmm." Her hum vibrates into my chest. "I think the two of you are similar. But you're also very different."

"How do you figure?" You'd have to look at our childhood photos to see how similar we actually look. As adults, gender differences won out.

"I'm only just getting to know her, but she doesn't seem quite as focused, or I guess, obsessive as you." Vivi's soft lips press against my throat, and I close my eyes, reveling in the sensation. "Is she color-blind too?"

"I don't think so. Why?"

"I noticed she wears a lot of monochrome colors. Like you."

"I think it's just her preference." In grad school, she began gravitating away from jeans and into what she called casual business wear. I always suspected she just wanted to differentiate herself from the undergrad students she was teaching. Or maybe she was simply more susceptible to Dad's influence. He liked to emphasize the importance of appearance.

"Maybe. But she's quiet like you. Contemplative. And her concern for those she loves...you, Dylan, Logan...I bet it rivals the care you give those in your life." I place a kiss on her temple. I love this woman in my arms, and I'd do anything for her. Is that what she means? "But maybe not. I doubt a security team is her go-to solution."

"Well, she's led a different life than me. But she married someone who leans toward security. He traveled with his handgun."

She sighs, and it sounds...sad.

"What's wrong?"

"I wanted this to be a break for you. A break from constantly looking over your shoulder. It's not healthy to always worry." But that's life at war. At any point in time, the enemy might attack. And when you least expect them is the best time for them to do so. Sun Tzu. Generals for centuries have followed his wisdom.

She presses her body over mine, and my already alert cock stiffens further. I shift away from her, as she needs rest.

"You've got to let it go. You'll go mad otherwise."

"You don't think I am already?"

"No. I think you've seen more than a normal person should have. I think your brain functions like a chess player. Always playing out scenarios, and unfortunately, in the game world you're currently living in, we don't have extra lives, and the potential scenarios don't all deliver the players to a higher level. I think the anxiety and stress force you to do some things that some of us consider irrational, but it comes from a place of preparation. Kind of like our players in Zeitgeist...we also set out on our quests fully stocked, as strong as we could make each player, with our trunks filled with gold, weapons, maps, and potions."

"Because that improved our odds."

"Exactly." She's wearing a thin silk camisole. The sunlight casts a seductive glow over the material.

"But you can't play nonstop. Remember? Players get stronger when you take breaks. When you step away."

"Have you forgiven me?" After everything that has happened, it feels like my identities don't mean anything at all. If anyone is going to understand, it will be Vivi. I was always real with her; the identity was meaningless.

"It was never a question of forgiveness. I understand. And I love you."

My chest detonates. It's a novel sensation, and I suck in air, absorbing it all. Whisper-soft light blue eyes. My lips fall to hers, and I kiss her with my everything. My all. Because she loves me, too.

# SMITHEREENS

Two Months Later

Erik is in a zone. He's lost to the monitor and the poetic code on the screen. It's with reluctance that I approach, but if we're going to ride together, he's got to wrap it up. I've got one hundred and thirty people arriving for my grandfather's birthday party, and as one of the hosts, I can't be late.

I brush my fingers through his hair. The muscles in his neck and shoulders are tight, and I dig my thumbs into them. His left hand leaves the keyboard, and his arm wraps around my waist. He presses a kiss into my belly then looks up.

"Time to go?" he asks. I nod.

"Making progress?"

He exhales before responding. "Yeah. We're getting closer."

He lets me go and powers down. Erik has been working closely with the FBI's Recovery Asset Team. He's convinced the best way to make the Internet safer is to eliminate the financial incentive. I think he's brilliant, and if anyone can do it, he can. And he's working with some of the most brilliant minds in the world to help make it happen.

Through his company, Arrow, he's not only hired talent from around the world, but he's also working in concert with the FBI and the NSA.

My skillset is nowhere near the level of Erik's. I'm more of a copy and paste coder. And, like Kairi, I can read people. People remain the weakest security link for any company. I've worked with Kairi on a few side projects now. It's not my full-time gig. I never wanted it to be. But like so many of the white hats out there, it's something I like to do on the side. It's doing my part in a twisted world.

"Did you see that something's getting delivered to our place tomorrow?"

"I did. Quite a few pieces of furniture are getting delivered. I arranged the timing so I could be there to meet the painters to review the punch list."

"Good. Wolf is coming up for a final inspection before our move-in date."

Of course he is. Erik found a spec home for sale with impressive views at the top of a hill. I like to tease him that it's more secure than Fort Knox. If the extra security allows him to live with his fear, then I'm all for it.

I still have The Bookery, but I plan to convert the upstairs into a comfortable lounge area for people to work and read and hang out. Wolf says he created an ideal space for employees to do the same thing in the warehouse down in Santa Barbara. We're going to visit once construction is complete, and if I like it, I'm going to hire his design team. If I don't like it, I'll put my designer's cap on.

When we arrive at Rossi Vineyards, preparations are well underway. The caterers set up in this portion of the vineyard regularly, and they require little guidance. To one side, I created an art gallery. A wedding party gave me the idea. They had photos of the bride and groom. But here, I am hanging photos of the valley over the decades. My grandfather has spent his entire life here. He's seen it transform from small farms to small vineyards to a tourist mecca and the home of award-winning wine. And here, in blown up black and white and colored prints, the story unfolds. Only, we all see enough of the landscape photos. They hang in restaurants, bars, and bed and breakfasts all over. I spent time collecting photos of his friends and our family. In most of the photos, Granddad is wearing jeans, work boots, and in many, he's got a drink in his hand. He's not one to love having his picture taken, but in some of them, the alcohol removed his edge, and he smiles.

There are also group photos of him gathered at tables with friends. Birthday celebrations, end-of-harvest celebrations, and Friday gatherings. There's one photo of him in a suit, and all the men around him are wearing similar black suits. I recognize the suit. It's the one he wore on the day of my parents' funeral. His daughter's funeral. He's not looking at the camera, and there's a glass of wine in his hand. But what stands out to me are the friends and neighbors surrounding him. Some of them are wealthy men who hire everyone to do everything. Some of them are land poor, meaning they struggle with bills every month, as all their money is wrapped up in land. And some only dream of owning land. It's an eclectic mix in our town.

Max and my grandfather approach, and I glare at my older brother.

"You had one job. One job."

He grins, shoves his hands in his pockets, and shrugs.

"Next time, you try corralling him."

Granddad places an arm around my shoulder. "You've done a great job here, Vivi girl. We could use you in hospitality." I roll my eyes but give his waist a squeeze. "Now, listen to me. This is the last big shindig you throw for me, okay? This isn't my scene. You may think I'm so old I can be bossed around, but that ain't so. You got it?"

"Yes, sir."

He narrows his gaze at me. "You really moving in with that guy?"

"I am." I brace myself. Granddad's a pretty liberal guy, but he's giving me a look that says he disapproves. "I love him," I add, in case that weighs the judgement pendulum in my favor.

"Just like your mother." He kisses my forehead as Erik approaches. "And here's the man who I have no doubt is going to make an honest woman of my grandbaby."

Erik's expression is one of a deer in headlights, and I crack up. So does Max.

The catering manager approaches and lets us know everything is set up, and that guests are arriving, and they have begun circulating appetizers.

"Well, that's my cue to go greet my friends. You kids have fun." He winks, and he's off. Max follows him, leaving Erik and me and the collection of photographs.

"You know, if your grandfather wants us to get married, we can get married," Erik blurts, and my mouth drops.

"Oh. Okay." My words drip attitude, but I can't suppress my amused grin. Anyone else would get my meaning…we're not going to get married because of my grandfather. Marriage isn't even specifically on my radar. Max was a year old before my parents got married. That's something they never specifically told us, but we put it together when we were old enough to do math.

"We can go ring shopping." He nods and scans the area. To Erik, that's just a to-do item. I shove him. The man is brilliant, but he can be dense.

"Erik." I say his name loud and enunciate each vowel. "No. That is not how you will propose to me. If I agree to marry you, it will be because it's something you and I want. Not because of my grandfather."

His brow furrows. He doesn't get it. He's probably also trying to figure out if I'm upset. I'm not, though. I'm amused. Erik and I are a good fit. I'm excited to move in with him officially and to start something new together. I can't imagine being with anyone else. Yes, he's it for me. But I don't need a ring or a marriage certificate. I have zero desire to navigate the prenup waters my grandfather would no doubt insist on. We're good. Doing it our own way.

My phone vibrates, and I get a text that Chloe and David are at the entrance wine table.

"Chloe's here. Let's go greet her."

"So, you don't want to marry me?" he asks. I take his hand and tug him in the direction of the entrance.

He follows along obediently. The bluegrass band I hired kicks up, and guests, mostly those around my grandfather's age, mill around. Many find seats at tables. A little later, the band will stop, and the DJ will begin playing from my grandfather's playlist, which mostly consists of rock music from the seventies and eighties.

"Hey, girl, thanks for coming." I pull Chloe into a hug. David stands behind her. He and I shake hands, and I introduce him to Erik.

Just then, Wolf, Trevor, and Kairi approach. Kairi stops. Something's wrong with her, but as I approach, Wolf picks me up, and my feet leave the ground, and the breath gets knocked out of me. The man is a giant who doesn't know his own strength. I pat his chest as he sets me back down, and then search for Kairi. She's snapped out of it and is taking a glass of wine offered to her from a tray.

When I return to Chloe, she's alone.

"Where'd David go?"

"He said the hospital paged him. Do you think you can hack his pager?"

"What?" I half-laugh at her. Yeah, sure, I'm happy to do research on strangers, but we know David. Like, he's Max's best friend.

"Why would the hospital page him?" she asks. "He works at a pediatric clinic."

"Why would he lie? You're at an event with free booze and food and lots of his old friends." And that's when it clicks. He and Kairi used to date. Did they not know they were both back in town?

"I haven't had the opportunity to bore him or repulse him. We just got here. You're right. I have to stop being so suspicious. You're a bad influence on me." She jabs my arm, and I grin.

"Only with the unknowns." An eyes wide open policy is a good thing. But it's not like I'm one who should judge. I'm moving in with a guy I met in a game. But the guys Chloe and I grew up with, guys like David and Max, we know them backward and forward. She's got a good guy in David, from what I remember.

The band kicks off a new song. It's a cover of an Avett Brothers song, and I tell our group of friends I like it.

Within seconds, I am dancing behind the bar tent, off away from the crowd. Erik listens to the words. He's dancing slow, holding me against him. It's not the way you're supposed to dance to the song, but we're out of view of the crowd. I loop my arms behind his neck and gently sway.

"What's the song called?" he asks.

"*Swept Away.*"

He hums the music. I've always liked these lyrics.

His lips are close to my ear, and it tickles when he says, "Your Granddad seems happy."

"Yeah. Now." The days leading up to this party, once the surprise was blown, were not particularly pleasant.

"It might not have gone exactly like you wanted, but I think it's gonna turn out pretty great."

The words of the song filter through my mind, and I smile as I make the connection.

"Like life. Our life."

Erik pulls back enough I can see the question in his eyes.

"When you were younger, did you have expectations for what Phoenix was like?" His question knocks me back to my younger years. I smile so wide my facial muscles stretch.

"Well, yeah. But my expectations varied over the years."

"How?" He nudges me, and his lips brush below my ear, then his teeth nip my earlobe playfully.

"Well, I suppose when I was thirteen, I might have imagined you looked like Justin Timberlake. Then when I was eighteen or nineteen, you might have transformed to Robert Pattinson."

His thumb grazes my tattoo.

"So, the vampire from *Twilight* is really the inspiration for that tattoo."

I can't hold back the giggles.

"I suppose. One could argue that point."

"And then who? Who did Phoenix transform into in your twenties?"

"A friend." I brush my lips against his chin and sway in time with the music. "I think I envisioned a nerdy gamer who had become a focused businessman and still kept in touch. I expected you might be married with a house in the suburbs and two-point-five kids and a cat."

"A cat? Not a dog?"

"Gamer." I shrug. I suppose I did have a vision of Phoenix over the course of our friendship. But the vision evolved as I evolved.

"Is that what you want, Viv? A house in the suburbs? A boy and a girl?" His dark eyes bore into me.

"One day." If you think about it, the secure house he bought on the hill

296

might count. There's no picket fence, but there's a tripwire around the perimeter and motion sensitive cameras. It's not exactly the dream house I envisioned, but it is my present day dream.

"Viv." He stops moving and waits for me to look him in the eye. "I want that, too. One day, with you. You blow every single expectation I ever had for Firefly to smithereens. I love you more than I ever thought I could love a person. It's a soul deep love. A love so powerful it rises above demons. More potent than any potion in Firefly's arsenal. Never doubt me. Never doubt us. I will never let you go."

# BRAVE NEW WORLD

The screen prompts the question, "Are you ready to embark on the sojourn of a lifetime?" Drums bellow through surround sound, thanks to speakers hidden away in corners of the ceiling. There's a mammoth television screen on the wall. I've always played this game on a much smaller device, like an iPad or on the much smaller television in our playroom growing up.

"The graphics are quite grainy at this size, aren't they?"

Erik sits beside me on the sofa. He's been bugging me to play ever since we created this setup in the guest room. There's a dog bed in the corner of the room, but no dog. Astra has yet to move in with us. Erik says Astra will be happier with Trevor because that dog is happiest on long runs, which Trevor does regularly. Erik prefers sprints, and the dog sits and watches. I don't like giving up his dog. It doesn't sit well with me. But I have zero plans to take up running, so if that's the dog's schtick, then I'll need to pack up the dog bed before Trevor moves down to Santa Barbara.

"Are you ready?" Erik's on the edge of the sofa, and his knee bounces up and down.

"Excited, are you?" I mock. He's so excited, but I had real reasons for backing off gaming. "If it gets bloody, I'm outta there. I'm warning you. I'll go sit outside in the den and listen to you play."

"Sit down. I told you, this is a new adaptation. Like Minecraft."

"That hit a little after my time. I never got into it."

"Veev. There's no way you didn't read about it. We're going to build our house and village. Like ROBLOX. Don't you think Firefly and Phoenix should have a house?"

Well, when he puts it like that. I join him on the sofa and cross my legs. He's said we're building a house, but with the controller in my hand, the urge to zap grows.

"Start this thing," I tell him.

"This version of the game allows for a force field. We can use some of those gold coins we're getting hassled to sell to buy a new force field." I watch as he takes over his control. His avatar has thick black locks and wears tights with fur boots. Hanging weapons crisscross his chest and waist. Firefly appears on screen.

"You changed Firefly?" he asks. He's stunned. I laugh because he seems somewhat affronted.

"I think she should've been a redhead. I've been thinking about dying my hair red. What do you think?"

"For real?" His facial expression says it all. He's not on board. Fine. That's the joy in an avatar. Erik is such a guy. He probably has no idea I dye my hair. My natural color is blonde, but platinum isn't one to find in nature. Not that the guy focused on the screen beside me is aware of that. His knee keeps bouncing.

"Are you nervous?"

"No." He's staring at the screen, holding the device out. It's like we're headed into war.

"Erik, you said there'd be no killing."

"Veev. Just follow me." He's annoyed. Whatever. We're supposed to be building. I press the forward button, and Firefly lumbers along behind Phoenix. It's been ages since I played this game, but it comes back to me lightning fast. I forgot how stilted movement is.

"When we build, I want to add a library for my sorcery books. Will the game let me store them in the house?" Erik is fixed on the journey through the forest. He said no killing, but the way he's locked on the screen, it's as if he's expecting an attack from the sides. He doesn't answer me. "I'd bet they'll stay in my cache."

But if the game is updated, there will be design options built in. I can see the room I want to build, with a roaring fireplace, and some massive painting over the mantel. I grin, eager to get to building.

Phoenix reaches a rocky cliff, and then his character jumps. Cool. I have not seen this landscape before. I'm pressing the toggle, and Firefly falls out of view. She's not moving forward, and I pound the red button. This handset is old. It must be short-circuiting.

The music changes to bluegrass. It's the Avett Brothers song for real, not a cover. I lean into Erik, shocked.

On-screen, Phoenix rises, his leather cape flapping around him, and he bends on one knee. Firefly comes into view. She's sporting her original black hair. That's odd. Her hand covers her mouth, and fire shoots from the base of her sandals, lifting her off the ground. I haven't touched my control. This is a video.

"Erik?" I ask.

On-screen, the words "Marry Me" appear.

"What are you doing?" I mimic my on-screen avatar, and one hand flies to my mouth. I can't quite believe what he's doing.

"You wanted romantic." He takes my hands. "Vivi, I love you. I can't imagine being with anyone else. I don't want anyone else. It's always been you. My spirit recognized yours the moment I entered your store, before I laid eyes on you. And you took up residence. I haven't been able to shake you from my thoughts. And I don't want to. My heart and my future belong to you. With or without marriage. But marriage is important to your grandfather. If my mother were alive, it would be important to her, too. And my dad, he and I don't talk much, but it's important to him. Maybe it's old-fashioned and archaic."

"A symbol of the patriarchy," I supply for him as the room blurs.

"Vivi, I don't need a ring. I committed to you the moment I saw you. It just took me time to comprehend it. I don't often listen to my heart. But you do. I need you in my life. Will you share your life with me? Will you marry me?"

"Yes." Tears stream down my cheeks. He leans up and kisses me, and we forget all about the game.

---

**Continue on the Twisted Vine with Breathe... Kairi's story**

Prologue

14 Years Earlier

"One." His teeth grazed the tip of my finger. "Two." He applied the same treatment to the next finger. "Three."

"And we're out of here," I exclaimed.

An abundance of stars twinkled in the dark night sky above us. I lay in his arms, in the back of a pickup truck, a light blanket across us. One more summer season and this small town would forever be in our rearview. Unfettered freedom stretched before us.

He rolled on his side with a carefree grin, his weight on one elbow. He twirled a strand of my hair around his finger. And then he drew back, thoughtful, remembering.

"What got you so upset earlier?"

"I wasn't upset." I really wasn't. Annoyed at the snide comments from a cheerleader who, if I was honest, I'd never been fond of. Two days away from graduation, I never planned to run into her again.

"Kare." He drew out my shortened nickname, the way he always did when he called me out or questioned without questioning.

The sharp ends of straw poked into my jeans, and I squirmed, snuggling into his wool sweater. He lifted my hand and kissed three knuckles.

The stars shone bright, high above. One smaller light flitted across the darkness. A plane.

"Do you think that's a big plane or a little plane?"

"Why don't you want to tell me?"

"It was nothing. She mentioned some stupid article. Said only one or two percent of high school couples stay together."

"She can be such a bitch."

"She was only telling the truth."

"How would anyone even know that? Like someone out there is keeping track of every single couple in the United States?"

"Statistics."

A crushing sense of sadness fell over me, which was ridiculous. In a couple of months, we'd both be headed to the same college. One year in the dorms, and then we planned to live together. Either officially or unofficially. We planned to make it work. I'd gotten into New York University, my dream school. Columbia too. But I turned them both down, because New York was simply too far from Minnesota, and I wanted to give David and me the best chance. If we only had two percent odds, I wanted to do everything I could to stack the deck.

He held my face in his hands. The outside temperature was cool enough his breath clouded the air.

"Statistics are meaningless. There's no other couple out there like you and me. I love you. More than anything. You and me, we're going to defy all the odds." He brushed his lips across my forehead. One of his cold hands slid up my sweater, and I flattened against him.

There was something else she said that bugged me. One last little dig.

David cupped my breast, ready to end our little discussion, but I stopped him.

"You don't think that one day you'll want to see what it's like with someone else? I mean, we were each other's first...everything." Of course, I had asked him this before. We had these discussions on and off. But that night, I needed to hear his answer.

"Kairi Anne Morrigan, all I want is you. I want you to be my first, my only, and my last."

His lips found mine and he gave me the David kiss. A slow kiss full of love and familiarity until it deepened to need. My palm flattened against his chest, pushing back against his building desire.

For some reason, maybe because of all the impending changes, what I needed that night was to be held. To simply be. And David, intuitive and tender, complied.

We sat in the back of that pickup, above straw and below a blanket, watching planes go by and wondering who was on the plane, where they were going, and what kind of lives they lived. He held me and gave me the comfort and warmth of love, with the promise of wide-open spaces far away from our small town. All we had to do was survive three more days and a life together was ours.

# ALSO BY ISABEL JOLIE

**The Twisted Vines Series**

Crushed (Erik and Vivi)

Breathe (Kairi and David)

Savor (Trevor and Stella) - Releasing June 23

**Haven Island Series**

Rogue Wave (Tate and Luna)

Adrift (Gabe and Poppy)

First Light (Logan and Cali)

**The West Side Series**

When the Stars Align (Jackson and Anna)

Trust Me (Sam and Olivia)

Walk the Dog (Delilah and Mason)

Lost on the Way (Jason and Maggie)

Chasing Frost (Chase and Sadie)

Misplaced Mistletoe (Ashton aka Dr. Bobby and Nora)

# NOTES

What's real? What's not? It's a question Sarina Bowen asked at the end of a book in her *Company* series, which also touches on cybercrime, and these days, it's a question worth asking.

Cybercrime is real. Sophisticated, corporate criminal syndicates are real.

Back in the day, cybercrime typically meant credit card theft. We in the United States have been slow to respond. In Europe, you don't hand over your credit card to the waitstaff - they bring the little credit card thingie right to you. In the US, we hand our card over all the time to the person at the gas station or to the waitstaff person - and you know what? It's a big source of credit card theft. In my day job (because in case you're curious, no, writing does not pay the bills), I sometimes have customers ask to give me their credit card information over the phone...as if that's somehow safer. They don't know me from jack, and they want to give me a number over the phone. What's to prevent me from hanging up and going shopping? No, no, no. As scary as it may be to enter it on a website, it's SO much safer. If you're on the right website (always read that URL at the top of the browser). Anyway, that's the end of this PSA.

Credit card theft is so 1995. The new wave of crime supporting a trillion-dollar worldwide industry does far scarier things than annoy us with unknown charges on our credit card statement. Case in point: Myanmar. Democracy was overthrown largely thanks to fake news spread via Facebook. There was a time, back when I was a kid, and you'd see an article about alien twins landing in Phoenix, and you'd think to yourself...ah, those *National Enquirer* people are so creative. When articles floated around about Hillary Clinton leading a sex ring from a basement in a pizza parlor, people BELIEVED it! And that propaganda sways elections.

It feels like we're *A Tale of Two Cities* redux. It is the best of times *and* the worst of times. We have so much available to us at the click of a keyboard. Yet, we have to use our minds. We have to question everything. And we do need to be safe. Be smart out there.

In doing the research for this book, I've read a number of fascinating books, including *The Hacker and The State* by Ben Buchanan, *The Art of Deception* by Mitnick, and *Hacking the Hacker* by Roger Grimes. I also thoroughly enjoyed *Tangled Vines* by Frances Dinkelspiel. Her book focuses on the wine industry and the plague of corruption and greed that has at times hit this seemingly pristine upscale world.

I've also reached out to real-life hackers (black, white, and gray). No, I don't know their real names. And none of them wanted to be mentioned in the acknowledgements. But I will say I found them all to be helpful, friendly, and real. Even without an identity or a face. There is a silent war in progress - all to keep our newest frontier safe and to cast light over the Dark Web.

# ACKNOWLEDGMENTS

My first draft of *Crushed* was beyond rough. Amy Claire Majer really ripped this one apart. The new version is so different from that very first draft, and it's all thanks to her unfiltered honesty.

My beta readers that followed include those from Hidden Gems, my author friend Evan Dave, and my husband. Now, so often, I read that one should never use your spouse as a beta, but he helped on this one a lot. All my betas helped me fine-tune the story—thank you.

This is my tenth book edited by Lori Whitwam. It's kind of shocking to me. Ten books! I'm always grateful to her for her patience and editing. Pretty much every time I review her edits, I feel like someone from the University of Chapel Hill is going to show up and revoke my Journalism degree.

The title *Crushed* has gone through an interesting journey. I was in a class with the head of the Codex Group, and he reviewed my tentative covers. He strongly recommended I test other titles. I tested "Firefly & Phoenix" as well as "The Man Who Loved Firefly." Ultimately, the basic, overused, one-word title won out. But I'd like to thank all my friends and my newsletter subscribers for weighing in on this. My newsletter subscribers are awesome. As are my close friends from way back, Sarah Mullen, Scott Gold, Heather Munday, and Katie Barker. Several writing friends also weighed in—Elle Greco, Cindy Smith, Tracy Brody & Michele Tsuki. It's so funny – everyone has a different opinion. Covers and titles are so subjective, and this exercise definitely proved that to me.

As always, a heartfelt thank you goes out to my ARC readers. You guys rock, and I so much appreciate your volunteering to be on the team and then going out and sharing your reviews. You make all the difference when it releases out in the world.

Most of all, dear readers—THANK YOU! Thank you for picking up this book and giving it a chance. I love to hear from readers. You can contact me through my website at www.isabeljoliebooks.com . Thanks again and again for your support!

# ABOUT THE AUTHOR

Isabel Jolie, aka Izzy, lives on a lake, loves dogs of all stripes, and if she's not working, she can be found reading, often with a glass of wine in hand. In prior lives, Izzie worked in marketing and advertising, in a variety of industries, such as financial services, entertainment, and technology. In this life, she loves daydreaming and writing contemporary romances with real, flawed characters and inner strength.

Sign-up for Izzy's newsletter to keep up-to-date on new releases, promotions and giveaways. Or stalk her on your favorite platform. And no, she's not on TikTok. Her teen keeps telling her to stay away...

Printed in Great Britain
by Amazon

37469961R00182